7X. 8/18.6/20

STARTUP

STARTUP

A Novel

Doree Shafrir

Little, Brown and Company
New York   Boston   London

Copyright © 2017 by Doree Shafrir

Little, Brown and Company
Hachette Book Group
1290 Avenue of the Americas, New York, NY 10104
littlebrown.com

First Edition: April 2017

Little, Brown and Company is a division of Hachette Book Group, Inc. The Little, Brown name and logo are trademarks of Hachette Book Group, Inc.

The Hachette Speakers Bureau provides a wide range of authors for speaking events. To find out more, go to hachettespeakersbureau.com or call (866) 376-6591.

ISBN 978-0-316-36038-8
LCCN 2016950681

10 9 8 7 6 5 4 3 2 1

LSC-C

Book design by Marie Mundaca

Emoji by Peter Bernard

Printed in the United States of America

For my grandparents,
who never went online

STARTUP

PROLOGUE

SAVE YOUR GENERATION

THEY CAME FROM all over the city in the predawn hours, a merry band of highly optimized minstrels in purple leggings and shiny headbands and brightly colored sneakers, walking the fifteen minutes from the L train or directing an Uber to the former spice factory in the no-man's-land between Williamsburg and Greenpoint. The neighborhood's normal early-morning crowd—the dog walkers, the construction workers, the marathon trainers—mostly looked upon them with amused curiosity. Nothing fazed them anymore.

Once they got into the club, they either headed straight for the dance floor or descended on the bar, which this morning was not selling alcohol but rather providing free sustenance in the form of granola bars and coconut water and green juice (all sponsored by an on-demand laundry app), which they drank greedily before, or in some cases while, slithering onto the dance floor.

This was the October edition of MorningRave, a monthly gathering devoted to the idea that the best way to start the day was with the excited energy of a clean-living dance party. It was a movement that in a previous generation might have been derided as corny, or Mormon. But this was a different New York. The cynical echo of Generation X had finally been quieted and, along with it, most of the dive bars, rent-stabilized apartments, bands, underground clubs, clothing boutiques, and fashion magazines that used to define the city. In its place had arisen a Promised Land of Duane Reades and Chase ATMs on every corner, luxury doorman buildings, Pilates studios and spin classes, eighteen-dollar rosemary-infused cocktails and seven-dollar cups of single-origin coffee—all of which were there to cater to a new generation of twentysomethings, the data scientists and brand strategists and software engineers and social media managers and product leads and marketing associates and IT coordinators ready to disrupt the world with apps. And today, like every day, they would work until it was dark again, and then they would go to dinner parties or secret cocktail bars or rooftop events, and most of them would end the night watching Netflix on their laptops in bed, perhaps in one of the new high-rises summoned directly from a marketing brochure—Doorman! Swimming pool! Rooftop cabanas! Yoga room! Unparalleled views and *the lifestyle you deserve!* Few of them lived alone, but most of them rarely crossed paths with their roommates. Everyone was just so *busy.*

Wherever they resided—Williamsburg or Bushwick or the Lower East Side or Bed-Stuy or Crown Heights—they embraced their neighborhoods' ready availability of acai bowls and yoga studios. They were all in agreement that adulthood could, and should, be *fun.*

It was truly a new Gilded Age.

At MorningRave, they danced alone and in pairs, with friends and with strangers. They danced on the stage and on the floor. One woman danced with a baby in a carrier attached to her torso. (The baby wore headphones.) A guy in a turquoise headband did a backflip into the crowd and landed on his feet. They cheered when the DJ told them to make some noise. They danced with the passion of people for whom nothing ever really goes wrong.

Twenty-eight-year-old William "Mack" McAllister was among them. Many of the sixty-three employees of his startup, TakeOff, were there too, and as he made his way through the crowd, coconut water in hand, it seemed as though every other person said hi. In New York's bustling innovation community, Mack was one of the anointed, at least if you went by consecutive number of times he'd been named to the TechScene 50 (three), the amount of money in seed funding he'd raised for TakeOff (five million; the industry's news site TechScene had reported it as six million, a figure he had not bothered to correct), his Twitter follower count (23,782), and how many women he had slept with since moving to New York City from his hometown of Dallas six years ago (fifty-one, and there would have been more if not for a three-month period of self-imposed celibacy when he was first launching his company). Indeed, by virtually any metric, Mack McAllister was crushing it, and he saw no reason why he would not continue to do so for the foreseeable future. He held up his phone to take a selfie, making sure to capture the crowd in back of him, and posted it to Instagram with a caption that read: *The best way to start the day: a massive dance party. #MorningRave #MorningRaveNYC.*

There was one person at MorningRave who did not post any selfies to Instagram. She was there to dance, and only to dance. Nor did she say hello to Mack. She knew who he was, but he was not yet aware of her existence. Katya Pasternack was at the party with her boyfriend, Victor, who himself was a founder of a small company called StrollUp. Katya was twenty-four years old, but ever since she was a child, people had said she had an old soul. From what she could tell, this mostly meant that she preferred the company of people older than herself. One of the exceptions was this party, which she loved. Katya weighed ninety-one pounds and had never gone to a gym a day in her life, but she danced at this party as though it were her job. Her actual job was as a reporter for TechScene. She took a break from dancing—Victor was at the bar, getting a green juice—squinted and scanned the crowd. Besides Mack, she recognized no fewer than seventeen startup founders. She took out her phone and noted all of their names, just in case she felt compelled to write something about any of them later.

At exactly 9:00 a.m., the music stopped, and the dancers cheered again. They held their phones up to record this moment, when the thick curtains on the windows of the club would be drawn back, and the crowd would recite, in unison, "Good morning, good morning, *great* morning!" and then a cheer, louder than before, would erupt. They posted this moment on Snapchat and Instagram, on Twitter and Facebook, anywhere that their message—*I was here*—could be loudly, clearly received.

Most of them still clutched their phones a few minutes later as they headed out into the morning. Although their eyes blinked as they adjusted to the sunlight, all of them had their heads down, looking at their phones. They needed to see how many people had liked their Instagrams, if anyone had viewed their Snapchat videos, how many likes and comments—*so jelly!!!!!; omg i can't believe i missed this; i'm here too! where u at*—they'd gotten on Facebook, how many people had retweeted their observation about this being the best party *ever*. Mack noted, with no small degree of satisfaction, that his selfie already had 129 likes. Katya pulled a long-sleeved shirt over her head, kissed Victor good-bye, and started walking toward the L train to go to work.

Neither of them knew it yet, but Katya Pasternack's and Mack McAllister's lives would be intersecting again very soon.

1

DO THE MATH

Two Weeks Later

MACK MCALLISTER EXITED his East Village apartment building wearing a royal-blue gingham-checked button-down shirt tucked into jeans and a navy blazer. He carried a soft brown leather briefcase with two buckles, given to Mack by his father when he graduated from the University of Texas and on which his initials—*WSM*, William Sumner McAllister—were embossed in gold capital letters. His dark brown hair was close-cropped, which highlighted his somewhat ungainly ears. Mack considered his ears his secret weapon in that they made him just *slightly* unattractive, a characteristic that he found made him irresistibly disarming to women.

This morning, Mack had agreed to give a breakfast presentation at Startup Boot Camp, an incubator that gave founders office space and access to venture capitalists and other successful entrepreneurs for one year in exchange for 10 percent of their companies. His Uber, a silver Prius, pulled up right as he put his headphones on and opened the MindSoothe meditation app on his phone. He hit pause as he confirmed his destination, an office building in the financial district, with the driver. Then the opening chimes played, and a soothing female voice said, "Welcome to your meditation session. For the next twenty minutes, you have granted your mind and your body permission to connect with the world of thought and feeling." He closed his eyes. Certainly an Uber in Manhattan at rush hour was not the most conducive atmosphere for meditation, but Mack had made it a goal to try to meditate in the most inhospitable environments. Anyone could meditate in a silent, darkened room, but could you find peace crawling down Broadway? *That* was the mark of true enlightenment. Meditation was relatively new in Mack's life, despite the fact that he had developed a workplace-wellness app. But the practice had become popular in the startup scene as a kind of self-improvement mechanism—supposedly even Zuck was a devotee—and it did seem like people at TakeOff were much more productive ever since he had begun offering guided meditation in the office once a week.

As the car inched along, honking every minute or so, he tried to focus on what the app was telling him—"Continue to bring awareness to the breath." But his mind kept drifting to his meeting with Gramercy Partners next week, where he was going to make a case to the partners that they should lead his next round of funding, his Series A round. He knew it was ambitious, but he was hoping for a valuation of six hundred million dollars, and then, maybe, just maybe, the *next* round of funding would value TakeOff at over one billion. In startup parlance, TakeOff would be a unicorn. Silicon Valley might have already been overrun by unicorns, but here in New York City, they were still a rare and coveted breed.

TakeOff had started as a company that promoted workplace wellness; at any point in the day, you could open the app and tell it what your mood was, and it would immediately give you something to help improve how you were feeling (Mack believed that even if you were in a great mood, you could always feel better). Sometimes it was a cat picture or a funny meme, sometimes it was an instruction to take a walk around the office, sometimes it was a song. Now he and his team were working on developing something even cooler, a new version that would go beyond the workplace and would *anticipate* your mood at any time of day or night, based on your past inputs but also on sentiment analysis from your social media accounts, emails, text messages, and IMs. TakeOff didn't actually *read* your emails, texts, and IMs or store them, of course; it just combed them for keywords and relevant emoji. Like if you were using the sad-face emoji too much or if you had the word *pissed* in your emails or texts more at a certain time of day, the app would take all of that into account and send you a notification when it perceived that you were feeling bad.

Even if TakeOff wasn't a unicorn quite yet, six hundred million dollars would be nothing to sneeze at. Six hundred million dollars would make his remaining 23 percent stake in the company worth approximately one hundred and thirty-eight million dollars. He said that number to himself a few times, just to get used to the sound. One hundred and thirty-eight million dollars. One *hundred* and thirty-eight million dollars. One hundred and thirty-eight. Million. *Dollars.* What would he even do with that much money? Maybe he would hire a personal chef and finally start that gluten-free paleo diet everyone was talking about. Actually, fuck it, if he had a hundred and thirty-eight million dollars, he could afford to buy a private plane and staff it with the personal chef.

"Take a long, slow, deep breath in through your nose." Pause. "And now release that breath out through your mouth. In and out. In and out. Slow your mind down and guide yourself into a new state of awareness." He had learned through meditation that it was important not to think too much about worst possible outcomes, because then that was what you ended up manifesting into existence. Instead, as his Uber picked up speed a bit, he brought himself to that new state of awareness in which he was a multimillionaire and *he* was the one turning down meetings with VCs.

"Sir?" He opened his eyes, startled. They had stopped in front of a glass-and-steel tower. "This the place?"

He hit pause and removed his earbuds. "Yes, sorry about that." He got out of the car quickly and, after handing over his ID at the security desk, took the elevator to the eighth floor.

"Hi," he said to the woman at the reception desk. "I'm here for—"

"I know who you are!" She stood up to shake his hand. He sized her up quickly: She was probably around twenty-two or twenty-three, wearing a floral dress and tights and bright red lipstick. Her light brown hair was in a bob with bangs. Not his type, exactly, but cute. "It's *so* great to meet you, Mack. We're so happy you're here! I'm Gina, I'm the office manager. I'll take you to the conference room! There's breakfast and some drinks all set up."

He followed her back through the open-plan office. It was a large room, packed with desks and computers. Small signs indicated each company's name at its workspace, most of which had three or four desks. People looked up as Mack walked by. Most of them smiled. A few stood up and followed him and Gina to the conference room, where there were already five or six people seated at a long table, including the guy who'd invited him, Peter Fernandez. Peter stood up as Mack came in. "Mack!" He made his way over and shook Mack's hand. "So glad you could be here this morning. Help yourself to a bagel or coffee." Peter was a former venture capitalist who had left the VC world two years ago to start this incubator. So far, seven of the incubator's companies had been bought, netting Peter around twenty million dollars in the process.

Mack poured himself a cup of coffee. "How's everything going?" he asked Peter.

"You know, Mack, everything is going great. We have a killer class right now—I'm just really psyched about the potential everyone brings to the table." He glanced around the room, which had filled up. "You ready to do this?"

Mack nodded. He had prepared his speech the night before, practicing in front of the full-length mirror in his bedroom. "Great. I'll give a short intro and then you can just go into it." Peter cleared his throat. "May I have everyone's attention?" The room quieted down. "I'm very pleased to introduce today's breakfast speaker, the extraordinary Mack McAllister." Everyone applauded. "He's a guy who needs no introduction, really—I'm sure you all have TakeOff on your phones—but I'll give him an intro anyway, just so we can be reminded how incredibly *awesome* this guy is. So Mack got kind of a late start in the startup world—he founded TakeOff at the ripe old age of twenty-five, which should give some of you here hope." Everyone laughed. Peter pointed at a tall guy leaning against the wall in the back of the room. "I'm looking at you, Sunil." Sunil saluted, grinned. "Sunil just turned thirty-two," Peter stage-whispered to Mack. "Anyway. In addition to founding TakeOff, which now has sixty-three employees, Mack's on the board of the New York Startup Series and he also founded Tech for Kids, which teaches children in underserved communities how to code. Oh, and he's run the New York City Marathon three times." Peter mock bowed down to Mack. "Really, dude, is there anything you can't do?"

"I never could master German." The room laughed with him. "Seriously, though, thanks for that intro, Peter. So…show of hands. How many of you, growing up, thought you were one day going to start a company?" Around half of the people in the room shot their hands up. "Wow, impressive. How many of you thought that you would one day work for a startup?" Another smattering of hands. "And how many of you thought that that startup was going to be in New York City?" This time, no hands went up. Mack grinned. "In the past few years, this city has experienced nothing short of a *revolution*. And it's all because of people like you, and you, and you." He pointed at a few random people in the room. "Heck, it's because of all of you! I moved to New York six years ago, and believe me, things were not the way they are now. The city was in a depression. And I don't just mean economically—I mean the whole city was *depressed*. Wall Street had basically imploded. New York was spiraling. Those point-zero-zero-zero-zero-zero-one percenters at the top, they never got rid of their Hamptons houses or their yachts, but a lot of people at their firms lost their jobs. So when things started to change, it wasn't Wall Street leading the way. You know who it was?" He paused for dramatic effect. "It was people like you and me. The tech industry. *We* were the ones taking leases on office space no one wanted. *We* were the ones hiring. And we were the ones trying to build a *community*."

Mack had moved to New York after getting a Facebook message from a college friend he hadn't heard from in a while saying that he was looking for people to work for his startup. A couple years later, the startup failed, but Mack decided to stay. He bounced around a few other startups before finally landing on the idea for TakeOff one day when he was running along the Hudson River, and after three months of all-nighters he'd raised one million dollars.

"Let me ask you something. Do you think Wall Street would have started a game-changer like the New York Startup Series?" He paused for effect. "Here's the answer: They had over a hundred years to do it, and they didn't. We've gotten over two hundred companies funding through the Startup Series. Because *we're* the visionaries in New York now. This is a new city. It's not about who your parents are or what school you went to anymore. It's about who you are and what you do, and what you can do for the greater good." He'd given a version of this speech at least a dozen times, and it never failed to make him emotional. "This means responsibility—great responsibility. But what could be better than giving your life to something greater than yourself?"

The room broke into applause. A couple people whistled. He waited for it to die down and continued. "Of course, there will always be naysayers about the tech industry. That just comes with the territory. There are always going to be the finance guys who think they can keep pretending they still rule the world. Then there are those types on the opposite end of the spectrum—you know, the ones who barely even know what the internet is? Once your companies begin to get off the ground and you start looking for office space, you'll understand this—there are people out there who will raise hell about a relatively small tax break for a tech company to stay in New York and create jobs." He shook his head. What he always wanted to add, but didn't, was how supremely annoyed he was by the entitlement of people who would fight tooth and nail to keep their rent-stabilized apartments even when they had country houses and sent their kids to private school. This was *basically* socialism. Meanwhile, his employees lived off subway stops in Brooklyn he'd never heard of.

"Now, look, I understand that there might come a time—well, let's say, there will *hopefully* come a time—when I'll find Wall Street and its access to capital markets extremely useful." Peter, and a couple others, laughed. "But until then, I will continue to argue that the tech industry is the best thing to happen to New York City since a Dutchman bought this whole dang island." The room erupted into applause.

Something else Mack always left out of his talk was how his dad had built an incredibly successful contracting company from nothing—but he had never forgotten that he'd been turned down by five banks in Dallas for a small-business loan when he was starting out. If he'd had the same access to capital that Mack had had, he'd probably be one of the richest men in Texas by now. But VC firms were built to understand and profit from this new world. So what if they ended up owning a chunk of your company? They knew that it took money to make money. In fact, it was considered a bad sign if your company was profitable too soon; you had to spend the money you were earning to build your business or else your investors would wonder if you were thinking big enough and taking enough risks. That was Startup 101.

Mack's dad still didn't totally understand what Mack did, or what the company did, or even really how VC funding worked or why Mack would take money from someone else and "let them get into your business like that," but he loved to talk about

how entrepreneurship was in the genes, and Mack had overheard his mother on the phone with one of her friends when he
was home for Christmas last year bragging that he was going
to be on the local news in Dallas talking about being a tech-
company founder. What they *really* didn't understand, though,
was why he was single. His younger sister, Hailey, had gotten
married three years ago, when she was twenty-three, to a guy
she'd met at SMU, and everyone at the wedding had seemed
surprised—Hailey's single girlfriends, pleasantly—that Mack
came unattached. He'd ended up hooking up with one of Hailey's sorority sisters *and* her best friend from high school, and he
was pretty sure that neither of them knew about the other and
that Hailey knew about neither of them. He still occasionally
got texts from the high-school friend; he responded if he knew
he was going to be back home for a few days. She was always
up for something fun.

His parents knew he dated around but didn't ask too many
questions. The closest they had come was when he was home
briefly at Christmas; he'd been watching football with his dad
and Hailey's husband, Colton, and when Colton got up to get
a beer from the kitchen, Mack's dad had said, quietly, "Your
mother's worried about you."

Mack's response was to laugh, a little nervously, until he saw
the dead-serious look on his dad's face. "I mean it, son, she's
worried about you. I know things are going well with the company, but she is just worried that...well, she'd just really like
you to meet someone, is all."

Mack had to laugh again to break the tension. If only they
knew..."Dad. Please, she has nothing to worry about. *You* have
nothing to worry about. I do fine." This seemed to do it; his dad
clapped him on the back and said, "Enjoy it while it lasts."

Still, they were old-fashioned in their way. They didn't want to meet any of Mack's girlfriends unless Mack felt like it was serious. And Mack would probably have to bring the girl to Dallas because his parents had yet to set foot in New York. Until very recently, he hadn't been with anyone he'd even remotely considered taking to Texas. But lately, the thing—he hesitated to put a more concrete label on it—he had with his coworker Isabel seemed to be getting more serious. They'd been seeing each other secretly, and nonexclusively, for the past year, neither of them willing to articulate anything that suggested a desire for commitment, but now Mack was starting to think he was "catching feelings," as they used to say in middle school. And he had probably felt this way for a while, if he was being completely honest with himself. Maybe the next time he and Isabel hung out, he would broach it.

He suddenly realized that the applause had died down and people were looking at him expectantly. "Are there any questions?" He took a sip of his coffee. In the back, Sunil raised his hand. "Yes?"

Sunil nodded. "First of all, thank you for coming today— your talk was truly visionary and inspiring. Second, my question has to do with scale and hiring. At what point did you need to add layers of, shall we say, administrative staff? You know, finance, HR, and the like. My company is obviously way too small to start thinking about this, but I've seen a couple of friends get tripped up by it and I was curious how you'd handled it."

"Sure. To be honest, we've been winging that stuff a little bit. Investors don't want to hear about you hiring a head of HR. They want to hear about you hiring engineers. So it's on our radar, sure, but not totally a priority."

"Thanks," Sunil said. He didn't seem totally satisfied with the answer but didn't ask a follow-up.

"Any other questions?"

"Where do you see TakeOff going from here?" This was from a woman sitting near the door. He'd noticed her on his way in—she was a little chubby, with curly blond hair. He'd dated girls like her in high school.

"I was waiting for someone to ask me that question." He smiled at her. Was she blushing? She was blushing. "What was your name?"

"Bella." She smiled back at him. Maybe she was cuter than he had initially thought.

"So, Bella, the goal right now—and by *now*, I mean, let's say, the next nine to twelve months—is to scale as fast as we can. We've got a new product that's launching very soon that I can't say anything more about, but as soon as that launches we're going to be kind of in a new phase. We're going to need probably a dozen new developers ASAP. And then, I mean, we're looking at international expansion, we're looking at a version for teenagers, we're exploring partnerships with some major companies right now...there's a lot happening. It's a very exciting time."

All of this was, of course, totally true, but also hugely exaggerated—but, he told himself, in a "fake it till you make it" kind of way. And it wasn't *completely* faking it—so far, everything he had "faked" he had subsequently "made." So he had no doubt that, even though it would mean everything going 1,000 percent according to plan, he would be hiring a dozen new developers, even if that depended on getting the money from Gramercy and being able to find a dozen developers. And he hadn't exactly *discussed* the viability of international expansion or a teenage version with anyone on his staff, but these were things that certainly *could* happen. The two most important things anyone needed for success were vision and willpower. And he had both. Now he caught Peter's eye, and Peter nodded imperceptibly.

"Okay, everyone, I think that just about does it for today," Peter said. "Let's give Mack another round of applause. And can people email you if they have additional questions?"

"Of course. I'm just Mack at takeoff.com. Thanks, Peter, and everyone, for having me." The group filed out, Peter lagging behind.

"Thanks, man, that was really great." He shook Mack's hand again. "I'll walk you out."

"It's a great space," Mack said as they left the conference room. "Hey, would you mind taking a picture of me?"

"Sure thing."

Mack handed Peter his cell phone and posed so that the entire office was visible behind him. He posted it on Instagram with the caption *Amazing time speaking to the new companies being incubated at Startup Boot Camp!* In the five minutes it took him to ride the elevator down to the lobby, go outside, and find his Uber, 46 of his 16,792 followers had liked it.

2

DRAG CITY

KATYA PASTERNACK HAD been at her job as a reporter at TechScene (motto: "Tech news straight, no chaser") since 8:00 a.m. and now, at 11:30, she realized she had been concentrating so hard that she hadn't even taken a smoke break. "What the fuck," she muttered to herself. No wonder she was starting to get a headache. smoke? she IM'd to Dan Blum. Dan was thirty-nine, with hair that was starting to gray at the temples and the stirrings of a belly under his rotation of plaid J. Crew shirts. He was the site's managing editor, but more important, he was the only other person in the TechScene office who smoked. He didn't respond. She stood up to try to catch his eye and noticed that he was wearing headphones and laughing at something on his phone.

It was probably that YouTube compilation of dog Snapchats that everyone had been tweeting about for the last four minutes. It was true that it was marginally better than most Snapchat compilations—because of the dogs, of course. There was, in particular, a six-second video of a black Labradoodle that looked exactly like Weird Al scarfing down its food while "Eat

It" played, and at the very end, the dog looked up into the camera and howled joyously—perfectly in time with the music—in a way that Katya found almost poignant. dog Snapchat = best Snapchat, she had tweeted, with a GIF of the Labradoodle and a link to the post. It had already gotten seventeen retweets and forty-two likes. There were other species of internet-famous animals, of course—superstar cats like Grumpy Cat, Lil Bub, and Maru, for instance—but dogs ruled when it came to the speed at which their antics spread online.

Stuff always spread through tech-reporter Twitter predictably: First, whoever posted it or found it would tweet it, and then, since everyone followed everyone else in the scene, Katya's TweetDeck would get clogged immediately with the same dumb retweets. The worst were people who manually retweeted the initial tweet and then added some inane comment like *Whoa!* or, worse, *Woah!* Katya had no patience for people who misspelled *whoa* or couldn't figure out the difference between *its* and *it's*. She longed to mute them, but sometimes they were actually important people whose tweets she had to follow, so she kept them all in her main timeline but also put them into a TweetDeck column she had labeled "Grammar Idiots" that she occasionally scrolled through when she wanted to feel superior. She didn't understand what was so hard about speaking English; she was an immigrant and she'd figured it out.

Janelle, her roommate in the Greenpoint railroad apartment where she'd lived since April, always laughed when she complained about stuff like this. "Katya, you gotta let it gooooo," she'd say, and then half the time she'd launch into a deliberately off-key rendition of "Let It Go" from *Frozen,* during which Katya would ostentatiously cover her ears. She'd met Janelle through Janelle's older brother, Trevor, the social media manager at TechScene. Growing up in a deeply Russian part of Brooklyn and living at her dad's while at NYU had left Katya with few friends who weren't still living with their parents and working as makeup artists or cocktail waitresses. Not that there was anything wrong with makeup artists or cocktail waitresses or living with one's parents, but Katya had a different vision for her grown-up New York life, and Janelle—with her job as a marketing manager for an organic beauty company, her podcast (*Say What!?*, which she hosted with her friend Fiona), and her fastidiousness when it came to keeping the apartment clean—fit into it more than her high-school friend Irina, who had suggested the two of them move into an apartment in Bensonhurst owned by one of her boyfriend's sketchy friends.

Katya went over to the desk across from Dan's so she'd be directly in his line of vision and waved her hands until he finally looked up. She pantomimed bringing a cigarette to her lips, and he looked relieved. "Yes!" he said, too loudly. He still had his headphones on. No one around him looked up, though, because they all had them on too.

Katya enjoyed smoking so much that she could imagine quitting only if she essentially became a completely different person. She couldn't imagine under what circumstances that might happen. She had made some small concessions to health in the last couple of years—going from a pack of Camels a day in high school and college to half a pack a day of Camel Lights—but now, smoking was as much a part of her as dyeing her hair platinum blond, wearing a nose ring, being rail thin, and speaking in a faint Russian accent that she could hear in herself only when she was transcribing interviews. And these days in New York City, smoking was an ongoing act of rebellion that she felt jibed so completely with her perceived and real persona that she never wanted to give it up. The smokers she knew—fewer and fewer these days—were, like her, stubbornly attached to this expensive, disgusting, delicious habit. Smokers had always set themselves apart, but now their numbers were so reduced and they were so beleaguered and resigned to their fate that she sometimes felt like they telegraphed secret, desperate messages to one another. She could immediately sense, if not smell, a real smoker nearby. The younger ones, like her, radiated a kind of jittery, nervous energy; she figured that at least half of the smokers she knew who were under twenty-five were probably also pill poppers of some kind. (She, of course, was not.) The older ones, like Dan, radiated a world-weariness she found comforting.

They weren't supposed to smoke right in front of the building, so Katya and Dan moved exactly seven feet to the left and lit up. They smoked for a minute before Dan broke the silence. "You're filing the Connectiv story this afternoon, right?" Katya was putting together a standard TechScene post called "Offices You Wish You Worked At," about Connectiv's new office, after getting an exclusive first look at the space. She was proud of the get; it signaled to the rest of the tech press that she, Katya Pasternack, was *real journalist,* as her father might say. TechScene was still in its relative infancy, launched a year ago by a now-twenty-seven-year-old media app entrepreneur named Rich Watson and a fired BizWorld editor, Deanna Stein, who immediately took what she'd learned at that site—a warp-speed aggregator and producer of business news of varying quality that got hundreds of millions of page views a month, thanks in large part to hundred-slide photo galleries—and applied it, hiring a gaggle of mostly inexperienced but hungry (often literally) reporters like Katya to produce content, and a couple of grown-ups like Dan to (loosely) supervise. As far as Katya knew, Dan was the oldest person in the newsroom.

Katya loved her job, which she demonstrated by working long hours and writing more than any other reporter. But she considered many of her coworkers to have a larger sense of entitlement than was healthy. The things they complained about! Food, mostly. When it came to food, TechScene was just like any other startup: There was way too much of it. Her coworkers grumbled that the snacks at TechScene weren't healthy enough and everyone was gaining weight, or that they were *too* healthy and people felt like they were being shamed into eating baby carrots and plain Greek yogurt. Or the brand of coffee wasn't the right one, or they were always running out of organic almonds, or they should be allowed to order their free dinner at six thirty so that it would arrive by the time they were hungry instead of having to wait till seven, which meant they might not eat until eight. She watched them eat snacks and she watched them eat pizza and she watched them eat huge orders of Thai food and she watched them drink beer after beer after beer, and then she heard them complain that they had gained the TechScene Fifteen. Katya's weight had stayed exactly the same during the ten months she'd worked there. She really cared only that the office fridge was kept stocked with Diet Coke and that there was coffee—*any* kind of coffee. She had also put in a special request with the office manager for Sweet'N Low.

Katya took a long drag and exhaled. "Yeah. I'm still waiting for some numbers from their PR but if I don't get them by tomorrow morning, I'm just gonna post. They're being annoying."

"Shocker," Dan said. She glanced at him as he took another drag of his cigarette. He was old, but it seemed like he still cared about how he looked—he made sure that he didn't come to work in the same plaid shirt twice in a week and he wore tortoiseshell glasses that gave his clean-shaven roundish face a more distinguished air—and even though he wasn't exactly her type (also, he was her boss), she could see how he would have been considered handsome at one point.

He also had strong feelings about the right way to do journalism. He had taught Katya that you should never, ever hold your best stuff, especially anything big or remotely time-sensitive. She operated under the assumption that if she had had an idea or gotten a story or talked to someone important, then someone else had had the same idea, gotten the same story, or talked to the same person. It was a lesson she'd learned quickly, a couple months into the job, when she had proudly relayed to Dan that she was going to be able to break the news that the founder of Calendr had been forced out. She'd gotten the information from her NYU classmate Tom, the founder's assistant, who had also reported that his boss was currently holed up inside his office and refusing to come out, which was made all the more awkward by the fact that his office was glass and in the middle of the room. But Katya had been slow to actually write the story; there were some details—what was he wearing? how had he been given the news?—that she was waiting to hear back from Tom about, and in the meantime, BizWorld published a post, and Dan had told her she was lucky he hadn't mentioned anything to Rich or Deanna about the scoop because they would have flipped out that BizWorld had beaten them. She was determined never to let that happen again.

So even though the Connectiv people had assured her that she was the only reporter they'd let into the building since they'd moved in two weeks ago—according to their head of corporate communications, "The *Times* was *begging* us for the story, but we decided to give it to you," which Katya neither totally believed nor disbelieved—she was still worried she'd get scooped if she waited too long.

"I mean, God forbid some idiot who works there tweets a picture of their new office. Good-bye, scoop! I love Twitter but, man, it really has ruined journalism." This was a familiar rant of Dan's, right up there with how young reporters today didn't know how to pick up a phone and instead got all their information online, how pointless journalism school was, and how many résumés he got each week from people his age who had finally figured out that print was dead and they should jump on this newfangled internet train. He liked to print these résumés out and theatrically rip them in half. He considered it a therapeutic waste of paper.

Katya secretly enjoyed listening to him talk like this; it made her feel like he was putting her in the category of "Not Completely Idiotic Young Person." She also didn't know anyone who worked in print or read anything in print beyond posting a copy of the Sunday *Times* or an image of an actual hardcover book on Instagram so that everyone knew how *intellectual* they were. She barely knew anyone who even read anything on a desktop outside of work. If it wasn't on your phone, it might as well not exist.

"Used to be, all you had to worry about was another site beating you by a few minutes on a story. Now, someone can ruin your scoop without your even having a story up. It's complete madness." Katya nodded as Dan continued. "That's why you see so many half-baked stories out there. People who don't have the whole story, just worried about getting scooped, putting some shell post up there and filling in the blanks later so they can say they were first. It's ridiculous."

Her phone vibrated and she glanced down at it. A Venmo notification that Janelle had paid her for the electric bill, which she'd annotated with several lightbulb emoji.

They took another few puffs in silence. "Actually," he said, and he seemed to be weighing his words carefully. "There's something I need to talk to you about."

"Okay." Hadn't they already been talking? She dropped her cigarette to the ground and stubbed it out with her boot.

Dan looked toward the door of the building as though to make sure no one was listening. He dropped his voice. "Rich and Deanna are going to do an audit."

"What kind of audit?" Katya asked.

"They're going to go through everyone's stories and score them—not based just on traffic, but also on how deeply people read them and their impact. So, like, how long did people spend reading your story, how many times did it get mentioned on Twitter, did it get talked about in other publications, did you go on TV to discuss it...that kind of stuff."

Katya felt an unfamiliar sensation in her head—not panic, exactly, but unease. "But this whole time they were telling us that traffic was the thing that really mattered." As she said this, she realized her voice was almost squeaking. *Embarrassing.*

"Well, yes." He was practically whispering now. "They've always said that traffic was the most important thing, but they also have always said they cared about who was reading and how they were reading. Now they're just going to actually quantify it."

Katya gave him a sidelong glance. "But what are they actually going to *do?*"

Dan sighed. "I don't know; Deanna apparently read some study that said that the only real way to motivate people and get them to do their best work is to always make them a little bit afraid of losing their jobs. Not *too* afraid, but a little bit afraid."

"Wait. *Are* people going to lose their jobs?"

"No." Dan took one last drag of his cigarette and stubbed it out. "I mean, not right *away*. At least, that's what they *say*. But they also said something about how it's good practice to always be getting rid of your bottom twenty-five percent of people."

"That seems harsh." Katya had never been known for her sympathy, but she now felt herself indignant at this sudden change in the rules. This wasn't how things were supposed to go! You had your job and people told you what it would take to succeed at it, and you did that thing and then everything was fine. "Why are you telling me this, anyway?"

"They're going to start doing the audit soon. I haven't gone through your stories yet, and I don't think you're in *danger,* exactly—I mean, your traffic is very high—but I don't know, Katya, we've talked about this, sometimes it can seem like you're doing *only* the quick and easy stories. Like this Connectiv post—I mean, it's great, but is it really going to move the needle?"

"What do you mean, move the needle?" she said. "And I ran it by you last week—why didn't you say anything then?"

He ignored the second part of her question. "Like, is it going to get people talking. Is it going to change the way people think about something. Is it going to be something that people are talking about on Twitter all day. Is it going to—"

"Okay, I get it. It seems like you're really on my case today. Besides, people don't talk about things on Twitter *all* day." She knew she sounded bratty, but this *attack* was coming out of nowhere.

"You know what I mean. I'm just saying, if there was any

time to publish a big story, now would be that time." Dan's phone chimed. He took it out of his pocket, unlocked it, and read his screen. He rolled his eyes. "Worst decision of my life was telling my wife it'd be great if she got a job in the same building." Dan's wife, Sabrina, worked at TakeOff, three floors above TechScene. Katya had seen her only twice and from a distance; both times she seemed to be in a bad mood. Dan was typing something back to her as he spoke. "Unlike her, I actually have *work* to do during the day, I can't just, like, drop everything because the nanny's not feeling well. I don't even know why she's bothering to *ask*."

He read out what he was typing back to her. "'Super... busy...today...can...you...handle.'" He put his phone in his pocket. "Let's go, just in case she comes out while we're here. She's been on my back lately about the smoking." Katya followed him wordlessly inside. Marriage seemed like a real bummer sometimes.

3

JUST BREATHE

SABRINA BLUM WAS TIRED. Their three-year-old, Amelia, had, God knows why, toddled into their room at five thirty a.m., even though she'd been consistently sleeping until six thirty, which was at least tolerable. But this morning she wouldn't stop whining about wanting to watch "toys," which meant the videos on YouTube of people unboxing or unwrapping toys; there was one with a little girl unboxing My Little Ponys and their various accessories that Amelia had watched probably seven hundred times. So even though she and Dan had a rule that Amelia was allowed only an hour of iPad a day, Sabrina got out of bed, retrieved the iPad from the kitchen table, parked Amelia on the couch, and let her watch videos until seven. Then Owen woke up, saw Amelia on the couch with the iPad, and started screaming that it wasn't fair that Amelia got to watch in the morning when Mommy only let him use the iPad in the afternoon after he'd had his snack. Her response was to stand in the living room of their Park Slope floor-through and let Owen scream until he finally just gave up and plopped down next to Amelia and watched with her until it was time to get ready for school. Dan usually got Owen dressed and made sure he had everything he needed in his backpack, and this morning he even poured Owen and Amelia some Cheerios and milk before giving each of them a kiss on the forehead and leaving on the dot of 7:45. "Have a great day, honey!" she said so forced-cheerfully that he jerked around at the front door and glared at her. The kids didn't notice, probably because they had started throwing Cheerios at each other. "Asshole," she muttered under her breath as soon as the door clicked shut.

Sabrina, who was thirty-six, had long ago resigned herself to the idea that marriage was, inevitably, death by a thousand little cuts; the problem was that the cuts—strictly metaphorical, of course—weren't as little as they used to be. They were more like gashes, deep wounds that required triage and left scars, and she and Dan both had become addicted to them.

Once she'd finally dropped Owen and Amelia off—Owen at the elementary school and Amelia at the Montessori preschool she went to in the mornings—she realized that it was actually one of those October days that made everyone forget, for at least twenty-four hours, that living in New York City could be a real slog. The sun was shining, the leaves were starting to turn, the air was crisp. And as much as Park Slope sometimes felt claustrophobic, its familiarity was also comforting. She didn't feel on display in the same way she did when she went into Manhattan, where suddenly her uniform of clogs and jeans and boatneck tees seemed woefully boring. When she got to the F train, she put her headphones on—she wasn't actually listening to anything, but this ensured that no one would talk to her—and closed her eyes. Even though she was surrounded by people, her commute was the only time when she felt blissfully alone.

They finally reached her stop, Twenty-Third Street, and Sabrina got off the train and emerged in front of the Best Buy. At 9:05 in the morning, standing at the corner of Twenty-Third and Sixth, she felt like everyone around her looked like a vaguely younger version of herself. Not that she looked *old*, of course—she credited her Korean genes and her mother's fanaticism about night cream with keeping her skin smooth—but lately she'd been watching the stay-at-home moms in leggings and Warby Parker sunglasses in her neighborhood, the ones who had nannies so they could go to Pilates and have "me" time, with increasing amounts of envy. But she had been one of those moms and hated it. After four years, she had turned into the worst kind of stay-at-home mom, one who thought she was too smart to be a stay-at-home mom *and* secretly judged all other stay-at-home moms for not working. (A couple of years in, her therapist had told her, "But you know you're really only judging yourself, Sabrina." She stopped going to therapy a few weeks later.) When she stayed home, there were days where she completely missed everything that was going on in the world because she was schlepping from playdate to playdate.

In her MFA program, Sabrina had been something of a golden child, winning scholarships and awards. It had not been hard to picture a fabulous literary future for herself. But everything changed after graduation, when Sabrina failed to sell her thesis, a novel about three generations of a wacky but endearing Korean American family living in Princeton, New Jersey, even though one of her professors, who had won a National Book Award, called it *brilliant* and *masterful* and a host of other adjectives that failed to move editors at every major publishing house in New York. (The feedback she got most consistently was that the family didn't seem "realistic," which she took to mean that they didn't think a Korean family could be funny and weird. Of course, exactly zero of the editors who'd read it were even Asian.)

So she'd abandoned fiction to take a string of increasingly grim magazine jobs for which she was both over- (she had a graduate degree!) and underqualified (she had no magazine experience!) and eventually quit altogether, after she had Owen, when the eco-crafting magazine where she'd been working suddenly folded with no notice and she didn't even get her last paycheck. Because Dan still had a job, it had just made sense for them to ride out the still-not-great economy, especially since child care was so expensive, and then she'd had Amelia. She wrote the occasional freelance essay about parenthood, but finally it was all just too much. When she started looking at job listings, Dan had laughed (not nicely) when she asked what a social media manager did, but she began applying for jobs nonetheless.

When she went in for the TakeOff interview, even though she had a pathetic seventy-six followers on Instagram and she didn't even have an active Twitter account, she was able to show them the viral article she'd just written for Scary Mommy—it was one of the bigger parenting sites, but they'd never heard of it—about what she wished she'd known before having a second kid. Maybe it was the article, maybe it was some kind of sincere yet misguided attempt at affirmative action for older people, but she was hired.

Sabrina was an Engagement Ninja—when she first applied, she'd thought this was a euphemism, not an actual job title—at TakeOff, whose offices were in a lofty Flatiron District building that a million years ago had been a garment factory and now housed, at any one time, approximately seventeen startups.

They were mostly tech-related, but there was a smattering of other companies, like the bespoke-baby-clothing designer on the second floor. (She'd wandered in one day, thinking about maybe having something made for Amelia's third birthday party, and had to pretend to be unfazed when the woman at the desk told her that their dresses started at two hundred and fifty dollars.) The entire building was run by ShareWork, a company that leased empty buildings around the city and then subdivided them into cool work spaces. Every office came with a customizable "employee-perks" package; standard was an iced-coffee kegerator, a Ping-Pong table, weekly chair massages, and building-wide lunchtime yoga classes in one of the shared conference rooms. When Sabrina had worked for the eco-crafting magazine, the break room was essentially a closet with a microwave, a dorm-size fridge, and a coffeemaker that you had to bring in your own coffee to use. At TakeOff, the employees had successfully rallied to get Stumptown back after the office manager had, out of nowhere, tried switching them over to Starbucks. After Stumptown returned, there had been an hour-long celebratory coffee break in the canteen, where a hired barista made espresso drinks for everyone.

The office itself was a big room where everyone sat at long tables. There were huge windows on the south side that made everything very bright much of the time. The other three sides were lined by several meeting rooms, a canteen, and a lounge with couches; on the walls were prints with cheeky inspirational sayings like I'M NOT HERE TO BE AVERAGE, I'M HERE TO BE AWESOME and DO EPIC SHIT. The only actual office was a glass-walled room in the corner with a comfy velvet sofa; it belonged to TakeOff's founder and CEO, Mack McAllister.

Sabrina made her way to her workstation. She sat next to

an intern on one side and her boss, Isabel, on the other. At the eco-crafting magazine, they'd been in cubicles, and Sabrina had initially found the level of closeness in the TakeOff office oppressive—and she still hated the very word *workstation,* which always made her think of an assembly line. Forget about private phone calls; you could barely send private emails! But now she was used to it, and besides, hardly anyone ever made phone calls here. All of the people at the level above Sabrina were called Heroes—there was an Engineering Hero, a Product Hero, a Sales Hero, and a Biz Dev Hero. Isabel was twenty-six, exactly ten years younger than Sabrina, but she had been at TakeOff for two and a half years, almost as long as the company had been around; she had started as Mack's assistant and been promoted rapidly.

Neither Isabel nor the intern, who came in three days a week, was there yet. Sabrina got to work before almost anyone else so that she could leave at five, which was practically midafternoon for most people in the office, but that had been a condition of her hiring that she had insisted on: she needed to be home before six so that she could let the nanny leave and eat dinner with her kids. Dan, who worked three floors down from her, had asked for no such concessions and usually didn't walk in the door before seven or eight.

Sabrina put down her still-unfinished coffee and her bag, took off her jacket, and woke up her computer. She sat and closed her eyes and breathed deeply. She'd been skeptical when Mack brought in the meditation guru, a woman named Carly with impossibly long and shiny dark brown hair parted in the middle who was bicoastal and alluded to her celebrity clientele, but Sabrina had actually found some of Carly's techniques useful, like just closing your eyes and breathing. "A little moment

35

for your soul to heal," Carly liked to say in her soothing voice. Sometimes that was all it took.

When she opened her eyes, there was TweetDeck on her screen, already scrolling automatically and furiously. Sabrina's job was to tweet from the TakeOff account and also to monitor anything being said about the TakeOff app on Twitter. She needed to start off the day with an innocuous tweet to the TakeOff account's 101,712 followers. She drummed her fingers on her desk and finally came up with

tfw u don't wanna get out of bed & then u see it's a perfect fall day

Beneath the tweet she put an animated GIF of a sloth poking its head out from behind a tree. Before she'd started this job, she'd barely known what LOL meant. Now she was entirely conversant in the lingua franca of people a decade younger than she was, which as far as she could tell consisted mostly of emoji, GIFs, and acronyms. When she was sure no one was walking by, she would sneak onto Urban Dictionary to look up new ones; it had taken her a week to figure out that tfw meant "that feel when" and not "too fucking weird," which, to be honest (or tbh, as her coworkers would say), made a lot more sense. (She didn't totally understand why tfw wasn't an abbreviation for the grammatically correct "that *feeling* when," but she kept that to herself.) Now and then, one of the acronyms would slip into her texts with her age-appropriate friends, and in response she would usually get back: ????? Dan was particularly scornful whenever she used what he called alphabet soup. "Just speak grown-up English," he'd said on more than one occasion. "It doesn't make you *cool*. It makes you seem like one of those people who just read an article about how to communicate with your teenagers using the new hip slang."

The TakeOff tweets didn't have to be specifically related to the app; in fact, Isabel was emphatic that the way to grow the account was through *not* always tweeting about the app. "Make it have a *personality*," she would say, which at first seemed a little ridiculous—*It's an app*—but over time, Sabrina came to understand what she meant. No one wanted to engage with a brand unless it felt fun; like a cool, sympathetic, wise friend. And a friend who always had a positive message. It definitely wasn't rocket science, but Sabrina had to admit that it had been oddly satisfying that on a day she'd been sick and the intern had taken over the account, they had lost 243 followers. On the days she tweeted, they always gained at least a hundred.

By the time Isabel showed up, at ten thirty, Sabrina had retweeted seventeen responses to her weather tweet and was screenshotting them to put on the TakeOff Tumblr. "Hey," she said as Isabel took off a plaid wool cape and put it casually on the back of her chair.

"Heyyyyy," Isabel said, smiling. "You will *not* believe what I got into last night."

"What did you get into," Sabrina said, still staring at TweetDeck.

Isabel was still smiling. "You know that guy Andrew Shepard?" Sabrina tried to remember whether Isabel had ever mentioned an Andrew. After concentrating on work all day and then having to deal with her kids, she had very little brain space left for anyone whose name was preceded by *that guy*.

"Um…maybe? Is he the…" She was stalling.

"He's one of the co-founders of Magic Bean," she said. Isabel looked at Sabrina expectantly. Sabrina had zero clue what

Magic Bean was but gave Isabel a noncommittal murmur of approval. "So last night—I mean, you know, I was like completely wiped after work yesterday; I had even decided I was going to skip yoga." Sabrina nodded. Last night she had rushed home to find Owen, who was five, screaming at the nanny that he wanted to watch another episode of *Peppa Pig* on the iPad and Amelia hiding under her bed, and then neither of them had wanted to eat the whole-wheat spaghetti with turkey meatballs that she'd made, so she ended up just serving them chicken nuggets. Organic, $8.99-a-package nuggets from vegetarian, grain-fed, free-range chickens, but still. "I just wanted to go home and *crash*. And then like *literally* the minute I get downstairs I get a text from Meredith, who works in Community at Magic Bean, and she's like, Isabel, you *have* to come out to Flatiron Social, *everyone* is here, and I'm like, Meredith, I am *beat,* I need to just go home, and she Snapchats me a pic of Andrew at the bar, and she had written on it 'Hey, girl,' and I'm like, well, this is interesting, because she *knows* I think Andrew is so cute."

Sabrina half listened as Isabel described telling Meredith that she'd be right over and that she and Andrew had ended up talking for hours just about, like, life. Isabel mostly amused her, though it was getting increasingly hard for Sabrina to even remember what it was like to be twenty-six and meet up with a guy you had a crush on. Obviously Snapchat hadn't existed when Sabrina was twenty-six. Facebook had barely existed! People were just starting to really use text messages! It was only ten years ago, but it felt like a completely different world. She and Dan had met when she was twenty-five and in grad school—she was getting her MFA and he was a friend of her friend Natalie, and the fact that he had a job in journalism seemed hopelessly exciting. Romantic, almost. She wished she could go back and tell her twenty-five-year-old self that there was nothing special about journalists and to say yes to the cute guy from the business school who had asked her out at least three times. She'd looked him up on Facebook recently and learned that he was a managing director at Goldman Sachs and had three children and a wife who looked like she spent a lot of time at Pilates. She briefly considered messaging him, just to say hi, but chickened out.

Sabrina was also fixated on a seemingly minor detail of Isabel's story, but one that—for someone whose formative years had been spent watching *Sex and the City* and absorbing the lessons of *He's Just Not That Into You* and *The Rules*—was particularly mind-blowing to her. When she'd been single—and even now, when she talked to friends her age who were still single—everyone seemed to have a firm grasp on the Right Way to Deal with Men in New York City, a world in which women never initiated *anything,* and straight men held every single ounce of the power, mostly because of the simple math that there were fewer of them. The idea of *just up and going to the bar to go after a crush* seemed completely foreign. Even though Dan could be a real dick sometimes, Sabrina nonetheless felt grateful that she had him. The thought of being single at thirty-six was too much. Even Natalie—gorgeous, brilliant Natalie, who was the author of a series of wildly successful *Hunger Games* meets *Gossip Girl* YA books about a clique of girls at a postapocalyptic prep school who have to simultaneously fight for popularity and for the survival of the planet—hadn't been in a relationship in three years. Maybe it was a generational thing? Isabel just seemed possessed of a self-confidence that Sabrina had never had. True, Isabel was very pretty, with long blond hair and impossibly clear skin and a seemingly year-round tan. But *still*.

"So now what?" Sabrina asked.

"He's hosting the New York Startup Series tomorrow night and I think we'll grab drinks after." Isabel grinned. "So...what do you think?" She shoved her phone in Sabrina's face. An unremarkably handsome guy on a ski slope stared back at her.

"Cute," Sabrina said. Isabel had, on more than one occasion, told Sabrina how great it was to have someone older and wiser in the office, a "compliment" that Sabrina accepted with a forced smile.

Just then, her phone vibrated with a text, and the notification on the screen said it was from Willa, the Pratt student from Australia she'd hired to pick Amelia up from Slope Montessori and Owen from kindergarten every afternoon. "Sorry, one sec, it's my nanny texting me." She unlocked the screen and read: hey S! Sorry for short notice but i'm feeling really crap today and think it's probs better for me to stay home. :(Don't want to get the kiddos sick! xo

"Oh, for fuck's sake," Sabrina said under her breath. When had Willa started calling her S and signing her texts *xo*? Was there *any* recognition that Sabrina was, in fact, her employer?

"What's up?"

"My nanny is sick."

"Oh, that sucks," Isabel said in the mildly sympathetic tone of someone for whom this was a recognizably bad yet wholly foreign problem.

"And we have that metrics meeting this afternoon, don't we. Fuck! Sorry." Isabel was looking at her with vague concern. "Maybe Dan can pick them up." She texted Dan: Hey, Willa is sick and I have imp mtg this afternoon—any chance you can pick A & O up and wfh the rest of the day? To Isabel, she said, "Kids make life complicated."

Isabel nodded. "I totally, *totally* get it," she said.

Dan texted back: Super busy today—can you handle?

Sabrina put her head in her hands. "Fuck!" she said, louder than she'd meant to. Isabel looked alarmed. "Sorry. I hate to do this but I'm going to have to leave in an hour or so—is there any way we could push that meeting to tomorrow? Or could I call in?"

Isabel scrunched up her face. "Hmm. I don't know?" Isabel glanced at her computer screen and made another annoyed face. She typed something on her keyboard. "Mack wants me to come by. Listen, do what you have to do, okay?" Isabel got up.

Sabrina sighed and texted Dan back: Not really, but I guess I have no choice. She waited a few minutes. He didn't respond.

4

DOWN THE RUNWAY

He needed to talk to Isabel. He clicked over to Slack, the chat client that everyone at TakeOff used to communicate with one another all day.

> Mack: do you have a second
> Isabel: what's up
> Mack: no I mean, can you come by my office
> Isabel: k

Mack shut his office door behind her, even though the interior was still visible to everyone. At least they wouldn't be able to hear what he was saying. There was a look on Isabel's face that he couldn't quite parse. It wasn't exactly confusion, but—impatience? No. He had to be imagining that.

"So what's up?" she asked. Her expression said *Can you hurry up because I'm in the middle of something really important.*

Okay. He wasn't imagining it.

The first year she'd worked for him, he'd kept her scrupulously off-limits. Isabel was one of those women who had never *not* been pretty, whose blond hair was always perfectly tousled, whose legs were long and taut from years of playing field hockey and now looked amazing in heels. And she exuded the kind of confidence you have only when you can wear an oversize sack dress to work ("fashion") and *still* look hot. In that year, every time he caught himself looking a little too long at her, he reminded himself that she was not only too young but also his assistant, which in and of itself meant there were a thousand reasons why it was a bad idea. Besides, he was seeing other people, most of whom were more on his level (among them a swimsuit model with a PhD in molecular biology and a former Miss America finalist who had gone to Yale and then started a nonprofit that taught entrepreneurship to kids in the Bronx).

But then one night, she'd stayed late to help him work on a presentation he had the next day, and she smelled really good, and she smiled at him in a way that made him think, *Oh, okay,* and before he knew it they were hooking up right there in his office. After that it just kind of continued in secret. They had never referred to themselves as boyfriend and girlfriend; they'd never even had any kind of a define-the-relationship talk. No one at work knew. Mack continued to see other people and he assumed Isabel did too, though he preferred not to think about it. Lately, though, Mack had started allowing himself to fantasize about what life might be like with Isabel in it, like for real, like Sunday-brunch-and-weekends-away-and-cooking-dinner-together for real. No more sneaking around, no more having to keep a Tinder profile up and go on halfhearted dates and have halfhearted sex with randos just so he could tell himself that he didn't *really* like her.

He realized they had been silent for at least a minute when she finally said, "So you wanted to talk about September numbers?"

He cleared his throat. "Yeah. Also...I'm finishing up my presentation for Gramercy today, and I was wondering if you might be able to...help me." He smiled in a way that he hoped seemed flirtatious.

The thing was, he really *did* need her help with the Gramercy presentation. Because last night, when he couldn't fall asleep, a troubling, persistent thought had entered his mind: Was there *any* possibility that he wouldn't get the money? The company was in the tiniest—really, the *tiniest*—danger of running out of cash in the near future. As in, the next-three-months near future. Five million dollars in venture funding just didn't go as far as it used to, especially when you were trying to launch a revolutionary new product and your investors were constantly on your ass. The new version of the famous *Glengarry Glen Ross* line "Always be closing" was "Always be scaling," but the problem with that slogan was that Mack still hadn't quite figured out how to constantly be scaling when the company was bringing in very little actual revenue. Bigger, faster; the more disruptive, the better. They were just weeks away from launching TakeOff 2.0, which was going to change the entire self-help field, he was sure of it, but in the meantime—somehow—the company was down to its last million. *Barely* one month of runway. The company could survive on lines of credit and called-in favors for a little while, true. But not *that* long a while.

The scariest thing was that he hadn't even realized how quickly the money was disappearing. But there were hiring costs, and salaries, and rent, and computers, and a launch party.

There was the team of cognitive psychologists they'd hired to consult on the app, engineers who needed huge signing bonuses because it was *impossible* to hire them in New York (all the really good ones were in the Bay Area). There was the design consultant who told him which desks to buy and where to put them. There were snacks and lunches and happy hours. There were all the things that came up every single day that he never could have anticipated. And now so much of the money was just...gone.

"Oh." Isabel seemed to be debating what to say. "I'm sorry, I don't mean to be rude, but I just got here and I have, like, a ton of stuff I need to take care of before the meeting at two, and Sabrina just told me she has to leave to pick up her kids because her nanny's sick or something." She sighed. "Can we talk later? I honestly don't think I'll have time to help you today."

He hoped his disappointment didn't show on his face. "Yeah. Sure. I'll text you." What he really wanted to say was *What the fuck is up with you?* Usually they texted constantly. At first their texts had been relatively mundane stuff like sup ;) that quickly turned into did anyone tell u that u look amazing today and can't wait to see u later, and then one day, when he was in a meeting with a potential client, Isabel Snapchatted him a topless selfie that she'd clearly taken in the office bathroom, and as he looked at his phone under the table he felt himself getting hard. From then on they traded nudes on Snapchat several times a week. He'd thought it might be distracting, but it actually broke up the day. But lately Isabel seemed to be taking longer and longer to respond to his texts—even when he could clearly see her sitting ten yards away from him. He'd been preoccupied by all of the money-raising stuff, but now that he thought about it, something *was* up. "Is everything okay?"

"Hm? Yeah. I'll see you later." She slipped out of his office.

As he watched her walk to her desk, he thought back to the last time they'd had sex, two weeks ago. Or was it three? In any case, it had happened the way it usually did; he was working late, and he'd sent her a selfie on Snapchat and written where u at on it. A minute later she'd responded, finishing up dinner, and then he asked her to meet him at his apartment, and she'd agreed. She'd stayed the night, which was unusual, and he had a moment in the early morning when he woke up and saw her lying next to him and was overcome by the urge to make her breakfast—although, given that he had no food in the house, it would have to be breakfast sandwiches brought to them by a Postmate. She'd stirred just as he'd reached for his phone to open the Postmates app, and then she'd groped around for her phone and said, "Oh, fuck, I didn't mean to sleep this long," and she'd leaped out of bed and pulled on her clothes and said, "Gotta run home, see you at work," and then she was gone.

And now he was kicking himself for being so fucking stupid about not locking it down. What had he been thinking? Isabel was *special*. Pretty, fashionable, ambitious girls in New York weren't hard to find, but Isabel was so much more; in private, she was charmingly silly and always surprising—she once showed up at his apartment wearing a sweatshirt and when she took it off she had on a T-shirt that said I ♥ FARTS. She'd worn it, she said, because she knew he would think it was hilarious, and it was, but partly because you'd never expect a girl like Isabel to be wearing a T-shirt like that.

There had been a couple of times in the beginning when they'd actually had sex in the office, which was, of course, incredibly risky but also incredibly hot. He'd pulled the couch away from the wall and they'd hidden behind it without even getting completely naked; he just pulled down her panties, and by then his dick was so hard that it probably could've made its way out on its own, and she was lying on the ground practically ripping his pants off. Both times he'd just plowed into her without a condom and she hadn't protested; she'd mentioned offhandedly one day that she was on the pill and didn't say anything when he didn't put one on. Of course he pulled out, but sex without condoms with a hot girl *in your office* was basically every guy's fantasy. Very few people knew about his trysts with Isabel, and he was careful that it never got around to anyone at work, but sometimes he just wanted to talk about it *so badly*. There was so little these days that was actually secret, and even though in a way that made it hotter—much hotter—it also made it seem less real.

He peered out into the office. Most people were at their desks, headphones on, staring at their two monitors. He felt a momentary swell of pride: *I built this,* he thought. *All these people are here because of me.* Then a thought occurred to him: Forget about sex; when was the last time Isabel had even texted him a nude? There wasn't really any way to check on Snapchat because the photos self-destructed after a few seconds, and he was always careful not to screenshot them because then Isabel would get a notification that he had. But . . . hmm. He left his office and walked to the bathroom, being careful not to look over to Isabel's work area, and locked himself in a stall. All he had to do was think about the last time they had fucked to get hard. He pulled out his phone, opened Snapchat, and took a picture. He was about to send it to her when he decided to write on it using the app's pencil tool. *We miss u,* he scrawled in red, and sent it off.

5

THREE'S A CROWD

WHEN KATYA GOT to work the next morning and wiggled her wireless mouse to wake up her computer, her TweetDeck—which she always had open on her second monitor—was scrolling furiously. *The TweetDeck never stops,* she thought to herself. There was an AM news radio station in New York called 1010 WINS that Katya's dad and stepmom always listened to in the car because it had traffic and weather on the ones. Katya had told them a million times that Waze was much better for traffic, but her dad's car didn't have Bluetooth and he found it distracting to have to keep looking at his phone all the time. One of 1010 WINS' taglines was "The news watch never stops," and Katya had updated the slogan in her head. And what the hell was a *news watch* anyway?

She clicked on the browser tab that had the post about Connectiv's offices that she had been working on. Did she really need to wait for their publicist to get back to her? She clicked over to Slack. The office was mostly empty, but Dan was already at his desk.

Katya: yo
Dan: hiya. long time no chat
Katya: ha. so I think we should go ahead and pub that Connectiv post, i can just fill in the other stuff when they get back to me
Dan: cool. anything you want me to look at?
Katya: nah. i think it's pretty straightforward.
Dan: k sounds good

Katya looked over her post one more time and then hit publish. As soon as it went up on the site, she tweeted it, then she pinged Trevor so he could tweet it from @TechScene and post it on TechScene's Facebook page. np, he wrote back. tweeting now and will schedule for FB in a couple hours. Katya set a calendar reminder to tweet it again in two hours. Now began the briefly exhilarating period after a story was published when she noted with satisfaction how many people—particularly other tech reporters—had tweeted the story. The need for approval from Twitter users was something that her younger self probably would have sneered at, but now she saw it as the cost of doing business. It was fine to get likes, but what she really wanted was either a retweet or, even better, a completely original tweet commending her for a job well done, preferably one from someone in the tech world whose work she respected and who, ideally, had hundreds of thousands of followers. If the only people who liked the tweet were "eggs"—people whose Twitter presence was so lame that they hadn't even bothered uploading avatars, or spambots, or both—she sometimes deleted the tweet.

Just as she'd hit publish, her phone had vibrated, and she had ignored it. Now she looked to see who it was: her

boyfriend, Victor. All the text said was sup. He never used
to check in with her like this, but now that Victor was out
of a job, he was bored and she got *way* too many texts
from him all day. He was out of a job because his company, StrollUp—"like Uber for strollers," she'd heard him say
approximately five thousand times—had gone out of business last week. Like most company failures, it had happened
slowly and then all at once. A few months after Katya and
Victor met, StrollUp was part of a cover story in *New York*
magazine about the city's hottest startups; it included the
company's origin: how Victor's business partner, roommate,
and best friend, Nilay Shah, had heard a mom pushing a double stroller complaining about how hard it was to schlep it
everywhere in the city, how her building wouldn't let her park
it in the lobby, how frustrating it was to fold it up to put it in
the back of a cab, and he'd had an idea, which he'd eagerly
relayed to Victor that night, that the two of them should start
a strollers-on-demand company. (Left out of the story they
told publicly was the fact that Nilay was eavesdropping because he thought the mom was really hot.) At the time of the
New York magazine piece, it seemed like things were going
well. At least, there was a warehouse somewhere in Long Island City with five hundred Uppababys that were supposed
to be their beta testers, they had just gotten seven hundred
and fifty thousand dollars in angel funding (half of which was
from Nilay's parents), and they had six employees in an incubator in the financial district. Then one night a few weeks ago
Victor had mentioned almost too casually that he and Nilay
had had dinner with one of their investors recently—he was
vague as to the exact timing—and it hadn't gone so well.

And now Victor was staying with her because he'd gotten

in a fight with Nilay over this very dinner because Nilay had gotten drunk and, when the conversation had meandered to discussing other startups in New York, had referred to a startup founded by one of the investor's best friends as "a seriously dumb idea," even as Victor was trying to tell him with his eyes from across the table to *shut the fuck up.* Nilay clumsily apologized over email the next day, but the investor never responded. Finally they got a call from the investor's assistant, who informed them that the investor was no longer interested in continuing the relationship, that he wished them the best of luck, and that they should cease contact immediately. And then the rest of the meetings they had lined up with VCs about their next round of funding were mysteriously canceled, and then suddenly they realized they wouldn't be getting any more funding at all, and they had to sell the warehouse full of strollers to a guy with a knockoff Babies R Us store in Bensonhurst called We R Babies who took everything away in a U-Haul.

But if she had to listen to Victor rant about Nilay one more time, she was going to tell him to find somewhere else to stay; Janelle had already not so subtly begun to hint that it was high time for Victor to either go back to his apartment or start paying rent. And preferably the former, because Janelle never would have agreed to move in with a couple.

The thing with the dinner and the investors—it *could* have all just been a coincidence. Even Victor didn't deny that StrollUp had been struggling, and they had started getting loads of contradictory advice about what to do. One of their advisers was pushing them to pivot to become a marketplace for secondhand baby equipment. Another wanted them to expand from strollers into other forms of transportation, like skateboards and bikes.

Katya was pretty sure that their indecision over how to fix the business was probably what doomed them, but Victor was convinced it was the dinner with the investor, and he held Nilay almost entirely responsible.

A Slack notification from Dan came up in the corner of her screen.

Dan: so let's talk today about what's on tap

Katya: ok. I have a couple stories on the lineup for next week

Dan: yeah I know. but we need to get you on something bigger

Katya: i know. i'm working on it

Dan: ok

Katya: what r u worried abt

Dan: the fact that you say "r u" instead of "are you" ;)

Katya: :-0

Katya: seriously tho is there something YOU ARE worried abt

Dan: thank u for using proper English

Katya: ok now ur just fucking w me

Dan: true story

Katya: is there something ur really worried abt or can I get back to work

Dan: no I'm not worried.

Dan: btw...you're the only person in the newsroom i'm giving advance warning about the thing we discussed yesterday

Katya: ok. i'm on it.

Dan: that's what I like to hear. and of course I'm around if you want to bounce any ideas off me. just think BIG.

She needed a smoke, and she needed it alone. She got up from her desk and, without making eye contact with Dan, slipped out to the street. The whole situation with Victor and his company put Katya in an awkward spot. A potentially huge story, filled with conflict and intrigue, and she couldn't write about it because Victor was her boyfriend and it would be the most massive conflict of interest, plus it would probably make him break up with her immediately. She scrolled rapidly through Twitter as she smoked, absorbing information and yet not totally processing it. There was one tweet, however, that caught her eye, from an account called @invisibletechman. She didn't follow the account, but it had been retweeted into her timeline by a Mashable reporter she followed. The tweet said: News flash to all startup bros: actually, we can hear you. Your silence speaks volumes. What did *that* mean? Katya wondered. She clicked through to @invisibletechman's profile. The profile picture was a black-and-white photo of a black man she didn't recognize, and the bio said: *Tryna make a dollar out of some 15-cent stock options. (For my white friends: That's Stokely Carmichael in the pic.) invisibletechman@gmail.com.* Katya googled Stokely Carmichael; her knowledge of the civil rights movement and the Black Panthers was limited to Martin Luther King Jr. and a vague idea about why Malcolm X was important.

Invisiblet Tech Man's account seemed to have started within the past few weeks, and most of his (or, possibly, her) tweets were about what it was like to be black in startup culture. Things like *Shit white founders say: "Stay humble." Nah, man, I'm good* and *Poll: how many POC work at your tech company? (1) <5 (2) #1 is the only possible answer.* He had around two thousand followers—respectable, but nothing mind-blowing. Clearly he (or she) was still trying to make a name for him- (or her-) self. She took a screen grab of the account and texted it to Janelle: you know anything about this? Janelle usually knew about anything on Black Twitter at least a week before Katya did.

Janelle texted back right away: Yeah everyone's talking about it & trying to figure out who it is...not sure if it's someone in SF or NY or even if they actually even work in tech. *Interesting,* Katya thought. She followed the account. You never knew where a story might come from; sometimes Katya got tips from the most random places. And if no one had written about @invisibletechman yet, maybe she could be the first. That might be something Dan would think would "move the needle."

That night, she got home at nine and found Victor sitting on the couch watching *South Park* on his laptop and eating microwave popcorn. "Hi," she said, plopping down on the couch next to him. "Is Janelle here?" He turned and gave her a kiss. "Hi," he said. "Nope. Haven't seen her all day." *Phew,* Katya thought. One less time Janelle would be annoyed about Victor being in the apartment when Katya wasn't there.

"So what have you been doing all day?" She tried to keep her voice neutral.

"You're looking at it." They were silent for a few moments. *South Park* blared from his computer. She found the characters' voices especially irritating.

"Mm-kay," she said. "Well...I'm going to do a little work out here. Can you put headphones on?"

"I don't know where they are. I'll just watch in there." He gestured toward the bedroom as he hoisted himself off the couch, leaving crumbs of popcorn in his wake. He was still wearing the sweatpants and T-shirt he'd had on when she'd left for work thirteen hours ago.

"Hey," she said just as he reached her bedroom. "What's going on with Nilay? I mean...have you guys made up yet?"

Victor rolled his eyes. "We're done. That's what's going on with him."

"Okay," Katya said. Was she going to have to spell *everything* out for him? "It's just that...you know, you've been staying here for a while."

Victor bristled visibly. "I didn't realize I was such an *imposition*. You *know* that if you were in the same situation I wouldn't even *think* about saying something like that to you. Are you seriously telling me I have to leave and go back to the apartment where the guy who totally screwed me over lives? Because if that's what you're telling me..."

She was starting to regret even bringing up Nilay. "I mean..." She tried to choose her words carefully. "Sorry if this is, like, awkward, but are you sure it was the dinner? I mean...are you sure that StrollUp was going to, you know, succeed?"

Victor glared at her. "What the fuck is that supposed to mean? You know we were close to getting that funding and then he just had to get wasted and run his fucking mouth. And really the worst part of it is he won't even admit that that's what happened. *He* thinks that we didn't pivot fast enough. We were pivoting so fast that I almost got whiplash." He shook his head. "It's *crazy* to think that what he did at that dinner had nothing to do with it. You know that and I know that." He went into her bedroom and slammed the door.

Well, then, she thought, and once again rued the fact that she couldn't write about it for TechScene. It had all the elements of a good story: a hot startup crashes and burns, co-founders not speaking. There was always the possibility that she could pass along the information to someone else, but she quickly dismissed that thought; she was ambitious, not psychotic, and besides, Victor would definitely know that she had been the one to tip off her coworkers. And if she was being really honest with herself, she didn't want to give a scoop to someone else at work—especially not now.

She and Victor had met in the line for a Vietnamese taco truck in Austin, Texas, at South by Southwest, the tech industry's five-day Super Bowl, prom, Oscars, and Coachella all wrapped into one, with breakfast tacos. By day, there were hundreds of panels inside the Austin Convention Center with titles like "Maximizing Mobile: The Next Frontier" and "Picturing the Future of Wearable Tech"; by night, the city's bars and restaurants—really, any open space where alcohol could be served—were overrun by the conference-goers, mostly men, who spent a maximum of fifteen minutes at each party before heading off to the next. The most exclusive parties used an elaborate system of online RSVPs, wristbands, and secret locations, and yet the lines to get in still snaked their way around the block of wherever they were held, everyone desperately texting the person he knew inside, who inevitably didn't have cell service.

Katya was doing a post on, among other things, the most popular food at South By (calling it by its full name was a sure sign you were a newbie) and was taking a picture of the menu with her phone so she could refer to it later when she overheard the conversation of the two guys behind her. "Tonight there's the Google Hangouts hangout, the Foodbox happy hour, the Spotify secret show, the BitForce party...am I forgetting anything?"

The TechScene party, Katya thought to herself. But she didn't even have to turn around to know that she didn't want to tell these guys about her company's party. They were clearly just your standard-issue startup bro dorks, the type who would obediently tweet from each party with the correct hashtag (#foodboxhappyhour, #bitforcesxsw, and so on) and get way too excited when they saw them show up on the real-time projection of everyone's tweets on the wall. This was Katya's first South By, but even before setting foot in Austin, she had already internalized a lot of the (exaggerated, she suspected) cynicism verging on outright disdain that so many people in the tech scene, particularly tech journalists, had for it. It was not cool to be a member of the media and be excited, in any way, by South By. The reasons were generally some combination of: it was the same damn story every year, no one besides the same two hundred and fifty people cared, there was no new way to cover things, there were too many journalists chasing too few stories about inherently boring startup people, and you got a distorted sense of what would excite real people in the real world because *every single thing* excited people in tech.

Maybe their conversation was something she could include in an "Overheard at SXSW" post? She casually opened the Notes app on her phone and started jotting down what they were saying just as one of them—she hadn't really taken a good look at their faces, but there was one who seemed to be more concerned about where they would be spending the evening than the other—was concluding that part of the problem was that the Google Hangouts hangout was a couple miles away from the Foodbox happy hour, but they wanted to hit both because they wanted to meet people at Google and there was a greater chance that the Foodbox party would have food, and it was at that point that Katya decided that this conversation was in fact too inane to record for posterity and turned around and said, as fake-sweetly as she could, "I'm sorry that you have to rely on free party food to survive. I didn't realize things were so bad out there." One of the two—the Indian guy, who she now deduced had been doing most of the talking—looked stunned, but the other one burst out laughing. "Yo, this girl is the realest person in this whole city!" Then he had stage-whispered to her: "You should see us at a buffet." Katya, who tended to be suspicious of most people's motives but especially men's, was unexpectedly charmed, and when he suggested that the three of them eat their *banh* tacos together, she agreed. By the end of the night, they had lost Nilay and were kissing in the back of a pedicab—which seemed to be the best way to get around Austin, at least until the driver turned to them with a flourish at the end of the ride and announced that their two-mile trip would be thirty dollars.

And now, seven months later, those tacos and that pedicab seemed like they had happened a million years ago.

After a few minutes, she went into the darkened bedroom and found Victor in the full-size bed lying on his side and facing the wall. She undressed to her underwear and got under the covers. She placed a hand on his naked back. "Victor?" she murmured, and it was then that she realized he was crying.

Katya was silent. She was not herself a crier, and she generally found people who cried to be weak-willed and sentimental, and she was particularly disoriented by men who cried. She had never seen her father cry—not even when her grandmother died, hit by a car crossing Ocean Parkway when she was going to buy groceries—and she had long been comforted by the feeling that Victor was not someone who would cry, ever. So now she sat up in bed, hugging her knees to her chest, until finally his tears dried up. He still hadn't said anything but turned to her and tried to get her to lie down and snuggle. She was stiff.

"What the fuck, Katya," he said.

"What am I supposed to say?" she said. She was finding herself, lately, having less patience for Victor's self-pity, because it was highlighting an uncomfortable truth about their relationship. Before StrollUp imploded, there had been an unspoken understanding that what he was doing was more important than what she was doing, that the pressure he was under dwarfed hers. But then their roles had shifted and now she was the only one with a job, and Victor couldn't handle the new dynamic. And, truth be told, maybe she couldn't either. She didn't even want to mention what Dan had said to her at work or that she too was under a lot of pressure. "So your company didn't work out. It happens every day! I *write* about it every single day. Most startups fail. That's just a fact. And it's better that it failed now, when you only put twelve people out of work, than later, when you'd have to fire hundreds of people."

Victor rolled back over and stared at her. "Okay, but not every startup that fails is your boyfriend's startup. I'm not one of those lame startup guys you're always writing about." Katya had no retort to that and in fact began to feel a little bad about what she had said. After all, Victor *wasn't* one of those lame startup guys, even though at first she had thought he was—well, not necessarily a lame startup guy, but one of those dudes who just ate, breathed, slept their companies. Which Victor did, but he was different. He talked to his mom every week, slipping into a Spanglish that Katya found endearing and familiar—even though it was in a different language, it was the same way she spoke to her parents in Russian. He played a weekly touch football game on Saturday mornings in McCarren Park with his college friends, guys who were lawyers and writers and teachers and bankers and doctors, and one Sunday, a couple months after they had started seeing each other, he cooked carnitas—his grandmother's recipe, he said—all day on the dingy, tiny stove she had never used but that he said was superior to his brand-new one because it was gas. She took his word for it and even though pork wasn't usually something she ate, she ate Victor's carnitas tacos until she felt more full than she ever had in her life, and that was when she knew that her stubborn (some, including most of her ex-boyfriends, might say cold) heart was beginning to open itself up.

That night, they slept deliberately not touching, but in the morning Katya got up at seven thirty and walked down the street to Brooklyn Label and got two black coffees and a bacon, egg, and cheese sandwich for Victor and woke him up by waving it in front of his face. He sat up and smiled and ate the sandwich in her bed, which normally she would have forbidden, the covers pulled up over his naked legs, and she sat up in bed next to him and drank her coffee and then when he finished the sandwich, she leaned over and kissed him. Then he was taking off her T-shirt and leggings and they were rolling around on her bed. Katya loved Victor's tight, smooth muscles; she loved the way he threw her down and kissed her everywhere. Then her phone trilled insistently. A text message. They ignored it and continued kissing, but then it went off again, and Victor stopped and groaned, and Katya, too, was distracted, and then *again* it went off and she realized that they both had the Pavlovian instinct to look at a phone when it buzzed—not even necessarily to respond, but to look, to find out who or what was so insistently trying to contact them—and so Victor rolled off her and she groped for her phone on the nightstand. She was now, in the light of day and the lingering smell of the bacon, egg, and cheese, feeling a little bad about how she had reacted the night before. She found her phone and turned it over to find three texts from Dan. The first one: hey. The second one: Been thinking about what we could get you going on. The third: Hope it's not weird that I'm texting you this early, just thought of it and was excited.

"What is it?" Victor propped himself up on his elbow.

"Nothing," she said. "Just a work thing."

6

KEEPING UP APPEARANCES

IT WAS A week later, and Sabrina still hadn't completely forgiven Dan for not picking up the kids that day. In the hierarchy of Dan's transgressions—which over the years had ranged from really significant things (like coming home drunk on her thirty-second birthday and flaking on their dinner plans) to everyday annoyances (like never putting the cap back on the toothpaste so it got all cakey and gross at the top of the tube)—it ranked fairly low, so she couldn't figure out why she hadn't been able to forget it. Maybe it was because she had finally realized that all the talk about her generation being so enlightened was bull-shit. Men were supposed to be (magically!) more willing to shoulder their share of household responsibilities, and yet if Dan disappeared, Sabrina would be able to take care of the kids without him, while the reverse was definitely not true. He probably didn't even have the nanny's number in his phone. (Although maybe that was a good thing.) She coped not by con-fronting him, but by taking refuge in the snack room, which was unlike anything Sabrina had ever seen—certainly not like the pantry at her parents', which was usually bare because her mother was always on a diet, or the break rooms anywhere else Sabrina had worked. But TakeOff seemed devoted to spending a significant amount of its latest round of funding on making sure its employees never, ever went hungry, as though the key to happy employees were bottomless bags of Baked Lay's. There were healthy snacks, like Greek yogurt and baby carrots and hummus, but most people went straight for the Sun Chips, Snickers, Pop-Tarts, and Oreos. There was a candy dispenser that had every kind of M&M in it and a make-your-own-sundae bar on Thursday afternoons, and there was always a special snack of the week, like Magnolia Bakery cupcakes. There was also a selection of shakes made with Soylent, the meal-replacement powder that the engineers liked to eat instead of food but that Sabrina thought was pretty disgusting. She reached for a bag of trail mix, willing herself not to look at the nutritional information—trail mix was usually a bad-for-you snack masquerading as a healthy snack—and went back to her desk, where Isabel was holding a piece of paper in her hand and beaming.

Sabrina didn't say anything to her. She just sat down, put in her earbuds, and started looking at TweetDeck again, but Isabel soon tapped her on the shoulder. Sabrina took one earbud out. "What's up," she said. Isabel showed her the paper she was holding. It was a handwritten note that said, in small block letters in the middle of the sheet of paper: THINKING OF YOU TODAY. That was it.

"Do you have a stalker?" Sabrina asked. "Isn't that kind of creepy?"

Isabel laughed. "*Hardly*. Andrew sent it to me using Errandr. I think it's really sweet." She positioned the note on her desk and took a picture. "You don't think it's weird if I put it on

Snapchat, right?" Before Sabrina could answer, Isabel tapped her phone a few times and smiled.

"What's Errandr?" Every day there was some new app that Sabrina had never heard of. How was it possible even to keep up, let alone use them all? Sometimes Sabrina rather liked being one of the oldest people in the office (there was a guy in sales who she was pretty sure was at least forty—he gave her a nod every time he walked by her, as if to say, *We're in this together*), because in most ways she was relieved not to be twenty-five anymore. But sometimes, particularly at work, it bordered on terrifying.

"It's one of those on-demand task apps. You pay like twenty dollars or whatever and they'll do a small errand for you." She paused. "Not to be cocky or anything but I think he really likes me." Her voice dropped conspiratorially. "I mean, *besides* the note. Did I tell you what he did last night? I was telling him about that new juice place down the street from my apartment, and he just took out his phone and Venmo'd me ten dollars so I could get a green juice this morning on my way to work." She gestured to an almost empty plastic cup on her desk streaked with mealy green remnants of spinach and kale.

"How…romantic." Isabel had gone back to staring at her phone and seemed oblivious to Sabrina's barely disguised sarcasm. "So you and Andrew are like…a thing now?"

She shrugged. "A 'thing,' I don't know. We're not, like, official or anything. What does 'a thing' even mean anymore?"

"Beats me," Sabrina said. "I've been married for six years and I'm still trying to figure it out."

"Wow." Isabel seemed genuinely impressed. "Six years! Crazy. What's that like?"

"Being married? Or being married for six years?"

"Both, I guess."

Sabrina wondered whether she should explain how, when she and Dan had bought their apartment right after they'd gotten engaged, she'd had visions of it being the perfect Brooklyn home—a washer/dryer, enough counter space to actually cook, a small patio off the kitchen where she planted herbs and where people could smoke when they had parties, and in a neighborhood where lots of their friends lived—but the herbs had died years ago, the counter was cluttered with toys and mail and stray pieces of fossilized organic fruit leather, and one of the reasons she'd taken this job was that she couldn't stand to be in there for one extra second. Not to mention that most of their friends had moved to Montclair, and to top it off, they weren't even in the really good Park Slope school district. And she hated having to think about things like being in the really good public school district. Another downside to working with people much younger than her was that Sabrina saw a vision of how her life might have turned out differently if she hadn't met Dan when she did. This whole time, she'd smugly congratulated herself on skipping the horribleness of being a single woman in her thirties in New York, but what if the real trap was being *married* in your thirties in New York? Or maybe, and this was something she tried not to think about, the real trap was just being married to Dan.

"It's good." She tried to keep her voice bright. "You know, we have our hiccups, like every other couple, but overall it's just nice." Could Isabel hear the insincerity in her voice? She hoped not. Because what she really wanted to tell her was to enjoy these years for as long as she could, before she had to worry about things like nannies and school districts and husbands who didn't do the laundry because you were "better" at it.

Not that her twenties had been so great, but Sabrina sometimes longed to go back to those first few dreamlike years in New York when everyone was young and attractive, and the rooftop parties and picnics in the park seemed like they would never end. She looked at Isabel and remembered those nights before grad school when she'd snort coke in the bathroom of a bar and then stumble home with whatever guy she'd been talking to all night and have exhausted sex on his mattress on the floor and then wake up in the morning and get Gatorade and bacon, egg, and cheese sandwiches from the bodega. But then those nights started being fewer and farther between, and then she met Dan, and the joys of a quotidian, grown-up New York life became more apparent: An apartment that didn't have mice or roaches but did have space for a kitchen table that sat more than two people. Taking cabs. Weekends upstate. She started to like the version of her life she'd graduated to; it was like she'd gotten a certificate that said she would now fuck only the kind of guy who had a nightstand and an actual bed, not a mattress on the floor or even one propped on the free metal frame. Dan, she had noted right away, not only had both items, but they were from West Elm. Even she hadn't totally abandoned Ikea yet.

But that phase was fleeting. Now she'd graduated to the I-neverhave-sex-so-who-even-cares-about-nightstands   phase. They hardly used the patio anymore; the last party they'd had was her baby shower for Owen. Almost six years ago! Owen and Amelia shared a bedroom that had been a dining room, so they'd put the dining-room table in the living room, which was theoretically fine, except now there was barely anywhere for the kids to play. Plus, prices everywhere had skyrocketed in the past few years, so even if they sold their apartment for a big profit, they wouldn't be able to afford anything bigger in the neighborhood, even in the still-good-but-not-PS-321-good school district.

Sabrina had been scrolling through TweetDeck for a couple minutes, trying to find a meme that people were talking about so she could retweet it from the TakeOff account, when she realized Isabel was talking to her again. "Sorry," she said, taking out her earbuds. "What's up?"

"Andrew's having a dinner party tomorrow night," Isabel said.

"Cool." Sabrina glanced back at TweetDeck. She couldn't remember exactly, but she thought the last dinner party she'd gone to was probably sometime in the last decade.

"You should come," Isabel said.

Sabrina turned away from her monitor to face Isabel completely. "Um. What? Did you just say I should come to Andrew's dinner party? You're kidding, right?"

"Why is that so weird?" Isabel looked genuinely offended. "You *never* come out to work things, so I thought a dinner party might be more your speed."

"I don't come out to work things because I have to get home to my kids." That said, Sabrina had never actually considered whether she *wanted* to go out after work with her colleagues. Also, her coworkers went out almost every night. Even if she *were* twenty-six, she highly doubted she'd go along on every single drinks excursion. It was shocking they weren't all in AA by now.

"I know. Duh. But you're, like, a cool mom." Isabel giggled.

"I'm not, like, a regular mom." Sabrina smiled.

"See!" Isabel said triumphantly. "You can quote *Mean Girls*. You're not, like, old-old."

"Um, well, thanks."

"Seriously, though, you should come. Think about it?"

"Okay," Sabrina said. "I'll think about it."

Sabrina couldn't deny that she was curious about Andrew's apartment, mostly because she was obsessed with seeing other people's apartments in the way that every New Yorker was always obsessed with seeing other people's apartments. Sometimes it was reassuring to see places smaller than hers. In those cases she was always intrigued by the concessions New Yorkers made: garment racks instead of closets, a desk under a lofted bed, a fireplace that had been retrofitted as a bookcase. But she really lived for moments when she somehow ended up inside apartments that offered a vision of a New York that seemed like it would forever be completely out of her reach. Like the time in grad school when Natalie had taken her to a book party in a huge Park Avenue apartment for an author in his sixties she'd never even heard of. The elevator opened into the apartment, the ceilings were eighteen feet high, and the bathrooms felt bigger than her entire place. Or the time she went out to lunch with one of her coworkers from the eco-crafting magazine and the woman said she just needed to pick something up at her parents' apartment, which turned out to be a huge Tribeca loft with Christopher Wool paintings on the walls.

She used to be perplexed by the nice apartments of people her age, but as she got older, she'd gotten more cynical about their sources of income. For every Natalie, there was a Hannah, another woman she'd gone to grad school with. A year or so after they'd graduated, Hannah was working as a freelance writer and dog walker and yet was living alone in a one-bedroom in a doorman building on Irving Place; Hannah's father, Sabrina later learned via Natalie, was the head of a huge pharmaceutical company. Certainly, Sabrina had taken money from her parents—they'd paid her rent all through grad school, but right after it they had cut her off. Well, except for helping Sabrina and Dan out with the down payment on the apartment in Park Slope. But comparatively, she told herself, what they gave her was nothing.

"Great," Isabel said. "When was the last time you went to a dinner party, anyway?" Sabrina laughed, hoping Isabel wouldn't wait for an answer. "And Andrew's friends are cool. They're tech guys, but they're not like..." She dropped her voice. "*Douchey* tech guys."

"Wait. What does that mean?" Sabrina thought of something else. "Also...you've already met his friends?"

Isabel ignored the second question. "You know. Just...those guys who think that, because they started a company, they've figured everything out."

"Ah," Sabrina said. She kind of knew what Isabel was talking about—from what she had observed working at TakeOff, these men had a confidence that translated into the arrogant belief that they knew what was right not just for themselves but for everyone else. Like the way that Mack had gotten the whole company into meditation—even if she had to admit, reluctantly, that she kind of liked it. At least the finance guys and corporate lawyers she knew had a certain degree of cynicism about what they did; they acknowledged that they were pretty much entirely focused on one thing, and that was making money, and in fact it was better if the average person stayed completely ignorant of what they did because then they could do the borderline shady stuff that would get them *more* money. Tech guys also loved making money but framed it in a way that suggested they were doing all this for the good of mankind, and sure, of *course* that was going to make them fabulously rich, but the money was just a by-product of disrupting things and improving the world, so it was okay.

Sabrina saw Mack coming toward their desks with what appeared to be purpose. "Got a sec?" he asked Isabel, and she stood up as he started walking back to his office. He had been showing up in their area more and more with what seemed to be invented reasons to talk to Isabel. Could something have happened between them? She quickly dismissed the thought. Still, as Isabel wordlessly followed Mack back to his office, Sabrina realized she was starting to notice something that she had never before seen in Mack, and that was the barely perceptible, yet distinct, scent of desperation.

A few hours later, the day showed no signs of winding down. Amelia and Owen were supposed to be in bed at seven, but now it was almost eight and they were still parked in front of the TV watching a Christmas episode of *Doc McStuffins,* the one where Doc has to help Santa fix toys at the North Pole. Every few minutes one of them asked for the iPad and Sabrina had to tell them that no, they had both exceeded their allotment for the day, and when Daddy got home he was going to be really mad if he saw them on the iPad. This quieted them momentarily, but Owen, in particular, seemed to realize this was an idle threat and said insistently, "But you never tell Daddy he's spent too much time on his phone." This was, of course, true.

Dan had texted to say he was working late, which was happening a lot more lately, and which she usually didn't mind, but it would be nice if *occasionally* he could help put the kids to bed. "Where's Daddy?" Owen said suddenly, climbing up onto the couch and nestling himself in her lap. She smoothed his hair and thought: *Excellent question.* She glanced at her phone: 8:07.

"He'll be home soon, sweetheart," she said and wondered if Owen could sense the lack of conviction in her voice. "But I think we should start getting ready for bed."

"No," he said, even though she could tell he was tired. Amelia was lying on the floor, her head in her hands. "Where's Daddy?" she said, echoing Owen. "I want Daddy to put me to bed."

She and Dan had never had an explicit conversation about Sabrina being in charge of almost everything related to the kids. Maybe it was because she *had* been a stay-at-home mom for a while, and they'd just fallen into this pattern that was growing increasingly difficult to break. Sabrina didn't blame Dan, exactly, for the way things were now, but she couldn't help but think that someone who was more supportive, more attuned to her needs, would have realized that even if she wasn't completely miserable, she was stuck in a rut that there was no escaping. Her sophomore-year roommate at Wesleyan had founded a huge flash-sale website and was worth millions. Every so often Sabrina ran into her in the neighborhood—she and her husband owned a penthouse apartment on Prospect Park West—and she would look at Sabrina with what seemed to be a mix of concern and pity. In college Sabrina had been the smart and pretty one. Now she was the tired one.

And the poor one. Yes, they technically had more money coming in than when she'd been staying at home, but somehow it seemed to get eaten up at an even faster rate. It felt like she was only working to pay the nanny and Amelia's school.

But there was something else, something that she had yet to confess to Dan or Natalie or anyone. Her shopping habit had started gradually, with things that the kids needed, like boots and winter coats. Then there were things, like clogs in three different colors from the No. 6 store, that she wanted. That she *deserved*. She didn't miss being a stay-at-home mom, but now that she was working, it was so easy to look back nostalgically on having time to do the laundry and go grocery shopping, even take the occasional yoga class or have coffee with a friend. The only thing that brought relief was going on her phone and clicking through on the dozens of emails she got each day from Madewell, or Saks, or Creatures of Comfort, or, really, *anywhere*. When they arrived, the purchases weren't hard to hide; she was always the first one to get the mail, and she quickly got rid of the packaging in the building's trash room. The clothes and shoes were quietly camouflaged in their shared, chaotic closet. And it wasn't like Dan would ever notice that she had a whole new wardrobe because she rarely actually wore most of the stuff she bought, the $120 super-soft Vince T-shirts and the $450 Rachel Comey ankle boots and the $55 Wolford tights so silky and sheer that she was afraid to take them out of the packaging. It just comforted her to know that they were there.

Shit. It was almost nine and Owen and Amelia were still in the living room. "C'mon, guys," she said. "Time for bed. Daddy will come say good night when he gets home." They were too tired to resist as she pulled them up from their seats and half dragged them into their shared bedroom. When they fell asleep, she allowed herself to entertain the idea of actually going to Andrew Shepard's dinner party tomorrow. Drinking a couple glasses of wine. Eating a delicious meal. Having conversations with people who weren't Dan or her coworkers, Isabel excluded. She was so comfortable in this fantasy that she didn't realize she had fallen asleep on the couch until she woke up with a start when she heard a key turn in the lock. "Who's there," she said with the confusion of the half-asleep.

"Ssshh," Dan said, slinking into the room and quickly closing the door behind him. She could smell the alcohol from ten feet away. He was walking toward her when he tripped on the pair of clogs she'd left in the middle of the living room, and she had to suppress a laugh. "Real funny," he said. "Would it kill you to put your shoes away?"

"Sorry. You're the first person who's tripped on them." He glared at her. "I need a favor, by the way," she said. "There's a work thing tomorrow night that I have to go to. Can you be home by six?" She hadn't realized how much she wanted to go to the dinner party until she saw her husband walk in the door, bringing with him every resentment toward him she'd ever felt.

Dan sighed. "I'm not sure. There's a lot going on at work."

"I have literally not once asked you to be home before me since I started work," she said. She was trying to keep her voice down because she didn't want to wake up Owen and Amelia, but she really wanted to yell at him and throw something, preferably a clog. "It's one time. Please?"

Dan was looking at her as though trying to judge how much he could push her. He sighed again—dramatically, she thought. "Fine. But really, couldn't you give me more notice next time?"

"It was a last-minute thing. Anyway, thanks, I really do appreciate it." Dan went into the bedroom without saying another word. She took out her phone and emailed Isabel that she was in for the party.

7

PITCH PERFECT

GRAMERCY PARTNERS WAS on the twenty-seventh floor of a glass-and-steel building facing Madison Square Park, and as Mack walked into the elevator that Thursday morning, he closed his eyes briefly, took a breath in through his nose, exhaled through his mouth, and repeated in his head: *Be the change you wish to see in the world. Be the change you wish to see in the world.* It was a mantra that reflected, he thought, the best of everything about himself. *Be the change you wish to see in the world.*

The numbers in TakeOff's bank account might have been rapidly dwindling, but an outside observer would have considered Mack to be calm and collected. And aside from his immediate money problems, he *was* calm. Getting Series A funding—after a seed or angel round, the first round was called Series A, and companies went on up through the alphabet until they had their exit (an IPO or a sale)—felt like a totally different animal than trying to get money out of the VCs initially. Now he had a track record. Now his company had more than sixty employees, and revenue, and a product that people actually used.

So what if they weren't making money off it yet? That would come. And Gramercy hadn't even been willing to take a meeting with him the first time he'd gone out for funding; he'd gotten a very polite but firm *Thank you for thinking of us* email from an assistant there, and he'd moved on. But this time all it had taken for him to get this meeting was his running into one of the partners, a guy around his age named Teddy Rosen, a few weeks back at a Ping-Pong fund-raiser for a charity that brought drinking water to remote villages in Southeast Asia. Teddy had asked him what was happening at TakeOff, and Mack had told him that, confidentially, he would probably be going out for another round of funding in the next couple of months because business was just crazy and they needed capital to be able to grow, and next thing he knew Teddy was inviting him in to give a pitch and had intimated—strongly—that he thought Mack should let Gramercy lead this round.

The elevator doors opened. Mack stepped into the foyer: dark brown herringbone floors; a jute rug; black leather couch on a wooden base; two low-slung leather chairs that looked like they'd be tough to get in and out of; a square wooden coffee table with a silver bowl of lemons, a terrarium, and three hefty art books in a stack; a couple of big black-and-white photos of bridges on the walls. Most VCs had blandly tasteful offices, but this looked like the lobby of a boutique hotel—one that Mack wouldn't mind staying in. A woman with dark brown hair in a low bun, wearing a blue silk jumpsuit, white blazer, strappy high black heels, black-rimmed nerd glasses, and bright red lipstick, sat behind a large wooden table and a MacBook Air. She smiled and came around to greet him as he walked toward her.

"I'm—" he began, but she interrupted him, already sticking out her hand.

"Mack McAllister," she said. She had the faintest trace of a British accent. "We're *so* glad to have you here. I'm Clementine. Teddy will be just a moment. Can I get you something to drink?"

"Oh, I'm fine." Mack took in his surroundings. "Love the décor."

"It's *so* great, isn't it?" Clementine said, her smile getting even wider. "Done by iDecorate. They're one of our portfolio companies."

"Oh, sure, of course." The app, iDecorate, took all your information from Pinterest, Instagram, Tumblr, Twitter, and Facebook, plus your Google search history, and made décor suggestions based on what it figured out your taste was and helpfully provided affiliate links to purchase the items. The basic package was something very cheap, like maybe around ninety-nine dollars, but if you wanted it to do a specific room, then that was another three hundred, and if you wanted real interior design services, like "tell me where the armchair should go" kinds of services, then the prices went up from there. Still, it was much cheaper than hiring an actual decorator, and he remembered reading somewhere that Gramercy Partners had invested because they felt it had the potential to completely disrupt the interior design industry, which was intimidating and expensive for most people. Mack knew firsthand that the iDecorate algorithm was eerily accurate; he had recently been at a party where the hosts, a couple in their early thirties who both worked in tech—he was a CTO for something involving health care, and she was in marketing at a restaurant-reservations startup—had enthusiastically told their guests that they'd used iDecorate for their very well appointed West Village apartment; the app had helped them design it in a look it called "urban-rustic." It felt very *them*.

"Whoever's profile it used has great taste, then," Mack said.

"It's all of ours. It processed everyone's information and did a composite. It was brilliant, really—it could have ended up such a hodgepodge, but instead it just totally *works*. Neat, isn't it?"

He nodded. Even neater was the fact that Gramercy had made a substantial first-round investment, something in the vicinity of three million dollars, which had paid off handsomely when the company sold for three hundred million to Crate and Barrel.

Clementine glanced at her screen and sat down again. "Teddy will be right out. You can have a seat if you'd like."

He sat. She turned her attention away from him and started typing intently on her computer. Mack pulled out his phone to go over his PowerPoint deck one more time. He had it stored in three places: in a Dropbox folder in the Cloud, on his phone, and on a thumb drive in his pocket. Everyone had heard the horror stories of people getting in front of a conference room of VC partners and not being able to present their deck, which of course meant no deal. If you couldn't even get a PowerPoint to work, how were you going to lead a company?

He looked up to see Teddy emerging into the foyer. "Mack, my man," he said as Mack stood up. Even though Teddy was a few inches shorter than him, he was more solid, and when he clapped Mack on the back, Mack felt like he would have been knocked over if Teddy had hit him just a little harder. Teddy was wearing a lavender-and-white gingham shirt tucked into dark jeans; his light brown hair was close-cropped. He held an iPhone and a folder. "How goes everything?"

"Ready to do this thing," Mack said. Teddy grinned and clapped him on the back again.

"That is what I'm *talking* about," he said. "You have a great energy, you know that, right?"

Mack just smiled in response as Teddy led him into a window-walled conference room overlooking Madison Square Park just to the north. The Empire State Building loomed large in front of him, and to his left he could see the Hudson River and, across it, New Jersey; to his right, the East River and its bridges. He was rarely up this high, with the expanse of Manhattan spread out in front of him like a map, except in planes. It was intoxicating to see everything so small and feel like you could sweep it all up in your arms.

"Mack McAllister," Teddy said. There were five other partners sitting around a reclaimed-wood conference-room table, with Gramercy Partners' famed co-founder James Patel at the head, in his trademark lavender cashmere sweater. Mack had never actually met him in person before, but everyone knew James's story: he'd started BitForce when he was a junior at Stanford, and later, in 1999, at the height of the first tech bubble, he had sold it to AOL for a cool $1.3 billion, then watched as AOL managed to cock up pretty much everything he had done. He'd then laid low for a couple of years, traveling the world, even living in a remote mountaintop cabin with no electricity for three months, and when he got back to the U.S. he wrote a book *(The Best Things in Tech Aren't Free),* and opened Gramercy Partners in 2005 with his co-founder, legendary investor Paul Yarrow, who was sitting to James's right at the table. These days, Paul, who was fifty-four, and James were known for making what turned out to be highly lucrative bets on under-the-radar companies; *Fortune* estimated James's net worth to be in the two-billion-dollar range and had named him number seven on its Most Visionary in Tech list. And everyone in tech read James's blog, *That VC Life,* which was a mundane yet surprisingly engaging account of James's day-to-day existence in

New York City: the renovation of his Tribeca loft, which he shared with his wife, Rachel, who herself had launched a Rent the Runway–type app for children's clothes and a nonprofit devoted to helping single mothers get jobs in tech, and their two children. He sat on the boards of six startups. He was forty-one years old. He had the life that at least 50 percent of the guys in tech in New York, Mack included, aspired to.

Mack cleared his throat, pulled up his deck, and began. The first slide was the company's logo circled by emoji displaying different feelings; #LIVEMOREMINDFULLY ran across the bottom.

"What if you could improve people's lives—before they even knew they needed them to be improved?" he said. He had practiced this dramatic opening in front of the mirror, with different words emphasized each time: "*What* if you could improve people's lives." "What if *you* could improve people's lives." "What if you could improve...people's *lives*." He had settled on a delivery that was a tad mysterious but definitive, with a slight emphasis on *lives*.

"How many of you have tried to get an Uber in New York City when it's raining?" Everyone's hand went up. "Now how many of you have been frustrated by the experience?" Only one hand went down. "Maybe surge pricing was so high that it made the cost prohibitive or there were no cars available because of the weather. But what if there was something that could *anticipate* what you were about to do and how you would feel about it—and prompt you to take preemptive action?" James Patel had a half smile on his face. *This is good.* He clicked to the next slide.

"Right now, TakeOff is based on input—what you tell the app about how you're feeling," Mack said. "We prompt you to check in throughout the workday so we can assess your mood. Based on how you say you're feeling, you get a suggestion or a tip about how to make it better, usually involving physical activity—anything from 'Take a walk around the block,' to 'Do downward dog in your cubicle for two minutes.' So if you tried to get an Uber in the rain and told TakeOff that you felt annoyed, we would have a mindfulness-based solution for you." *Click.* "The problem, we found, is that despite the prompts, we were relying on people to recognize when they needed us—and people need us the most when they *don't* realize it. In other words, we asked ourselves, How can we recognize when people are *going to be* feeling bad? We started processing huge amounts of data about what our users had been telling us about their moods and when they felt they needed to use the app. We also initiated a beta test with some of our power users that allowed us to have read-only access to their social media accounts, text messages, email, calendars, browsing and app history, and location—"

James interrupted him. "Mack, my obvious concern is, this seems like an awful lot of information to ask of your users. I want to hear more, but I'm already skeptical about privacy issues."

Mack smiled. He had been anticipating this. "Of course," he said, clicking to the next slide. "So, two things that I think are important to keep in mind that I was just about to get to. First, when I say that our access is read-only, what that actually means is that we are simply scanning all of this data for keywords and, often more crucially, emoji that we will be constantly tweaking as we get more data. So we look for words or phrases like *pissed off, annoyed, bummed,* and *shitty,* and any emoji that indicate sadness, anger, or frustration. We don't store people's data, nor do we allow our employees to access people's data. It's entirely algorithmic." He paused and looked around the room. They seemed attentive so far. "Second, and this is just the reality of the world we live in, but we are accessing barely more data than what Facebook or Google, just to give a couple of examples, already have access to. And the data shows that consumers prefer convenience over privacy." *Click.* "A recent study by researchers at the University of Michigan found that when an app asks for access to social media accounts, only three percent of consumers decide not to download the app because of privacy concerns. Three percent! That's down from fifteen percent a year ago and fifty percent three years ago. And the generation that's in their teens right now—whatever we're calling them—their only concern is that they maintain control over *the people they know* who get to see their accounts. They're worried about their parents seeing the picture they just texted their girlfriend, not about whether an app knows too much about them." Mack paused again. "Does that address your concern?"

James nodded and smiled. "I hadn't seen that Michigan study, but that's a great data point," he said. "Continue, please."

"So let's go back to Uber in the rain," Mack said. "Before you even thought about calling Uber, TakeOff would process that, one, it's roughly around the time that you typically leave work; two, that it is raining in New York City; three, that you have a dinner on the Upper West Side in twenty minutes; four, that you just texted your wife 'Looks pretty brutal out there'; and, five, that half an hour ago you tweeted about how New York shuts down in the rain. We would send a notification that says something to the effect of 'Hey, it's raining out there—you should probably get that Uber now. And by the way: Take a deep breath. You've got this.' And we'd put a smiley emoji at the end of it. It makes people feel like there's someone looking out for them."

"A question," James said. "Won't constantly scanning people's feeds take a huge amount of server capacity?"

"Correct, it would," Mack said. "Right now, we have it set up so that it checks in with people five times a day: when they usually wake up, an hour before they typically get lunch, midafternoon, right before they leave work, and about an hour before they go to bed. We've found that those are the most common pain points."

"When people wake up?" Teddy asked.

"That's right," Mack said. "We're able to look at data from their sleep apps, so we'll know if they had a good night's sleep or if it was more restless. And we can see if any texts or emails came in overnight that they'd see first thing that might cause stress—say, something from the boss asking why the TPS report wasn't done." A few people chuckled at the *Office Space* reference. After all, *Office Space* was the ultimate movie about office drudgery, about working somewhere that offered you zero intellectual or creative fulfillment. For people like him and, he assumed, everyone in the room, work was usually the most rewarding part of the day. "Just think about how life would have been different at *that* office if they'd had TakeOff," he said, to laughter.

"TakeOff started by wanting to help improve people's lives at work, and we've succeeded." He clicked to the next slide, showing a chart of the app's month-over-month growth in the past six months. "As of today, the hashtag workmoremindfully has been tweeted one hundred seventeen thousand, three hundred and forty-eight times, and that's in just six months of the app being available." He paused to let that sink in. The men around the table were all scribbling in their notebooks; Teddy gave him what looked like it could have been a wink. "And our research shows that eighty-five percent of TakeOff users report that their workdays have improved since they got the app.

"We currently have fifty thousand active users, but as you know, we're still in beta. We need to acquire users rapidly to reach our goal of one million by this time next year. So this round of funding would launch the new version of the app and triple the headcount in the next six months, with the goal of doubling it again within the year. I want to acquire the top data analytics team in tech," Mack said. "There is no one in the world who can't benefit from it, whose life won't be improved by using TakeOff. As more people start using us, more people will *need* to use us. Because if you're not using TakeOff, you'll be at a psychological disadvantage. Think of us as being like technological Wellbutrin, with none of the side effects." Out of the corner of his eye he saw Teddy nodding. "We're talking infinite scale. And more than that, we're talking about *improving people's lives*. After all, isn't that what this is about?" He paused, allowing everything to sink in, then clicked to the final slide. It was the same as the first slide, except that all the emoji were happy now. Teddy was grinning. "We've been working more mindfully. Now let's live more mindfully. Any questions?"

The room burst into applause. Mack tried not to look too pleased with himself, but inside he felt triumphant. If Gramercy led this round, that sent a message to other VCs, to the engineers he so desperately needed to recruit, to TechScene, to—hell, to *everyone*, that TakeOff was a force to be reckoned with. That he was for real, that TakeOff would probably be joining that elite club of billion-dollar startups—unicorns—*very soon*. His company had everything that VCs loved: a great product, low overhead, potentially infinite scale, a charismatic founder.

James looked up from his Moleskine notebook, where he'd been jotting things down as Mack spoke. "You're at fourteen engineers right now, is that right?" Mack nodded. "To be honest, that seems low for what you're proposing. I'd like to see you scale even quicker, staffing-wise." Mack nodded again, barely able to contain his grin. "And what about product?"

"We're at nine on that team," Mack said.

James shook his head. "Way too small," he said. "I mean, it's impressive to see what you've accomplished with that headcount, but it's time to really be aggressive about growth."

"Right," Mack said.

"Who's leading that team now?" James asked.

"Casper Kim. He's been with us for a year and a half or so."

"What's his background?" James said.

"Harvard undergrad, hired as a summer intern by Foursquare before his senior year and launched a new product for them. We recruited him that summer, waited for him to finish school. He's young, but he's the real deal—great at anticipating growth and where the pinch points might be." James nodded; this answer seemed to satisfy him.

"Are you at all concerned about the effect on company culture as you scale?" Paul Yarrow asked.

Mack smiled. "I don't think I'd be concerned about that even if I got to five hundred this year," he said, and the room laughed.

Another partner, who Mack recognized as Scott Nathanson from his periodic appearances at the New York Startup Series, leaned into the table. "What are the drawbacks of being entirely consumer-facing?" he asked.

Mack answered quickly. "The only drawback is that right

now we can't grow fast enough," he said, and the room laughed again.

"Have you thought about bringing in a co-founder?" James asked. Mack winced inwardly; this was a touchy subject. So many successful startups *did* have two founders—usually one was a hard-core tech guy and the other was all business, with the idea that they would complement each other. But Mack was wary of getting a partner; he liked the highs and lows of doing it himself. The risk was greater, but so was the reward.

"I have," Mack said carefully, "and I've decided that I'm better served by a strong senior team than by bringing on another co-founder."

"Well, we can discuss," James said, and everyone smiled. "One final question. Why *shouldn't* we invest in TakeOff?"

Mack took a moment to think about it. "Well," he said, "if you want to invest in a company that's just looking for someone to tell them what to do, then we're not for you." He smiled. "If I think your advice is bad, I won't be afraid to tell you that, even if you are giving me millions of dollars." Everyone laughed. They hadn't asked about cash on hand, or about how he was going to make the next payroll, or about any of the other potentially uncomfortable issues he had been dreading.

James stood up. "Thanks for coming in, Mack. We'll talk soon," he said, and he left the room. The rest of the partners filed out after him, nodding to Mack on their way out. Teddy lingered behind; he had an excited gleam in his eye. As soon as the last partner had left, he closed the conference-room door and, again, clapped Mack on the back.

"You fucking *nailed* it," he said. "Nailed. It. I haven't seen them this excited about something in ... fuck, I don't even know. Look, man, you're going to have a lot of options this round, but you really want someone like us leading it because that's how you're going to get the best valuation. Once everyone sees that we're leading it, it's just like, *bam*. They want to be a part of it and then you have the upper hand, you can pick and choose. Plus, you want a firm that can really help you grow the business and is going to be able to give you strong, actionable advice and guidance when you need it. We're not going to be obsessing over every number and every decision you make. But we love what you're doing and we think you have a smart board, and—"

Mack interrupted him. "So you think it's a done deal, then?"

"We're having a review meeting early next week," he said. "We'll just look over all the numbers, cross the *t*'s, you know, all that stuff. But I'm sure I'll have good news for you."

It wasn't until after the meeting, after he and Teddy had shaken hands and he got down to the lobby of the building and walked outside into the crisp fall air and almost did a jig down Twenty-Third Street, that he saw the text from Isabel. All it said was Gotta talk to u. He texted back: Can it wait? Just got out of Gramercy mtg. He hoped she would respond quickly, ask him how it went, but a few minutes went by with nothing. Then, just as he was about to put his phone back in his pocket, a vibration. He looked at it eagerly, but no text from Isabel, just the TakeOff beta that he and a few other employees were testing. Hi, Mack! We thought you might be feeling a little ☹. Here's a little pick-me-up! it said. He didn't even bother opening the app, just shoved his phone back into his pocket and kept walking.

8

HOLD THE PHONE

THE WEST VILLAGE block where Andrew Shepard lived—brownstones, black streetlamps, trees turning vibrant shades of yellow and red and orange—was straight out of a New York tourism-board ad, Katya thought as she checked the numbers on the elegantly imposing buildings. When you grew up where she had grown up, it was hard to believe that people in the same city lived this way. It was also somewhat hard for her to believe, still, that she, Katya Pasternack—who hadn't really learned English until she was seven, whose father had been an engineer in Russia but drove a cab in New York City, who had grown up surrounded by other Russian immigrants in a huge, anonymous apartment building in a section of Brooklyn that most of her colleagues at TechScene wouldn't have been able to find on a map—had been admitted into this exclusive world.

His email had said that the party started at eight, but she had stayed late at the office and now it was approaching nine. Not that she particularly minded being late—if she missed the cocktail hour, so be it. She had bought a Snickers bar at the newsstand by the office and eaten it on the subway down to the West Village, and that, plus the cigarette she'd lit as she stepped off the subway at West Fourth, would keep her sated for a while.

The streetlamps gave the block a warm glow; Katya detected the pleasant scent of burning firewood in the air as she hurried to Andrew's house. In some corner of her brain, Katya acknowledged that living like this would be nice, but it also felt like it would be too easy. Katya's memories of the one-bedroom apartment she, her brother, her parents, and her grandmother had been crammed into for the first few years they lived in New York were still too vivid for her to romanticize poverty, but wasn't the struggle part of the point? What did you have to strive for if everything was easy? Katya certainly didn't think she *wouldn't* enjoy living in a huge West Village brownstone with heated bathroom floors, decorated tastefully with midcentury modern furniture, but that didn't mean this version of herself was one that her present self would loathe.

Katya knew Andrew as well as she knew most of the successful twentysomething founders in the startup scene, which was to say, both not very well and rather intimately, all at once. She didn't really know Andrew Shepard, *person*. But she *knew* him, just like she knew practically all of these guys. They were runners and foodies and cyclists; they all wore fitness trackers and competed with one another about who had run the most miles or slept the optimal 7.5 hours. They donated money to charities started by their friends that taught underprivileged kids how to code but voted against raising taxes to make those kids' schools better. They participated in hackathons and marathons; they climbed mountains; they loved South by Southwest. They thought everyone, including themselves, were where they were entirely because of hard work and innate creativity, and if you weren't successful, that was because you hadn't tried hard enough. They didn't understand people who weren't just like them.

Katya rang the bell, and she wasn't surprised when Teddy Rosen, a young venture capitalist who periodically texted her tips—like this is so off the record but one of our companies that rhymes with shmy mecorate is about to sell and i want you to be ready—opened the door. His firm had been an early investor in Andrew's company. "Heyyy, you made it," he said, wrapping her in a hug, a level of familiarity that she wasn't quite prepared for.

"Hi, Teddy," she said, carefully extracting herself. Teddy wasn't much taller than she was, and stocky, and she felt he was trying to hug her a little too long. "Victor's here already, right?"

Teddy's smile seemed a bit forced. "He is," he said. "Come on in. Oh, you can leave your coat here." There was a rack set up outside the door, already stuffed with jackets and a long, belted camel-hair coat. Teddy helped Katya out of her black wool coat. She was suddenly self-conscious that it was slightly threadbare.

They walked into Andrew's apartment. The ceilings must be sixteen feet high, Katya thought. There was a fire going in the living room and the logs crackled pleasantly. She turned around and Teddy had wandered off, so she peered into the rest of the apartment. In the dining room was a huge walnut table set for eight, with a couple of small floral arrangements as centerpieces. One wall was dominated by a mural-size painting that looked like it had been done by a graffiti artist, all loops and tags and bright colors. In the open kitchen, Andrew was holding a drink and talking intensely to Victor and a woman whom Katya didn't recognize. There was a tray of cucumber slices topped with crabmeat on the counter flanked by two cheese boards, and a full bar was set up in the living room. A couple of people were pouring themselves what appeared to be rather complicated drinks involving fresh mint. A tall black woman and a shorter white woman—both beautiful and thin and wearing oversize sacklike dresses—were bustling about in the kitchen, putting spices on sliced fish on baking sheets and chopping vegetables. They periodically checked on the appetizers, freshening up the cheese or bringing out a few more pieces of cucumber and crab. Katya mentally cataloged everything—the cucumbers and crabmeat, the fireplace, the mural—so she could report it all to Dan tomorrow. He loved hearing about shit like this. "Welcome to Startupville, population douchebag," he was fond of saying.

Victor was deep in conversation with Andrew. She finally caught his eye and gave him a nod, and he smiled at her. She decided not to interrupt and instead helped herself to a club soda in a little glass bottle, sat on the edge of the midcentury modern sofa, and opened Twitter. Nighttime Twitter was different from daytime Twitter only in that the content shifted from people in her timeline making dumb jokes about tech news to people making dumb jokes about TV. Katya rarely watched TV except when Victor was over, and she had never really understood the appeal of getting "into" a show. And people who said that they watched shows ironically or as "guilty pleasures" she understood even less. Life was short. Why waste it on something that made you feel like you had to explain yourself?

"Hey." There was suddenly an older Asian woman sitting next to her who hadn't been there before, carefully holding an overly full tumbler of ice and alcohol. A sprig of mint peeked out from atop the rim of the glass.

"Hi." Katya closed Twitter but kept her phone in her hand.

"Sabrina." The woman extended her hand. Sabrina? Wasn't that Dan's wife's name?

"Katya." She shook Sabrina's hand. "How do you know Andrew?"

"I don't, really," Sabrina said. She took a sip of her drink. "I'm here with his...girlfriend, I guess? Isabel. We work together at TakeOff. You know...we're the 'work more mindfully' people?"

So it *was* Dan's wife. How odd that she would be here. "Oh, yes, I am familiar," Katya said. "I've seen you around. I work with your husband at TechScene. Dan likes to say that they used to just call 'working more mindfully' a smoke break."

Sabrina grimaced, and Katya remembered, too late, that Sabrina disapproved of Dan's smoking. "So you must be the bad influence on him." Katya tried to keep her face impassive. Sabrina cleared her throat. "What do you, ah, do for TechScene?"

"I'm a reporter." The dinner was technically off the record— and Victor had made it very clear to Katya that if she published anything she heard at the dinner, she was potentially jeopardizing any future employment or investment opportunities he would have with Andrew or Teddy Rosen or whoever else happened to be there. StrollUp's demise had been quiet, although she assumed that the news would have traveled by now, at least to people like Andrew and Teddy. But Victor had made it very clear: She was not to discuss StrollUp at this party. "What are you doing here, anyway? I mean, not to be rude, but from what Dan says, you guys don't venture out much." Sabrina tilted her head to one side. Katya quickly amended her remark. "I mean, I *assumed* that from what Dan's said. He didn't, like, actually say that."

"Hm. Well, it's true that *I* don't venture out much," Sabrina said. "Dan...Dan ventures out a little more than I do. But Isabel invited me to this and I figured, what the hell, I haven't gone to something like this in *years*."

Katya was still trying to process what was happening: This was *that* Sabrina, the woman that Dan complained about during at least half of their smoke breaks and about whose marriage Katya knew way too much. But she was having trouble reconciling the nagging control freak Dan had told her about with this perfectly pleasant, if a bit anxious, woman sitting next to her. It was unsettling.

"So what else has Dan said about me?"

"Not a ton," Katya lied. Dan was constantly paranoid that Sabrina was going to come downstairs to the building lobby and catch him smoking. "You know, just that you guys live in Park Slope and stuff."

"'And stuff,'" she said. "I guess that accurately sums everything up." They were silent for a moment. "Why are *you* here? Are you friends with Andrew?"

"No, I don't really know him. My boyfriend, Victor"—she gestured with her head in the general direction of the kitchen—"knows him from startup stuff." Sabrina nodded. "Will you excuse me for a moment?" Katya said.

She had to get away from Sabrina, at least for a few minutes, because the conversation was freaking her out more than she wanted it to. She'd glimpsed Sabrina a couple of times in the building, but she'd never had a conversation with her. It wasn't that Katya had taken everything that Dan said about Sabrina as gospel, but she had definitely internalized Dan's perspective on their relationship. And, she realized guiltily, she'd always tacitly encouraged Dan to vent about his wife. It seemed harmless. But now, presented with this woman in the flesh, she felt embarrassed.

And besides, she wasn't here to talk to Sabrina Blum. Even though Victor had insisted that the dinner was off the record, she was hoping she'd be able to at least pick up a couple of tidbits that she could spin out into stories. There was nothing stopping her from pursuing rumors—she just had to get them confirmed *on* the record. But this was how careers were made. During their smoke breaks, Dan had told her a million times about the scoop that had changed his career—he had broken the news that Google had offered thirty million dollars to buy the old social network Friendster, at which point in the story Katya always reminded Dan that she had barely been in middle school when this had happened, and he invariably took a much bigger drag on his cigarette. Also, after a few of these conversations, it had slowly dawned on her that Dan brought up the Friendster scoop so frequently because it was at that precise moment in 2003 that he felt like he peaked, and that everything since—even this job, which Katya figured paid a lot of money and was reasonably prestigious—paled in comparison. That was *not* going to happen to her. "Get them to notice"—here he would gesture vaguely above his head to indicate, she assumed, Rich and Deanna—"and then you'll have people banging down your door to hire you. Not that I want to lose you, but you're not gonna want to stay here forever." And then Katya would always reassure him that she wasn't going anywhere, at least not yet, but she would do her best to get as many scoops as she possibly could, and he would look momentarily glum at the prospect of losing her and then get distracted and want to go back upstairs.

As she stood up, about to walk away, Isabel Taylor came over, plopped down next to Sabrina, and put her arm around her. "You're Katya, right?" Isabel said, looking up. She laughed. "Your boyfriend's Victor? He's cute." Katya felt herself blushing. *What a weird thing to say to another woman you've just met.* She never knew how to interact with girls like Isabel, the ones who had a seductive combination of being pretty, rich, and completely, blithely confident of their position in the world. And they took all of it for granted. Nothing really, truly bad ever happened to these otherworldly girls, and if it did, it seemed so very inconsequential. Even in this city, which would grind you down and make you hate it as much as you loved it, they seemed to exist in an uncomplicated universe of trust funds and museum parties and Hamptons summers. After college they lived in their own apartments in doorman buildings that their parents paid for; they spent $125 on yoga pants; they married rich and powerful men and had children who did the whole thing over again. She supposed she couldn't really *blame* Isabel for coming from this world or taking advantage of her position in it, but it all just seemed so patently unfair. And yet, here they both were, at one of the more exclusive dinner parties happening in the city at the moment. *Worlds collide,* she thought, more than a little triumphantly.

"Um, thanks," Katya said.

"Sit down!" Isabel laughed again, and Katya realized she was already drunk. "Have you met Sabrina? Sabrina is my coworker. I'm her *boss*." She giggled. Definitely drunk. Isabel put her phone and her drink on the coffee table. "She's the *best*." Sabrina had a frozen half smile on her face. "Seriously, Sabrina, you *are*."

"I try," Sabrina said. "When are we eating, do you know?" It was almost nine thirty.

"I'm not sure. You know what, I'll go ask Andrew." Isabel stood up, wavered, and then walked toward the kitchen. Sabrina raised her eyebrows at Katya as Isabel's phone, which was still on the coffee table, vibrated. Both women's eyes went to the phone.

And so it was that Katya saw a string of texts from Mack pop up on Isabel's lock screen.

i'm still at the office. it's lonely here w/out u
where are u

And then:

don't tell me u don't miss this

And there was a small, but distinct, picture of an erect penis. And then another one. And then one more.

"Oh my God," Sabrina whispered. "I...I wish I hadn't seen that."

"Um." Katya's mind was racing. "I'll go give this to Isabel. I won't tell her we saw anything." Sabrina nodded. Katya picked up the phone and walked toward the kitchen. She glanced back to see if Sabrina was looking at her, but she wasn't—she seemed to be staring at the opposite wall. Katya slipped into the hallway and snapped a picture of the screen of Isabel's phone with her own.

She wondered if Sabrina knew that Dan was particularly scornful of Mack McAllister. He had gone on a long diatribe about him one afternoon when they were taking a smoke break, and SXSW had come up. "You have to understand, it used to be this small, friendly, useful conference for people in tech. And the people who went were actually cool! It was like a fun reunion every year. And then slowly it shifted from being this kind of open secret among people who weren't douchebags to being this, like, huge conference almost exclusively *for* douchebags. Seriously, Katya, the douchebag to non-douchebag ratio at South By is probably the highest on the planet."

Katya had contemplated this for a moment and then asked, "Isn't that pretty much the whole startup world?"

"Nah. There are cool, smart people in tech. They've just been overrun by the Mack McAllister types."

Katya snorted. Dan's antipathy for Mack was something that Katya both understood and, on some level, didn't totally grasp. It had something to do with what Dan had explained was Mack's status as the "ultimate startup bro," a guy whose company did something that seemed wholly unnecessary and yet had gotten millions of dollars in funding, and the rest of the tech press had gone along, lemming-like, agreeing that Mack was the Next Big Thing. Mack was always speaking on some panel or other, earnestly representing New York tech, which just garnered him more adulation. Still, he and his company made it onto TechScene relatively rarely—Dan didn't exactly have an edict against it, but as he put it, the bar was "especially fucking high" for someone like Mack McAllister, who in the manner of George W. Bush "was born on third base but thought he'd hit a triple," and wouldn't you know it, they were both white guys from Texas? Katya was pretty sure it also had to do with the fact that Mack was a known player when it came to women while Dan was married (to Sabrina! The woman who had just seen inappropriate texts her boss's boss was sending to her boss!) and had two kids in a Park Slope one-and-a-half-bedroom (Dan had told her a thousand times about how they'd converted the dining room into the kids' room), which he said they were staying in for the foreseeable future "because the neighborhood has gotten so fucking expensive that we'd probably end up in a smaller apartment and out of the decent school district," and

Katya made a mental note never to be trapped in a Park Slope one-and-a-half-bedroom with two kids just because of a decent school district.

She clicked on the button on Isabel's phone to make her screen go dark and went into the kitchen. She tapped Isabel on the shoulder. "Hey, you left your phone." Katya held it out to Isabel, who seemed to barely register that she had forgotten her phone and that Katya was here giving it back to her.

"Oh...thanks." Isabel took the phone and turned away from her. Katya waited a moment—would Isabel look at her texts?—but Isabel just put her phone in her pocket and put her other arm around Andrew.

9

MORE MONEY, MORE PROBLEMS

IT WASN'T UNTIL Mack woke up the next morning and saw the text from Isabel time-stamped 12:03 a.m.—wtf is wrong w u—and his previous messages (starting with don't tell me u don't miss this with a picture of his dick, and then another picture of his dick, and, God, had he really sent a *third* picture of his dick?; then really, ur not even gonna respond, time-stamped seven minutes later than the third picture; and, finally, three minutes after that: bitch) that he started piecing together everything that had happened the night before. He had seen Isabel leave work with Sabrina around seven—she hadn't bothered to say good-bye—and he'd been sitting at his desk thinking about the first hires he was going to make with the Gramercy money, but soon the office had emptied out completely and he started thinking about Isabel and then he was drinking from the bottle of Bulleit someone had sent to him that had been sitting, unopened, on his bookshelf for six months. He rarely drank, because he liked to keep himself sharp and present at all times, so it hadn't taken long for things to go downhill from there. He didn't remember sending any of those texts, but there they were. And he hadn't responded to Isabel's last message because by that point he was sound asleep, in his clothes, in his bed; he had apparently gotten in an Uber at 10:40, according to the receipt in his email, but he had no recollection of that either. But now Isabel probably thought—fuck, what *did* she think? And why had he sent her a picture of his dick in a text, not on Snapchat? He must have been wasted. This was *not* in character for him; he couldn't remember the last time he'd been drunk, let alone gotten drunk at work, alone, upset about a *girl*. What was *happening* to him?

He didn't notice anyone else in the office when he got in at eight thirty the next morning, but he'd barely turned on his computer before getting an email from Casper Kim asking to talk. Casper had been working on the new version of TakeOff. He'd been expensive and had insisted on a vested stock grant—ballsy for someone so young, but Mack had decided he was worth it. Mack messaged him on Slack that he could come by any time before nine thirty, and within one minute, he was standing at the door. He seemed to be dressed as a unicorn, in a plush onesie with a hood hanging down his back that had a big unicorn horn on it. Was this some kind of sick prank? Like Casper throwing it in Mack's face that TakeOff was not yet, in fact, a unicorn? Before Mack could ask him why the hell he was dressed as a unicorn, Casper sat down and said, "Mack, you know how much I appreciate everything you've done for me and how great an experience I've had at TakeOff," and then Mack thought: *Is he quitting?* And then he thought: *No no no no no, please don't be quitting,* and then Casper said, "And I'm really proud of everything we've built here and feel like we're in such a great spot with the new version," and Mack thought,

Fuck, don't be quitting in a unicorn onesie, and then Casper said, "Which is why I feel like it's a good time for me to be moving on. I got a job offer and I know this is a cliché but it's really an offer I can't refuse, and I want you to know that I wasn't looking to leave TakeOff at *all,* this just happened to land in my lap and, really, I can't refuse it," he repeated.

Be calm, Mack thought. *Stay cool.* If Casper Kim quit—right when they were on the cusp of getting new funding and hiring a shit-ton more people and launching new versions of the app—they would be not completely and utterly fucked. But they'd be *pretty* fucked, at least temporarily. He didn't even want to contemplate the possibility that Casper wasn't telling the truth, that he actually *had* been looking for another job because he was for some reason dissatisfied with TakeOff. *Could* that be a possibility? Mack thought he did a pretty good job of realizing when people were unhappy, and he did everything he could to prevent that. It was of course important that you felt fulfilled at work and felt like you had a good work-life balance. But the way people, Mack included, worked now, work *was* life. They expected their work to be fun and their fun to be work, and they didn't differentiate between "work friends" and "real friends"; they assumed that the way things had been in college was the way things were in real life. So he gave his employees money for a kickball league in the summer—Casper was a team captain—and sponsored a bar trivia team and paid for happy hours and free lunches and snacks, so many snacks, and in the midst of all that, they were supposed to also be getting work done, which, for the most part, they did.

"I'm sorry, I want to talk about this, but—are you dressed as a *unicorn?*"

Casper glanced down at his outfit as though noticing it for the first time. "Oh! Yeah. It's Onesie Day in product."

"Onesie Day? Did I know about this?"

Casper shrugged. "Maybe? Was I supposed to tell you?" *I guess not,* Mack thought. "Anyway, it's just, like, a fun team-bonding thing, you know? We're going to take pictures in Madison Square Park at lunch." So it *wasn't* a comment on being a unicorn? This made it somehow worse. "Chelsea got a Pikachu one. I think Joe is going to be a kangaroo—"

He seemed like he wanted to keep going but Mack cut him off. "That's...great. Really, great idea." He hated that he actually meant this—it was a smart team-bonding exercise—even while he wanted to rip that dumb unicorn horn right off. "Are you unhappy?" he asked. "Is there something we can do to make you happier here? I guess I'm just confused—like, doing Onesie Day doesn't really seem like something that someone who's unhappy at work does, you know?"

Casper shook his head. "No, really, I love it here," he said. "It's just that, you know, sometimes things come along that you feel like you can't say no to." He added, "I'm only twenty-three."

"Right," Mack said. Was he just playing hardball? Could he be seduced with more money? "Well, can you tell me a little more about the offer?"

"Umm," Casper said. "Not really. I signed an NDA."

Casper signing a nondisclosure agreement didn't necessarily mean anything. At some companies, hell, you had to sign an NDA if you were just visiting a friend there. But if Casper wouldn't even tell him what company had made the offer, Mack wouldn't really be able to get a sense of whether the offer was from a place that Mack could theoretically compete with or if he was going to be completely outgunned. This job offer could be a lot of things—it could mean a new product at a Google or a Facebook, or that a new company was bringing him on as a founder, or something in between.

"Casper," he said. "Did I ever tell you about the time I almost took a job at Facebook?" Casper shrugged noncommittally. Mack knew Casper must have heard this story—it was part of TakeOff lore—but he kept going. "I'd started TakeOff a few months before and things weren't great. We had some funding, but it was disappearing real fast, and I was beginning to worry that I was either going to have to lay some people off, borrow money from my dad, or do something pretty drastic that I didn't want to do." Casper was staring at the ground, but he nodded. "So one day, I'm out for a run and I start thinking about how we could do certain things so much better." Casper nodded again. "I had been thinking of TakeOff as a *general* improve-your-workplace company. And I realized it needed to be more focused. So I stayed up all night writing a new business plan, and literally not a day later, I get an email from a Facebook recruiter. I'd sent them a résumé months before, when I had been out of work for a while, for a job I didn't even remember applying for, and so just when I had come up with the idea that would ultimately save us, *now* they're contacting me." He paused. "So you know what I did?"

"You...didn't take the job at Facebook?" Casper said.

"Well, right, I didn't. But I took the meetings and I got the job offer, and it seemed like the least risky option. We didn't have that many employees yet—maybe ten or so—and for a few days, I really debated taking the job and winding down the company. It would have been the safe thing to do. But I decided, you know what, I want to build something. And that something became TakeOff. If I had abandoned ship then, I would've just been another cog in Facebook's machine, and none of this"—he gestured to the rest of the office—"would have happened. None of this"—he pointed to his wall, where he had several framed, letterpress prints of positive comments they'd received about the app—"changing people's lives for the better, would have happened. None of—"

Casper cut him off. "I have the opportunity to build something new," he said. "I just want something that feels like *mine*, you know? I came on here when you guys already had the beta up and running, and it's been cool to see it grow but it's not *mine*. You know?"

They were both silent for a minute. "Yeah. Yeah, I do know. Listen, Casper—" He suddenly felt very, very tired, but he was going to try for a Hail Mary. "Confidentially, we're about to close a new round of funding, and—well, look, it would just be really important to me and to the company if you were able to stick around and see this thing through. If you want more money, I can give it to you. If you want more of the company, I can give it to you. I can't picture TakeOff without you." *Nor do I want to,* he thought. "Can you please consider reconsidering?"

As soon as Casper didn't respond right away, Mack knew that his Hail Mary had bombed. "Mack, I can't even tell you how much I respect you and what you've built here, but I have to say no. It's just—" He hesitated. "I don't quite know how to put this, but..."

"Put *what*? Whatever it is, tell me. This is valuable feedback, Casper." Even as he said it he could feel himself cringing inwardly. The only truly valuable feedback would be Casper deciding to stay.

"Well...it's just that the tech problems we're trying to solve here..." He paused. He seemed to be struggling with whatever he was about to say. "They're not really interesting enough for me," Casper finished.

What the fuck, Mack thought. And then before he could help himself, he actually said, "What the fuck does that mean?" And quickly, because he saw Casper's face: "Sorry. I'm just a little surprised to hear you say that."

"I like a challenge," Casper said. "And what we're doing now—it's kind of...basic."

"*Basic.*"

"Yeah. I mean, we're essentially just gathering data at this point. From a product and dev perspective, it's not particularly challenging." Casper paused. "Congrats on the funding, though, that's great news." He stood up. Mack stood up too and stuck out his hand. No sense in burning a bridge. Then again, if ever a bridge deserved to be burned, it was probably this one. Leaving two months before the new beta was supposed to be released! Who did that? Assholes, that was who. Selfish assholes who only thought about themselves and not the good of the company that had supported them, not to mention paid them handsomely.

As Casper shook his hand, Mack said, "Well, like I said, thanks for the feedback. It's...useful." *The fuck it is,* he thought. "Actually...can you just do me one favor?"

Casper looked at him and didn't say anything.

"Can you stay on for the month? At least help us get the new beta ready to ship."

Casper sighed. "They want me to start December first, and I was really hoping to take a couple weeks off and go to India. Now that I'm into meditation, there's this really cool-sounding retreat—"

Mack cut him off. "I get it. I really do. But—and pardon my language, Casper—we are utterly fucked if you leave sooner. I'll... I'll give you a bonus if you stay till the end of the month."

"How much of a bonus?"

"Five grand." It was a random number that seemed big enough to be enticing but also extremely reasonable, given how much he needed Casper to stay. "On top of your regular salary, of course."

Casper sighed. "Fine. I'll stay a month but not a day longer."

"Thank you." He simultaneously wanted to hug Casper and throttle him. "So let's keep this quiet for now, okay? We can tell your team in a week or two and then make a broader announcement, but I don't want to panic anyone quite yet."

"Okay. That's fine." He turned to leave, stopped at the door, and turned back to Mack. "And, uh, thanks for everything." He shut the door behind him.

"Fuuuuuuuuuck," Mack said under his breath. He wanted to scream. He wanted to punch something. But there he was, in his fucking fishbowl of an office, where even if no one was actually looking at him at that precise moment, it *felt* like everyone was looking at him. The glass had been his idea—he had read in some startup-management book that it promoted transparency. But right now he would have given anything for one of those offices behind opaque, solid walls with a thick door.

This was supposed to be a triumphant—euphoric, even— time for him, the day after a great meeting with Gramercy Partners. He was about to get a shit-ton of money for his company! He was about to be rich! On paper, but still. But no one really understood how hard—and how *lonely*—it was to be a founder sometimes. Sure, it was exciting to stand in front of a company that you had created and see all those eager faces looking at you, taking in your every word, feeling inspired and moti-vated. But whenever something like the conversation he'd just had with Casper happened, there wasn't really anyone he could talk to, no one to whom he could explain how *hard* it was, day in and day out, to keep a smile on his face and a spring in his step and act like everything was *just fine.*

And he couldn't stop thinking about what was happening—or not happening—with Isabel. The downside of work being life and life being work was that there was no shutting it off, and the downside with hooking up with someone at work was there was no escape. He'd never been in this position before; usually *he* was the one cutting things off with a woman he worked with, taking her out for a drink afterward just to make sure there were no hard feelings. Usually he was the one who caught an ex staring at him from across the room or heard that she had been crying in the bathroom. And now that it was hap-pening to him, it sucked.

He *knew* he and Isabel weren't exclusive. He *knew* they were allowed to date other people. He *knew* this was a casual thing. But the note sent to her *at the office* that she'd put on Snapchat—he was still looking at her stories on there; he couldn't help himself—felt like she was just taunting him. *She* was the one who hadn't wanted to be in a relationship, and now all of a sudden it was like she was fucking married. It was true that he had never actually *said* he wanted to be exclusive, but he knew that he was getting to the point where if it had come up, he definitely would have. And now she had to go and throw it in his face like that.

What made it worse was realizing how much Isabel's cold shoulder bothered him. He was stung by the rejection and dou-bly stung and embarrassed by how much it had hurt him.

He had never wanted to be, or thought he would be, in this position. There was one night, not long after he'd gotten TakeOff's first seed funding, that had seemed especially, exhilaratingly pregnant with the possibilities that were to come. He and Victor Vasquez and Nilay Shah, the StrollUp guys he'd met when they both gave presentations at the New York Startup Series, and a couple of their friends had gone to dinner in Williamsburg, where they had started off the evening with absinthe drinks and dozens of oysters. Mack had quickly arrived at a place of happy and confident drunkenness, and the five of them had heatedly debated whether New York or Silicon Valley was the best place to launch a startup. The other two guys at the table, Dinesh and Kyle, were friends of Victor's, and were about to move their six-month-old company to San Francisco.

"You have to look at it this way," Dinesh said. He was a cheerful, slightly overweight guy who was apparently some kind of programming whiz. Mack guessed he was around twenty-five. "The access to capital in the Valley is unparalleled. But the only way you can get that access, really, is by putting yourself in front of their faces. And they like to know that their investments are close by; they want to be able to keep tabs on you."

Kyle jumped in. "Not only that, but the talent pool—there's just no contest." Kyle spoke with a flat Chicago accent, and Mack could tell that he would be bald by thirty. "You're telling me that you can get the same caliber of engineers in New York as you can in SF? Bullshit."

Victor smiled. "I like to think of it this way. Silicon Valley might be baking the cake, but we're making the frosting. And everyone knows the frosting is the best part of the cake." Everyone laughed. "And those people in the Valley... are they people you would want to have drinks and oysters with? We've all been to SF. We know what it's like there. Everyone looks like they came right off the assembly line at the engineer factory. All anyone cares about, all anyone talks about, is tech. And don't even try to tell me that the girls in San Francisco have anything on the girls in New York. *That's* where there's just no contest."

As if on cue, two women appeared at their table. They were both short and skinny with long brown hair. One was wearing a crop top and high-rise jeans, the other was in a vintage-looking flowered dress. "Victor!" Crop Top gushed, enveloping him quickly in a hug. "We *thought* that was you."

Victor paused just a millisecond too long and Mack realized that his friend had forgotten the girls' names. "I'm Mack," he said quickly, standing and offering his hand to the woman in the dress.

"Erika." She shook his hand.

"And I'm Sam," said Crop Top, extracting herself from the hug and shaking Mack's hand.

"Very nice to meet you both." Mack felt himself almost bowing to them. Victor seemed to have recovered; he stood up and, smiling, said, "And this is Kyle and Dinesh," and they stood up to shake the girls' hands as well.

As the seven of them stood around semi-awkwardly, Victor asked, "So what are you all getting into tonight?"

It turned out Erika and Sam had gone to Barnard—Victor, who had gone to Columbia with Nilay, had met them in an art history elective he took senior year—and they had just finished dinner and were about to meet up with a few of their friends, and then they were all going to head to a loft party in Bushwick, and would the boys like to come with? And thus, three hours later, Mack found himself making out with Erika on a worn velour couch, a familiar position even if the exact surroundings—a makeshift bedroom in a loft overlooking a noodle factory—were a little shabbier than he was used to. An hour after that, he was in a cab with Erika, Sam, and Victor (they had somehow lost the other three guys along the way); half an hour after *that,* Erika was pulling him into the back bedroom of a fourth-floor railroad apartment in the East Village and shutting the door. She had kicked off her shoes and proceeded to take off his pants and his shirt, so he took off her dress, and then he took off her bra, and then she had whispered, "Do you have a condom?" And, well, yes, he did just happen to have a condom—not that he necessarily made a habit of keeping a condom in his wallet, but he had, lately, figured out that it was always better to be prepared than, well, not. It took him a couple tries to get the condom on his penis, which was not really as hard as he would have liked, but Erika was lying on the bed, eyes closed, and kind of moan-laughing, and then she reached for his dick and with a couple of strokes had not only gotten him legitimately hard but also managed to slide the condom on, and then she guided him into her. He remembered she had surprisingly large breasts, big, fleshy orbs that lolled to either side of her body and jiggled manically as he thrust into her, and when he flipped her over—his preferred position to finish in—they'd almost touched the bed.

Early the next morning he woke up with one of the worst headaches he had ever had—ugh, absinthe—and Erika was still asleep, so he found his boxer-briefs on the floor of her bedroom and tiptoed into the kitchen and poured himself a glass of water and saw, through the open door to the other bedroom, Victor and Sam, both lying on top of a patchwork duvet completely naked, and he drank the water in one gulp and tiptoed back into Erika's bedroom and pulled on the rest of his clothes and left. He'd gotten a text from Erika later that day—come back soon ;)—and meant to respond, but forgot. (He did, however, remember to add her to the list of women he'd slept with since moving to New York that he kept on his phone. She was number thirty-nine.)

That was—fuck, that was almost two years ago! Did he even keep condoms in his wallet anymore? He took his wallet out and looked into it: just a few singles and his credit cards and driver's license. No condoms. Just one more thing he was going to miss about Isabel.

From his office he could just see Isabel's desk. She was talking to Oliver from sales, who was leaning over her shoulder and pointing to something on her computer screen. He saw her laugh. His stomach felt hollow. *Allow yourself to feel at peace,* his meditation app always said, but how the fuck were you supposed to feel at peace when the world was conspiring against you?

10

THE HUSTLE

KATYA YAWNED AND stretched and gave herself a minute before rolling out of bed. Victor lay curled almost against the wall next to her, still sound asleep; he probably wouldn't wake up for another couple of hours. It was seven thirty in the morning and she was wearing only a pair of black lace boy shorts, and so when she opened the door of her bedroom and stepped into the living room, she almost screamed when she saw Janelle sitting at their two-person table, her phone set up on a tripod, an array of beauty products in front of her. Janelle's head whipped around when she heard Katya, and then she sighed. "Damn it, Katya, I almost had it." She looked Katya up and down. "And you need to eat a sandwich."

"I'll make a note of that." She stood there, hip jutted out, not covering her chest. Janelle had seen her naked before—it wasn't like Katya's skinniness was any surprise to her. And, actually, it was kind of rude to tell her to eat a sandwich. She didn't even *like* sandwiches. "What are you doing up so early, anyway?"

Janelle gestured toward the windows. "The light in this place is best in the morning. I gotta get this video up before I leave for work." This was Janelle's latest attempt at "building brand awareness," or, as Katya thought of it, "trying to become famous." She was posting videos to Facebook and her YouTube channel, Black Girl Beauty. "This is 'the easiest smoky eye.'" She batted her eyelashes. "See?"

"Mmm," Katya said.

"Oh, by the way, I asked around about your invisibletechman. No one knows who it is." Janelle picked up her phone. "But he's kinda funny. Like look at this one." She held out the phone.

Founder: *pats my hair* I like the new 'do! Me: *quietly casts voodoo spell on him*.

"Like, that is *real*." She shook her head. "You know that your founder or whatever he is patted my brother on the head?"

"Who, Rich did that?" Katya said. Janelle nodded and rolled her eyes. "Well, he probably just doesn't know any better."

"Well, that's because he hasn't made it his business to ever be around black people before." Janelle had a point, Katya had to admit. Trevor was one of two black employees at TechScene; the other, Kiana, worked in sales. "And guess what, it's not my brother's job to teach him how to behave. So I don't *hate* this invisibletechman, whoever it is, if it makes the Rich Watsons of the world stop petting my brother like he's some zoo animal." Janelle sighed. "Anyway. I need to see how this new lip gloss looks on camera." She turned her phone around to look into the camera, pursed her lips, and snapped a photo.

Katya stared at Janelle. It was *way* too early for all of this. "The lip gloss is pretty. Um...I'm gonna take a shower."

"Okay...but can you make it quick? Sometimes my phone picks up the background noise."

"Uh, yeah, sure." When they'd first met for a drink after work, Janelle had assured her that she "worked hard, played hard," was rarely home, didn't mind if Katya had overnight guests but personally preferred to "sleep out" if there was a gentleman or a lady in her life, and would pay her rent on time. Basically, the perfect roommate. Katya's previous roommate, Alicia, was always asking Katya to hang out and seemed offended when Katya made plans with other people that didn't include her. Katya had enough to worry about without having to wonder whether she was hurting her roommate's feelings because she'd gone to a concert with someone else. It was, frankly, too much hassle. These were Katya's first roommate experiences—she lived in her bedroom at her dad's during college at NYU, which had actually been a better experience than she was expecting; her dad was so proud that his daughter had gotten a scholarship (partial, but still) that he and her stepmother, Larisa, pretty much left her alone, and she didn't have to live in one of the overpriced, overcrowded dorms, and she still got to come and go as she pleased. It was a long commute into the city every day, but she always got a seat on the B train and used the forty-five minutes to study. She'd kept living at home for those first few months after graduation when she was interning at Mashable by day and bartending at night, trying to save enough money to move out. Finally one of her professors from NYU put her in touch with Rich, and after he'd canceled several times, they eventually met for coffee and she was hired on the spot. Two weeks after Katya moved out, her dad announced he and Larisa were moving to a nicer apartment in Brighton Beach because Larisa's best friend and her hair salon were there.

Katya showered and got dressed quickly—Victor was still sleeping. Janelle paused her smoky-eye tutorial just long enough to remind Katya that Victor had officially overstayed his welcome, and so Katya left the apartment feeling anxious and annoyed at the situation she now found herself in. As she walked down Greenpoint Avenue toward the G, which would take her to the L to get into Manhattan, she thought about whether she should tell her parents she was dating someone. Lately Victor had started dropping hints that he thought it was a little weird that Katya's parents lived so close to them and he hadn't met them yet, and she didn't want to tell him that her parents didn't even know she had a boyfriend. And the longer she waited, the more awkward it was going to be when she finally did tell them, because they'd ask her how long it had been and she'd have to answer truthfully, and then they'd wonder why she hadn't introduced them, and then she'd have to tell them he was Mexican, and she didn't want to see their faces fall when she said that. She didn't want Victor to be exposed to their old-world racism. They didn't seem to care that she was living with a black woman, probably because they weren't sleeping together. When she was feeling generous toward them, she thought of it more as ethnocentrism than anything else. Almost their entire world—home, work, friends, the stores they shopped in, the restaurants where they ate, the newspapers they read, most of the TV they watched—was Russian. Her dad and Larisa, as well as her mom and her boyfriend, rarely ventured out of Brighton Beach, and when they did, it was to see friends in other Russian enclaves in Brooklyn and Staten Island. They disapproved of her living in Greenpoint, a Polish neighborhood, even though she had told them dozens of times that lots of different kinds of people lived there now, "even Russians!" They hadn't believed her, and it only got worse the one time her father and Larisa had come to visit her and observed that the nearest bodega, coffee shop, grocery store, bank, and nightclub were all

Polish-owned. "I don't even go to nightclubs! And World War Two is over, you know," Katya had hissed at them, and her father had shrugged, a shrug that implied that this was about so much more than World War II, it was about generations and blood and traditions that someone like Katya, raised as she was in the United States, could never hope to understand. It was then she realized that they were stuck in a Russia that they had psychically transported to Brooklyn, and introducing them to her Mexican boyfriend was only going to make things more complicated for everyone. So it had been easier to deflect their questions for the past few months about whether she was dating, and who, and try to avoid letting them set her up with one of their friends' sons, who were invariably named Boris and had thick necks and vague jobs and drove their BMWs way too fast down Ocean Parkway.

She got to work just as the weekly TechScene editorial meeting was about to begin. Everyone had taken a bagel and was standing in the kitchen expectantly, waiting for Rich or Deanna to say something. They had these meetings every Monday morning. When Katya started, they went through a dozen bagels in a meeting. Now, because they'd hired so many new people, they were up to three dozen, none of which Katya ever ate, although she would occasionally avail herself of a spoonful of scallion cream cheese and lick it surreptitiously at her desk later.

"Good morning, everyone," Rich said. No one responded, but the chatter gradually died down. "I *said*, good morning, everyone!"

"Good morning, Rich," everyone replied, a chorus of voices in various stages of enthusiasm. Katya glanced around at her colleagues. Dan was standing toward the back, looking at his phone.

On Friday, the day after Andrew's party, Dan had messaged her on Slack when he got into the office.

Dan: sooooo... I heard you met my lovely wife last night.
Katya: yup.
Dan: she said she had fun talking to you.
Katya: yeah she was cool
Dan: what'd you guys talk about? just out of curiosity
Katya: ummm idk, I don't really remember

It was at this point that Katya had a creeping sense of panic and stopped responding. Had Sabrina told Dan about seeing Mack's dick pics? What had Sabrina said about her? Katya hadn't yet decided what to do about the photo of Isabel's phone screen that she'd taken, but she knew that the second she said anything to Dan, he'd want her to write something about it—and she figured that if Sabrina *had* said anything to Dan, then he would have said something to her. Katya decided that the best way to navigate the situation and buy some time was to try to avoid Dan as much as she could. It had almost killed her, but she'd taken only one smoke break that day, and she made sure to do it when he was in a meeting with Rich and Deanna. But today, he was probably going to want to smoke. And talk.

Katya tried to turn off this line of thinking and pay attention to Rich. The co-founder of TechScene was a media-app prodigy who'd managed to find himself in several right places at several right times even as the wider media world was in various stages of collapse or, as people liked to euphemistically call it, "transition." At Harvard, he'd started a company that sold online ads via an app, a business bankrolled in part by his dad, the formidable Silicon Valley attorney Chip Watson.

He'd moved the company to New York right after college and sold it two years ago for a reported $235 million, taken a year off to backpack around Southeast Asia, and met Deanna Stein, one of the early proponents of the importance of teaching journalists to code, when he got back to New York. Deanna had been fired from BizWorld after clashing with the founder and was trying to launch her own media company, and Rich had the cash. Now Rich was generally the public face of the company, while Deanna was more reserved and more intimidating. As had been related in dozens of articles and blog posts about Rich and his new company, they ended up launching a few months ahead of schedule at SXSW, where they'd broken the biggest news of the conference, that Mack McAllister had just secured six million in funding for his workplace-wellness startup, TakeOff. Breaking *that* news had in turn led TechScene to attract more funding on top of what Rich had already put into the company, which Rich had strategically leaked to the tech gossip site Valleydirt just as he was trying to recruit journalists to come work for him.

Now it seemed as though Rich spent just as much time on TV and giving speeches as he did at the company. In fact, Katya's dad had been completely skeptical about TechScene altogether until he saw Rich as a talking head discussing Snapchat's valuation on CNBC, which was on at all times on the TV in the kitchen in his apartment (the TV in the living room was usually on one of the Russian channels they got via satellite).

As Katya watched Rich—clad in his standard outfit of an untucked button-down, dark jeans, and high-top Nikes—talk, she couldn't stop thinking about the screenshot that resided in the Photos app on her phone. She hadn't told anyone, even Victor, about what had happened at Andrew Shepard's house. She was simultaneously thrilled by her daring and incredibly guilty about what she had done, and since Thursday, she had replayed that moment what felt like hundreds of times in her mind, along with the ways that things could have turned out differently if only one tiny thing had changed. Why had Isabel come over to talk to them? Why had she left her phone on the table? Why, why, why.

But what she always kept coming back to was, if Mack McAllister weren't a disgusting pig, he never would have sent that text in the first place, and then none of them would be in this position.

Still. She may have been conflicted about what to do about the photo, but she knew she needed to safeguard it, so she had backed up her phone to her laptop when she got home from Andrew's party, taking care not to let on to Victor that she felt the *really urgent need* to back up her phone on her computer at that moment. She wasn't sure what she was going to do with it but she *was* sure that she didn't want to decide right then or, worse, have Victor make the decision for her. There was no way he would be cool with her keeping the photo, let alone writing anything about it. He probably wanted to hit Mack up for funding for whatever his next company was. And that had been their deal: Everything at the dinner was off the record. And this wasn't just off the record, it was *private*. It had not even been meant for her eyes. It had been an accident, a fluke.

Katya had also thus far avoided thinking too much about the true ramifications of the photo and what could possibly happen if she did anything about it. There was something about speaking truth to power that had attracted her to the idea of being a journalist in the first place—wasn't that a journalist's job? To shed light on the nefarious, seedy underbelly of how the sausages of the world got made? And certainly, the Mack McAllisters of the world were the sausage kings, so secure in their positions that they felt it was within their rights to send pictures of their dicks to their employees. It was her job as a journalist to tell the world what a gross human he was. She had never given much thought to gender politics—she didn't have time, she told herself, to worry about whether she was or wasn't getting ahead in life because she was a woman—but for the first time she had the thought that maybe it was her job, as a woman, to expose him.

"Deanna is going to say a few words about traffic and goals," Rich said, as the room applauded, and Katya realized she had completely zoned out for the past few minutes.

Deanna came to the front of the room. She was a small woman with frizzy black hair that she usually wore in a bun at the top of her head, and her outfits always looked like they could have walked off the set of *Reality Bites*. Today she was wearing a long-sleeved black baby-doll dress, purple tights, and black Doc Martens boots. Her nails were painted bright pink. She looked like a Goth elf. Deanna dressed like she had been shopping in Urban Outfitters since the early '90s and just never saw the need to go anywhere else. She lived with her wife, a music teacher, and their two kids in a brownstone in Prospect Heights, where they'd hosted last summer's TechScene barbecue in their backyard.

"So, traffic." Deanna's voice was low and a little raspy. She was older than Rich, but no one knew exactly how old she was. Katya figured she could be anywhere between thirty-two and forty-two. "Great week. Overall we broke three million uniques, which was our best week since WWDC." WWDC was the Apple Worldwide Developers Conference, the annual event where Apple unveiled new products and the tech journalism world exploded; it was an all-hands-on-deck situation, with everyone in the office covering various aspects of the conference. This year had been Katya's first and she had written five posts in one day, more than anyone else on the team. "And we're beating Mashable *and* BizWorld for the month on Twitter mentions and retweets." The room applauded.

"So. Yes," Deanna said, trying to speak above everyone and mostly failing. "Good job, everyone, but the month's not over." The room quieted down. Deanna smiled. "Thank you. I also wanted to say a few words about how we'll be evaluating things going forward." She cleared her throat. "Up until now, we've been primarily focused on traffic. And traffic's good. Traffic's great, in fact. We love traffic. But traffic can be cheap. Traffic can be fickle. Traffic is not always your friend." The room laughed, a little nervously. "Along with Dan, Rich and I have been coming up with a new metric to measure success that takes into account not just traffic, but also things like Twitter mentions and inbound links. In other words, how influential is your work? How are you driving the conversation?" Dan caught Katya's eye and raised an eyebrow as if to say, *See?*

"So what does this mean for you?" Deanna continued. "Well, it means that original reporting, even if it doesn't get as much traffic as, say, Thirteen Things You Never Knew Your iPhone Could Do—great post, by the way, Brian—is going to be more important. We want you on the phone, we want you meeting sources for lunch. We want to be breaking news all over the place. And when I say breaking news, I don't mean being the first person on the internet to post news from a press release or a statement, or from a conference, or panel, or whatever. We're talking something that *you* break yourself."

Rich spoke up again. "Now, of course, this doesn't mean that things around here are going to *change*. We'll still be the awesome tech news site we've always been." He grinned, but Katya could practically see her colleagues' minds racing. So many of them thought that *news* meant posting something that another site already had with the words slightly rearranged and a different headline. Well, they were in for a rude awakening. But how would Deanna and Rich assess impact, exactly? They hadn't really addressed that. It seemed subjective in a way that made Katya nervous. At least with traffic, the raw numbers were right there for everyone to see; there was no questioning them, no way for someone to make the case that actually, no, they deserved another twenty thousand views or Facebook shares or whatever. The traffic was what it was. She didn't even really understand how journalists functioned in the days before you could see exactly how many people were reading your stuff. If something was just buried in the middle of a magazine, who cared how many people subscribed to the magazine? You had no idea how many people were actually reading *your story*. Katya thought this would have driven her absolutely crazy. She also didn't understand people—true, mostly old people—who bemoaned the quantification of journalism. If the whole point was to have people reading your stuff, wouldn't you want to know how many people were doing that? They were just scared, she decided, to know how *few* people were actually reading their work, so it was easier just to criticize the whole endeavor.

Maybe that was a good enough reason to go after the Mack story—to show everyone she worked with, and everyone in the industry, that she was not to be fucked with, that she would go after the tough stories even if they might make some people feel bad.

"Thanks, everyone," Rich said, and everyone started talking

again, a low murmur that felt more charged than usual. And—fuck, this presented a whole host of other problems related to the picture on her phone. And what Sabrina had or hadn't told Dan. She needed to be alone to think, but Dan was making a beeline for her.

"Everything okay?" he said.

Ugh, I must look upset, she thought. She smiled quickly. "Yeah, everything's fine, why?"

"Just thought you looked a little...I don't know. Never mind. Want a smoke?"

"Yeah—just let me run to the bathroom," she said. Dan nodded and walked toward the front door. Katya scurried to the bathroom and, once safely in a stall, pulled up the picture of Mack's text again. She just needed to make sure it was still there.

11

HOUSE OF CARDS

DAN TEXTED AT seven to say that he was working late, a text Sabrina didn't see right away because she was giving Amelia a bath, and when they came out of the bathroom—Amelia in her pajamas with her dark brown hair combed back and ready for bed—Sabrina was confronted with an entire box of Cheerios whose contents were now on the kitchen floor, where Owen was sitting and shoving handfuls of the tiny Os into his mouth.

Sabrina didn't say a word, just yanked Owen up from the floor so hard that he immediately started crying and dragged him into his bedroom, where Amelia had retreated and was sitting on her bed with a slightly scared look on her face. Sabrina shoved Owen down on his bed and turned him over and spanked him, hard, on his bottom. He turned and stared at her and then started screaming even louder.

Shit. Shit shit shit. Before her kids were born, Sabrina had lots of notions about good parenting, one of which included never, *ever* spanking her children. That had gone out the window around the time Owen turned three and was a complete monster, and she couldn't figure out any other way to make him listen to her. Until the one time he got in trouble at nursery school and started crying and asked the teacher if she was going to spank him "like Mommy," and Sabrina got a phone call from the school director reminding her that Slope Montessori had a no-physical-discipline policy, and that applied to what went on at home too, and so Sabrina had promised it would never happen again. She didn't tell Dan about that phone call; he would have gone on a rant about how they were paying thousands of dollars a year to have someone who saw Owen for two hours a day, three days a week, tell them how they should be raising him, and even though she didn't really disagree, she also couldn't fathom not having those six hours a week, when Amelia was napping, to herself.

Since that phone call two years ago, though, she had kept her promise—she hadn't struck Owen or Amelia once. His sobs grew louder. "I was hungry, Mommy!"

"If you're hungry, you tell me." Out of the corner of her eye she saw Amelia lie down and turn away from her, putting her hands over her ears. "You do *not* try to get the box of Cheerios down from the cabinet yourself. Do you understand?"

Owen just cried louder.

"I said, do you understand?" He finally nodded. "Okay," she said. "I'm going to read to Amelia now and you're going to go into the kitchen and clean up all the Cheerios." It was Owen's turn to look confused and frightened. "Put all of the Cheerios into the garbage can. I don't want to see even one Cheerio when I come out there or you're going to be punished again."

It wasn't until she'd read *Cloudy with a Chance of Meatballs* to Amelia, and Owen had cleaned up the Cheerios and brushed his teeth and gotten into bed, and Sabrina had turned out the light and gone back into the living room and poured herself a full glass of red wine that she finally checked her phone and saw the text from Dan. By now it was eight thirty, and she just texted back ok and turned on the TV, and so by ten, when she finally got into bed, she had gone through an entire bottle of wine. She passed out for half an hour or so and then woke up and realized it was now ten thirty and Dan still wasn't home.

Sabrina hadn't told Dan about what she'd seen at Isabel's party. When she'd gotten home on Thursday night, slipping through the door at midnight, he had been awake, sitting on the couch working on his laptop.

"So, how'd it go?" she asked.

He shrugged. "Fine? Owen didn't seem to care. Amelia seemed confused. She just kept saying, 'This is Mommy's job.'"

"And they went to bed without freaking out?"

"Yeah? They were probably asleep around eight thirty." *Okay, not terrible,* Sabrina thought. "So does this mean you'll be on daddy duty more often, then?"

Dan laughed. "You act like it's a choice! I'd be happy to put them to bed more, I just can't. This job is only getting crazier."

"I met someone you work with, by the way."

"Yeah? Who?"

"Katya? Skinny girl, bleached-blond hair?"

She could have sworn she saw Dan do a double take. But when he spoke, he sounded totally normal. "Oh, yeah, Katya. She's great. One of our best reporters."

"Really?" Sabrina couldn't picture this girl being a killer reporter. She was so...skinny. "How old is she? She seemed like a child."

"You know, twenty-five or something? They're all like that. They're not like how we were."

"How were we?"

"I mean, we were ambitious. But not like them. It's like they were born with their life goals already imprinted onto their brains."

Sabrina had snorted. "Yeah, I see that. Well, anyway, she seemed nice."

Now, as she lay in bed, vaguely wondering where Dan was but also not really caring, she thought back to this conversation. Truth be told, she hadn't been able to shake what had happened at Andrew's party. Not just the texts from Mack to Isabel—which she had yet to confront Isabel about—but also the way all the guests had seemed so convinced of their own importance. The party had dislodged something in her, reignited some long-dormant spark. She remembered that she used to think that if she wasn't exactly destined for greatness, she was definitely at least destined for *significance*. And there was little, if anything, that felt important about what she was doing now. If she stopped tweeting for the TakeOff account, no one would miss her. No one would likely even *notice*. She just wouldn't be getting a paycheck anymore.

Somewhere along the way, she'd lost her ambition. Somewhere along the way, it had just seemed easier to fade into the background, to become unmemorable. It was probably when she had stopped being Sabrina Choe and started being Sabrina Blum. At the time, she had just turned thirty, and changing her last name didn't seem like such a big deal, even if, when you looked at her, she was clearly more of a Choe than a Blum. Maybe if she'd been able to get her book published, she would have felt different—if she'd actually made a name for herself as herself, then perhaps the stakes of becoming someone else would have felt higher.

She patted the bed next to her, looking for her phone, and

finally found it under her pillow. There was a notification from Chase, alerting her that the payment on her Visa card was over thirty days late. She frowned as the words swam in front of her briefly, then squeezed her eyes shut for a moment and reopened them. Better. Now if she could only remember which Visa that was...For a while she'd managed to keep track of everything, opening store cards to get the 10 percent discount and keeping the balances on their other cards low enough that Dan wouldn't notice—she was the one who paid the bills anyway—but lately, she was starting to think that maybe things had gotten a wee bit out of control. First the Barneys card had been suspended because she'd forgotten to make the minimum payment, and then she'd been turned down for a J. Crew card—a *J. Crew card!*—when she'd applied, and she knew she needed to make a minimum payment on the Delta SkyMiles AmEx by the fifteenth or that card was going to get shut off too. It was at the point where she preemptively cringed when her monthly statements arrived in her inbox, because she knew the money in their actual checking account was dangerously low and she had to make sure their mortgage payment would clear. Somehow, miraculously, Dan hadn't caught on yet. But she needed to figure out a way to make more money, and quickly. Soon she would just swallow her pride and give that woman she knew from grad school who had a big job at *InStyle* a call and see if she had anything—*anything*—to assign her. Because soon the only thing she was going to be able to write was a personal essay called "I Made My Family Go into Debt Because I Resented My Husband and Couldn't Resist That Really Cute Isabel Marant Dress (Hey, It Was on Sale!)," which she'd probably have to publish on the *Huffington Post* for free.

When she was Katya's age, the parameters of "success"

seemed much more clearly defined. Or maybe there were just fewer options. When she first got to New York, all she wanted was to make enough money to be able to pay rent without overdrawing her account or taking a cash advance from a credit card or asking her parents for money. But with each stage she reached, it seemed like there was something else on the horizon, just one raise or one new job away—that soon, she could be someone who owned clothes that required dry cleaning and got weekly mani-pedis and shopped at Alexander Wang sample sales and took Pilates classes and had an apartment that allowed pets that was also big enough to have people over for dinner or throw a party, and she could afford to hire someone to come clean the apartment every two weeks and rent a share house in the summer and go on yoga retreats in Tulum. Then when she had kids, it was like a whole new edition of the New York Olympics, one that she felt she was definitely not medaling in.

She had a few Facebook notifications, so she opened the app and saw that there were new posts in a private group she'd joined a few weeks ago called YUNG MILFS NYC. It was a group of a couple thousand women, most of whom seemed to be five to ten years younger than she was, who all had kids in New York. Her friend Penelope, who she had secretly categorized as her prettiest and coolest mom friend, had added her. And they really were MILFs—lots of them seemed to be actresses or models or just extremely attractive women who had married young. They weren't boring Upper East Side women either; most of them lived in Williamsburg or Bushwick or Greenpoint, and there was a lot of talk about how *judgmental* the older moms were. (Sabrina felt dangerously close to being put into this category.) The first couple of new posts were standard YUNG MILF fare—crafternoon playdates, a humble-brag disguised as a question about a four-year-old who was reading already—but then there was one that made Sabrina sit up in bed so quickly that her head started spinning. She took a deep breath and closed her eyes again and then opened them after a few seconds and read the post:

> Ladies, so I'm in a bit of a spot at the moment. The hubs lost his job a few months ago and I've been looking for some ways to pick up extra cash from home. Anyone have any suggestions that aren't illegal? Or at least, not so illegal that I could get in actual trouble. ;)

She scrolled through the first few comments, all of which said something to the effect of "Sooo sorry to hear that! Thinking of u!" but a post a few lines down caught her eye.

> Hey girl, was totally in the same boat last year. Sucks. But let me tell you, you'll get through it!!! Don't be grossed out, but I started selling my dirty underwear on Craigslist. It's super easy and you can probably make $400 to $600 a week depending how much time you want to put into it. Message me if you want more details! ♥

Now the original woman's post had been hijacked by commenters debating whether it was okay to sell their underwear; some women were saying it was anti-feminist, while others were worried about what would happen if their husbands found out. Some were convinced it was too dangerous. But others—several others, Sabrina noted—were asking for more information. Finally the first commenter replied:

I sell on Craigslist for anywhere from $50 to $75 each plus shipping, depending on what I'm selling. I write something short and dirty where I talk about how I'm sooooo hot and how I get soooo wet (lol) and I post a pic of myself in the underwear I'm selling—I have one pic of me in a thong that I use and one pic in boy shorts. Those are the most popular ones but every so often you get a guy who's really into granny panties so you might want to have some of those on hand too. You can get cheap ones online. Usually I say I'm a hot MILF but sometimes I'll do other characters, like college girl. Sometimes they'll ask you for more pictures, up to you if you want to send them a face shot. Once they pay you, you get the underwear dirty (however you want to do that...), put them in a Ziploc bag, and send them off. That's pretty much it! Let me tell you, it was a total godsend when we were in a tight spot. I don't do it so much anymore, now that I have a full-time job, but I do have a few loyal customers who I'll make special arrangements for. ;)

Sabrina stared at the comment. She went to Craigslist on her phone and typed in *used panties* in the search field and watched dozens of ads come up. *Holy shit.* All this time, a super-easy solution to her problems had been right here in front of her, and all she had to do was take a selfie and post an ad.

Dan still hadn't shown up or texted—she probably had at least half an hour until he came home. She turned on all the lights in her bedroom and rummaged through her underwear drawer until she found a black lace thong. She couldn't remember the last time she'd worn it, and as she put it on she felt a thrill. She stood in front of their full-length mirror, turned her butt to it, and snapped a picture of herself. It was blurry. She tried again, positioning the phone so it was angled more toward the mirror. *This would be easier with a selfie stick.*

The next one was better. She opened the photo and made sure her face couldn't be seen and that she hadn't inadvertently included any images of herself or, God forbid, anyone in her family in the photo. Was she really going to do this? She was. She sat down on her bed and opened the browser on her phone, went to Craigslist, and selected "Post an Ad."

Sexxxxy Asian Mom Selling Sweet Used Panties $40.

Start low, she told herself. She also needed a new email address for her new business. She went to Yahoo and opened a new email account, sweetpanties4u@yahoo.com, and went back to Craigslist and posted her ad. She got excited when she got a notification that an email had arrived at her new address, but all it said was *Your ad has been posted!* A few more minutes went by, and still nothing. Were all the used-panty fetishists asleep for the night? She felt giddy, like she was extra-drunk. Then, all of a sudden, the emails started coming in.

hi beautiful im looking for 2 prs, need to have strong odor
will u cum in the panties before u send them?
Will pay extra for an in-person meeting

Hi, sexy, she typed in response to the first email. *Just let me know exactly what you want. I'm here to please you. :)*

She had just hit send when she heard the lock on the door click and the sound of Dan shuffling into the house. She quickly logged out of the Yahoo email and closed the Craigslist tab, so when Dan came into the bedroom she was just looking at the website for Amelia's school. "Hey. You're still up?"

"Just looking at the new parent portal for Slope Montessori." Dan started undressing. "Why were you at work so late?"

Dan sighed. "Just typical Deanna and Rich bullshit. They want us to be publishing around the clock, but they haven't hired someone to be an overnight editor, so we're there till God knows when editing and scheduling posts to go up all night."

"Huh. That *is* annoying."

"Plus, we're getting ready for this year's TechScene Fifty, and they want to do breakout posts on a few founders, which I could not be less excited about."

"Why?"

He didn't answer her, just sighed dramatically and went into the bathroom and shut the door. She heard running water, then the toilet flush, then running water again. She closed her computer and placed it on the floor next to the bed. Dan came back into the bedroom. "Why do they even have an executive editor if they're never going to listen to him? I told them there is *no* point in giving someone like Mack McAllister more press, the guy has barely done anything and we write about him like he's Steve Jobs." He paused. *"Sorry."*

Sabrina usually mounted a halfhearted defense of Mack whenever Dan launched into a diatribe about him, but now she was silent.

"The tech world builds these people up like they're gods just because they got some VC funding and they're *somewhat* good-looking, and then it just perpetuates the cycle because they go to South by Southwest and talk about how great their app is but no one ever bothers asking if anyone is actually using it or if the company is making any money. No one *cares,* though. That's the crazy thing. It's basically all a house of cards waiting to fall."

"I'm really tired," Sabrina said. "Can we talk about this later?"

"Do you really *like* working there?" Dan got into bed. "Like, really. If the company closed down tomorrow, would you be sad? Would you miss your job? Would you miss your coworkers?"

"What a thing to say, Dan." She refused to meet his eye.

"Look. I'm glad you have a job. I really am. I just...I just wish it was with someone else, okay? To me he just represents everything that's wrong with startup culture."

"But you *work* at a startup!" Sabrina said. "TechScene *is* a startup."

"That's not the point. I think Rich and Deanna are actually good people. And we're building something necessary and important."

"Don't tell me you really believe that bullshit. Now you sound like the rest of them." Dan was silent. "I'm turning out the light." She clicked off the table lamp next to her side of the bed and the room was in darkness. She waited for him to respond—he always wanted the last word—but instead he just turned over onto his side, facing away from her, and soon she heard his breathing become slow and rhythmic.

12

BOUNDARY HUNTER

yo

The notification flashed across the top right-hand corner of her screen. It was Dan, direct messaging her in Slack. She sighed. It was 6:23 p.m. and she was so close to finishing a post about a new app for New York apartment listings that was billing itself as the "Tinder for apartment listings"—you swiped through photos of apartments the app preselected for you based on preferences (size, location, et cetera), and if you chose one, you'd find out immediately if you were qualified to rent it based on information the app had saved about your income, roommates, guarantors, and so on. If she finished soon, she might be able to leave by seven. What could Dan possibly want? She clicked over to Slack and typed:

Katya: hiya. what's up?
Dan: almost done here?
Katya: yeah just finishing up this one thing
Dan: cool, lmk when you're done. i'll walk out with you.
Katya: you don't need to wait for me

Dan: it's fine, i have a couple emails i need to send. just ping me when you're almost done

She sighed again. Now she felt like she had to hurry things along because Dan was waiting for her. She halfheartedly typed a sentence into her post, then deleted it. She sat for a minute, drumming her fingers on the desk—a nervous habit that she tried not to do when there were other people around—and finally typed:

> FindMyPad is entering an already crowded market for apartment rentals in New York City. Billing itself as the "Tinder for apartment listings" is a canny attempt to cater to the demographic it wants to serve. The only thing standing in the way of success is its ability to keep an updated database of listings and keep out the spammers. If it can do that, Craigslist might finally have a worthy competitor for our hard-earned security deposits.

She read over the last few sentences again, gave a little nod, and hit save.

It had been two weeks since she'd taken the photo of Isabel's phone, and so far, Katya had done…nothing. Every time she thought about contacting either Mack or Isabel to ask them about it, she started feeling nauseated. And the Sabrina complication was another layer that made it even more awkward. Katya was usually unwavering in her conviction that she was doing the right thing—not always the easy thing or the predictable thing, but the right thing. She was confident, too, that the bad guys and the good guys in this scenario were entirely clear—Isabel was dating Andrew now; one of the texts

had said *don't tell me u don't miss this,* strongly implying that
they were unwelcome. So why was she having so much trouble
actually doing anything about it? Instead she was spending her
time on posts like this one—posts that would get her points for
breaking something exclusive but that weren't anything truly
ambitious. The FindMyPad news had landed in her lap, thanks
to a well-timed text from Teddy Rosen, who told her that
Gramercy had just made a seed investment and they were about
to launch their product.

Katya: wanna go over my post before I publish it?
Dan: that was fast!
Katya: ha I guess. i've been working on it all afternoon.
Dan: ok what's the link? I'll take a quick look and then let's
get out of here.

Three minutes later, Dan messaged her back:

looks good. go ahead and pub.

She reopened the post and hit publish, waited to make sure
the post was actually up, tweeted it, sent it to Trevor to post
from @TechScene, and then unplugged her laptop and put it in
her messenger bag. She shoved her phone in her back pocket,
double-checked her bag to make sure she had her headphones
and wallet, and stood up, pulling on her black leather jacket.
Dan was already standing at the end of her row of desks. The
office had started to empty out, but she saw Christina staring
intently at her screen a few desks away, and Brian, headphones
on, typing so hard on his keyboard she thought it might break.

When they got downstairs, Dan already had his cigarettes

out. "Smoke?" Katya nodded, taking the offered cigarette out of his pack and allowing him to light it. She inhaled. It was dark out, and starting to get chilly. The early signs of New York winter, when it was never still light out when you left work. She'd have to remember to wear her fingerless gloves tomorrow.

"Let's get a drink," Dan said suddenly.

Katya glanced at him. "I'm kinda tired," she said, even though as she said it, she wasn't sure if it was really true.

Dan laughed. "How can you be tired," he said. "You're, what, twenty-three years old?"

"Twenty-four," she said.

"Right. Same thing, really." He took another drag of his cigarette and looked at her sideways. "There was this one night, I must have been around your age, maybe a little older, and we'd gone out drinking after work and then all of a sudden they'd locked us in because it was four a.m. and technically they were closed, but they let us stay, and then they finally kicked us out when the sun started to come up. I went home, slept for an hour, showered, and came into work. It was *fine*."

"Sounds pretty crazy," Katya said. The thought of staying out until sunrise was nauseating.

"Well, it was nothing compared to having kids. You don't know tired until you've had kids."

Couldn't thirty-nine-year-olds just be old and tired and not talk about it constantly? Having children didn't feel like something she had to start thinking about for a long time—maybe ever. She was rarely around kids—every so often she'd see some in her neighborhood, either teenagers causing trouble or well-dressed toddlers who looked like miniature versions of their parents, wearing Converse sneakers and Fleetwood Mac T-shirts. She was hardly ever even around parents, come to think of it, except for Dan, who was not exactly positive about the effect that children had on one's life.

"I wouldn't know, I guess," she said.

"Look, I love my kids, but…let's just say, try not to have any before you're at least thirty-five."

"Noted," Katya said. Thirty-five seemed about as far off as fifty, or a hundred. She would *die* if she was still working at TechScene when she was thirty-five. Actually, if she was still working at TechScene when she turned twenty-six, then something was probably wrong.

"One drink," Dan said. "I don't really feel like going home yet, to be perfectly honest."

Katya took one last long drag of her cigarette and ground it into the sidewalk with her boot and ignored Dan's second comment. "Okay," she said. "One drink. I know I don't have kids, but I really am tired." That was suddenly true; maybe it was all the talk of kids and getting old that just made her want to go home and lie down on the couch. "Hold on, let me just text Victor."

She took out her phone and typed out: gonna grab a drink w work ppl. A few seconds later, a text came back: cool.

Dan looked relieved. "Let's go to Old Town," he said, and so they walked south on Broadway for three blocks until they got to Eighteenth Street, where they took a left. The neon Old Town sign was lit; inside, even though smoking had been banned in bars in New York since 2003—right around the time Katya had had her first cigarette, a Newport she stole out of her mother's purse—Old Town still felt like a smokers' bar, and it kind of smelled like one too. Maybe it was the smoke from all the people taking smoke breaks outside, or maybe the scent had just permeated the walls and floorboards.

The crowd at the bar was already two-deep by the time Katya

and Dan showed up. They walked all the way to the back room, saw that it was also packed, and they had just turned around to take another lap of the room when two people got up from stools in front of the ancient dumbwaiter behind the bar, which was still used to transport food from the kitchen. Katya had come here a few times when she was at NYU; it was a favorite of some of the more pretentious guys who worked on the school paper. There was also an upstairs seating area, but it didn't have the same energy. Downstairs was where everything happened.

"What do you want to drink?" Dan asked, a little too loudly. It was crowded, so he was sitting close to her. Their knees were practically touching.

"Vodka soda, please," she said. Dan ordered a vodka soda for her, gin and tonic for himself, and told the bartender to run a tab. "You're opening a tab?" she asked. "I said one drink! I really do have to go home."

"I'm not expecting you to keep up with me." Dan grinned but his eyes seemed sad. The bartender set their drinks down, and as if to demonstrate he meant what he'd just said, Dan took a big swig of his gin and tonic, downing practically half of it in one gulp.

"Okay, then," Katya said, taking a much smaller sip.

"Crazy day, huh?" Dan said.

"I guess?" Katya said. "Was it any crazier than any other day?"

"I mean the leaderboard," he said.

"*Oh*," Katya said. "The leaderboard, right." The leaderboard was new, a screen on the wall in the middle of the newsroom that showed a constantly updating stream of everyone's traffic and impact score. For a few seconds it would show where everyone ranked in total traffic and impact for the month. Then it would flash to the totals for the week, then for the day. When Deanna unveiled it that morning, she'd said that it wasn't meant to be threatening or scary, but motivating. "Healthy competition, people!" she said, and Katya glanced up and noticed she was in fifth place for the week, which stung. She was used to being at or near the top, but now, under this new system, her impact score was lower than she would have liked. She had spent so much time over the past few months learning how to get a lot of traffic; she hadn't necessarily been trying to get mentioned on other sites or influential Twitter feeds, although that was always a bonus. She usually operated under the assumption that quantity tended to beget not only quality, but also traffic. The more you wrote, the more you figured out what people liked to read, and then you could just write more of that, and presumably each post would be better than the last one. And there was definitely a point where, if your posts got really shitty, people stopped reading. The secret was learning how to churn out posts that were just good enough quality-wise, and do a lot of them. But under this new system, that wasn't working as well.

Every so often she'd see a reporter complaining on Twitter about how far the quality of journalism had tumbled, thanks to the internet, and that journalists with *real skills* and *experience* who knew how to write *original stories* were getting shoved aside in favor of young people who leeched off the hard work of these allegedly hardworking journalists, and it was all because their greedy overlords were obsessed with clicks and traffic—again, at the expense of "real" journalists. *Aggregation* had become a dirty word, and the people who suffered were the readers, who were now faced with piles of online news dreck, according to this line of thinking, and every story was the same, and no one checked sources, and eventually everyone was just going to die under a pile of clickbait, which was the dirtiest word of all. TechScene was regularly accused of publishing clickbait, and what Katya didn't understand was why everyone seemed so upset about stories that people actually wanted to read. Was the success of quality journalism in the old days measured by how *few* people read your work? Katya felt like the people doing the most complaining were the ones who didn't have jobs, so they had time on their hands, or who couldn't keep up with the way that the world was changing, so they felt like they had to cling to how things used to be. Whatever the case, she would be fine with never hearing from them again.

"I don't know," Katya said. "I'm not really concerned about the leaderboard. I think I'm in third place, or something?" She said this knowing full well that she was in fifth.

Dan put his drink down on the bar—a little too forcefully, Katya thought. "Actually," he said, "you're in fifth. And, to be honest…I'm a little concerned."

"You are?" Dan had never told her he was even remotely concerned about the quality of her work or how much she was producing. In fact, he was usually making fun of her for taking work *too* seriously.

"I just…" He took another sip of his drink. "I just don't want Deanna and Rich to start…noticing."

"What would they have to notice? I'm fifth, not *last*."

"I know," Dan said. "But you've been on a downward trajectory, not an upward one."

"Ouch," Katya said. "Wow. Tell me how you really feel."

"Oh come on." He punched her lightly on the arm. "You know I'm telling you this for your own good. I'm not taking Christina out for drinks to tell her she needs to step it up."

Fair point, Katya thought. "Why are they doing this?"

"Well, you can never really know what Rich and Deanna are thinking, but from what they've said to me, they feel like we should be competing with the *New York Times* and the *Wall Street Journal,* not just, like, Mashable. And to do that we need to be writing bigger stories. So they really only want to keep people on staff who can write those kinds of stories."

"So they're going to fire people?" Katya asked. "Like, a lot of people?" TakeOff was her first real job; everywhere else she'd ever worked—the jewelry store owned by her mom's friend, a short-lived stint as a hostess at an Applebee's in downtown Brooklyn—she'd seen people get fired, but the idea of mass layoffs was new and somewhat terrifying.

Dan shrugged. "I don't know for sure. But the numbers I've heard them toss around are around one-third of the staff."

One-third! How would they be able to publish *anything* if they fired a third of the staff?

"Fuck," she said. She took a big swig of her vodka soda and realized she hadn't eaten since lunch, when she'd had a Kind bar and a bag of Baked Barbecue Lay's at her desk. She should pace herself.

"Yeah." He stared straight ahead and took a final sip of his drink, then beckoned the bartender over. "Another round, please."

"Whoa," Katya said. "I said *one* drink."

"I know. But you seem to be taking this news hard."

"I'm just a little surprised, is all."

Dan smiled. "I don't think I've ever even seen you surprised. Katya Pasternack is usually the calmest, the coolest, the most collected. You're a tough nut to crack."

"And what is that supposed to mean?"

"I don't know. You're Russian. You're tough, you know? You don't take anyone's shit."

"Well...thanks, I guess." She took another sip of her first vodka soda as the bartender brought another.

"It's a compliment. Anyway...I just want you to know that whatever happens, I'm on your side. So if you need help deciphering what Deanna and Rich mean or whatever, you just ask me, okay?"

"Thanks. Sure. Okay, I will. Thanks."

"I know you're the best reporter in the newsroom, full stop. I just want to make sure that everyone else knows that too." He paused. "I especially want to make sure *you* know that."

Maybe it was the vodka soda, maybe it was Dan's little speech, maybe it was this unfamiliar, unwelcome feeling of anxiety—but suddenly, she wanted to confide in him.

"So...remember when I met your wife?"

"Ha, yes, I do. Why?"

"Something happened at that party that I haven't told you about that I actually think could be a big story." She took a sip of the second vodka soda. "A *really* big story."

"Yeah?" Dan said.

"It's about Mack McAllister." She watched as Dan's eyes grew wide. "I'll give you the abridged version, but basically..."

When she had finished telling him the whole story, he sat in silence for a minute, sipping his drink. "Okay. Okay. This is big. This is huge. This is...wow. I mean, I can't believe you waited this long to tell me, but fuck, Katya, we have to *move* on this! Tomorrow, you call Mack and you try to get him to say something, anything, about it or about—what's her name again?"

"Isabel. Isabel Taylor."

"Right. Okay. We can't sit on this any longer." He put his arm around her shoulders and pulled her closer to him and kissed the top of her head.

She froze. Was there a protocol for when your boss kissed the top of your head at a bar? Her head was swimming. Could the drinks be affecting her that quickly? *Pretend nothing happened,* she thought. She pulled away and glanced at her phone. "I should take off. It's getting late."

"I guess I should too." Was he not going to acknowledge that he had just kissed the top of her head? Was she supposed to think this was normal? "Wow. Mack McAllister is going *down.*" He looked at her again—was there a hopefulness in his eyes, or was she just imagining it?

"I'll see you tomorrow." She slid off the bar stool and walked out of the bar without turning around. On the subway, she sat slumped against the window, her eyes closed.

When Katya got home, Victor was sitting on the couch with Nilay, and the apartment reeked of pot. Victor and Nilay had made up? When had that happened? And why were they smoking in her apartment? *Please don't let Janelle be home,* she thought.

"Hey, Katya," Nilay said. "I was actually just about to leave." She didn't respond.

"Where'd you go?" Victor asked.

"I told you, just out for drinks with some work people." She wasn't totally sure why she wasn't telling Victor the whole truth. Even though she knew she hadn't, technically, done anything *remotely* wrong, she still sensed that Victor might react badly.

Victor patted the couch next to him. "Come on. Sit down. Do you want to smoke? Nilay brought some over."

Normally, she wasn't opposed to smoking pot and generally didn't mind when Victor did, but there was something about coming home and finding Victor in *her* apartment with Nilay, and the weed, and it was late, and Dan had kissed her on the head...ugh. "Where's Janelle?"

"Dunno," Victor said. "She hasn't been around." Nilay was looking increasingly uncomfortable. Victor glanced at him and back at Katya, and then he slapped his thighs and stood up. "Okay! You know what? I'm gonna stay at my place tonight. Just need to grab my bag." He went into the bedroom and Katya could hear him throwing stuff into his backpack. She gave Nilay a strained smile.

"How you been, Katya?"

She didn't know Nilay very well, even though he was her boyfriend's roommate and his company's co-founder. He'd gone to Columbia with Victor, and whereas Victor had a scrappy outsider vibe—he'd grown up in LA and gone to private schools on scholarship—Nilay just seemed like a spoiled guy who'd never really had to work for anything.

"Fine." She stood in front of him, arms crossed. "What have you been doing?"

"Not a ton, to be honest," he said. "I kind of just came to terms with the fact that StrollUp isn't coming back."

She snorted. "Yeah, that's probably a good thing to come to terms with."

Victor reappeared in the doorway. "All right, I guess we're outta here." He looked at her plaintively, as if to say, *Are you sure you want me to go back to my beautiful apartment?* He walked over to her and gave her a hug and nuzzled his face in her ear. "See you tomorrow," he whispered.

"Actually—can I talk to you for a sec?" Katya said. Victor glanced at Nilay, who was looking intently at his phone. *"Alone."* She pulled him into her bedroom and shut the door. "Were you going to tell me you and Nilay made up and you're going back to your apartment? When did all this happen?" She was trying to keep her voice down but these walls were so thin—Nilay could probably hear everything.

"Yo, chill." Victor sat on her bed and put his backpack on the floor. "First of all, you told me I've been texting you too much at work. So I just figured I'd tell you when you got home. And second of all, I thought you'd be happy! You've been on me for a week to get out of your apartment and now I'm leaving and you're all pissed?" He shook his head. "I can't win with you."

Katya looked at him through narrowed eyes. Was it even worth trying to make her point? "*Fine.* I mean, I *am* glad you're leaving. Not because I don't want to see you, but, you know." Victor nodded. "But it's weird that you didn't tell me ahead of time! What if I'd gotten home and you were already gone?" She felt her face flushing.

"Why do you think we were waiting around? I was just waiting for you to get home." She was slightly mollified by this. "And Nilay and I 'made up' this morning. The fight was stupid." He shook his head. "Like, he's my boy, you know? I just needed some time to chill out about everything." Katya was still silent. "Is that acceptable?"

"Yeah," she said. "Okay. I'll see you tomorrow."

He looked at her one last time and shook his head as he picked his backpack up off the floor. "You are tough," he said, and he kissed her. "That's what I like about you."

13

COMING TO TERMS

THIS TERM SHEET summarizes the principal terms of the Series A
Preferred Stock Financing of TakeOff, Inc., a New York corporation
(The "Company"). It does not constitute a legally binding agree-
ment...

There it was, in ten-point Arial font on the five inches
of his phone screen: the term sheet from Gramercy Partners,
which had come through via email from Teddy Rosen, as
promised, that morning. *Beyond pumped abt this,* the email
said. *We've never gotten a term sheet together so
quickly—can't wait to get going.* And there, right after all the
preamble and legal boilerplate, were the numbers Mack had
been awaiting:

Amount: $20,000,000
Price per share: $3.41
The purchase price is based on a post-money valuation of $600
million.

The rest was a stream of legalese that he skimmed, and then he read the important part again to make sure he hadn't gotten anything confused, and he grinned. He hadn't gotten anything confused. "Fuck. Yes," he said to himself. Gramercy Partners was investing twenty million dollars in his company. The lawyers would look it over, of course, and there would probably be some more back-and-forth, but as of right now, it looked like Teddy Rosen and James Patel and the rest of Gramercy Partners were about to make him very, very rich. On paper, true. But very rich nonetheless. He pinged Jason Schneider, TakeOff's COO, who sat directly outside his office.

Got a sec? I have something I need to show you...

He could see Jason get the message, and he watched as he got up and came to the doorway of Mack's office. "What's up?" he said. Jason had been at TakeOff for only a few weeks, but Mack already felt like he had become a crucial part of the fabric of the place. Jason had approached Mack at a Startup Series panel on how to raise a seed round that Mack had moderated a few months ago and told him how much he loved the product—he credited TakeOff not just with increasing his productivity at work, but also with improving his performance at the gym because he was able to recognize when he would be most energized—and they made plans to have breakfast, and then Jason told him that he was feeling restless at the ad tech company where he'd been director of operations for three years, and a lightbulb went off in Mack's head. "We can't pay you what you're making there," he had told him. "At least, not *yet*."

"I got some news I think you're going to like," Mack said

now, grinning. "Close the door?" Jason closed the door. Mack turned his phone toward Jason.

"Hooooooooly shit," Jason said. "Holy shit! Mack, this is fucking *huge*." They fist-bumped. "Twenty mil from Gramercy? You crafty motherfucker. You said you were going for ten from them."

Mack shrugged. "Well, you know how it goes."

"Fucking A I do," said Jason. He banged on Mack's desk. "Damn. This is the best news I've gotten in a long-ass time." They grinned at each other. "You ready for the managers' meeting? Are you gonna tell them?"

Shit. He'd actually completely forgotten about the weekly managers' meeting. And of course, that meant sitting in a room with Isabel. After the night he'd gotten drunk and sent her what he now thought of as *the texts I can't take back*, he'd sent her a few more texts—first apologizing, and then apologizing again, and then just a text that said we have to work together, and I am still your boss, so let's keep it professional going forward, and she had responded, yeah our relationship was always so "professional." It stung but also made him angry. Who the fuck did she think she was? He had given her the kind of work experience you couldn't pay someone to get. Hell, if she wanted to, she could march into probably any other startup in the city and get a job in about three seconds.

Which, come to think of it, wouldn't be the worst idea in the world.

"Yeah," he said in response to Jason's question. No need to tell him that he'd forgotten about the meeting—better to play it like this had been his plan all along. "But I also have to give them the news about Casper."

"I've been thinking about that whole situation." Besides

Brandon, who was going to be filling in for Casper while they looked for a replacement, Jason was the only person Mack had told that Casper was leaving. "It's not really as dire as you think it is."

"Tell me why," Mack said. "Because right now it's feeling pretty fucking dire. Gramercy specifically asked about product and I went on and on about how great our product lead is, what a genius, visionary, blah-fucking-blah. I just feel like they're not going to be thrilled. It makes it seem like I can't keep my best people. And they're going to wonder how we're ever going to ship the new beta on time. And—"

Jason interrupted him. "You're spiraling," he said. "Let's take this one step at a time." Mack nodded. He hadn't realized exactly how much he was unloading on Jason. "First of all, you are under no obligation to tell Gramercy anything before that term sheet gets signed."

"What if they find out?"

"They might." Jason shrugged. "They also might not, if we move things along fast enough. I'm going to advise you, as your chief operating officer, that the news about Casper is strictly on a need-to-know basis. Don't ask, don't tell."

"Okay." Mack felt bad about not telling Teddy Rosen, in particular, but he also felt that Jason probably knew what he was talking about. "So, wait. Why do you *not* think this is so dire?"

"Casper's good," said Jason slowly. He seemed to be choosing his words carefully. "But...it seemed like he sometimes thought a little...*small*."

"What do you mean?"

"I've seen this happen at a couple other places," Jason said. "Early employees come on because they like the excitement of building something, but they also get used to being the underdog. Sometimes they can't handle it when the company gets to the next level. They don't always love when people with more experience come in and start telling them how to do things. Like I don't think it's a total coincidence that he's leaving just a few weeks after you hired your first COO. You know? So it's not really surprising to me that Casper wants to leave to go somewhere that's just getting off the ground. That's who he is. He'll never be at a company that's doing huge stuff. He'll always leave before that happens because he never wants to go above the ground floor."

"Wow. That's...that's a really useful insight." *Do* I *think big enough?* Mack wondered.

"That's what you're paying me for." Jason smiled. "Anyway, let's hit that meeting."

As they walked the ten feet to the conference room, Mack mulled over how he was going to break the news about Casper's departure. He had to tell the managers while also emanating a reassuring I've-got-this-all-under-control vibe. And after Jason's little speech just now, Mack was also thinking that he needed to be not so subtly communicating that they had to start stepping things up. He'd make it clear, of course, that he was including himself in this directive. It was always better for morale when people felt like they were all in this together. As he approached the door to the conference room, he closed his eyes briefly and repeated to himself: *Be the change. Be the change.*

The five department Heroes were all sitting around the table. Oliver Brandt was the Sales and Biz Dev Hero, Jon Liu was the Engineering Hero, Isabel was the Engagement and Marketing Hero, Morgan Vickers was the Recruiting Hero, and Brandon Fisher was the temporary Product Hero. Jason took a seat next to Isabel. Mack didn't *think* that Jason knew about him and

Isabel—how would he?—and seeing them next to each other was making him a tiny bit jealous.

She was looking down, as though deliberately avoiding making eye contact with him. Still, he couldn't help but notice the way her sweater revealed her collarbones, and then gently outlined her breasts. Ugh. Those breasts. Those perfect, perfect breasts. Was it really possible he might never see them, touch them, suck on them ever again? It couldn't be. How could it be? Not only was she blowing him off, but she was clearly involved with Andrew Shepard, at least if her Snapchat was to be believed. And Andrew Shepard was so *annoying!* He had very ostentatiously not taken any venture funding for Magic Bean, and he gave interviews where he talked about how important it was to him and his co-founder to maintain complete control over their company and to grow at a rate that felt reasonable to them—the implication being, of course, that taking venture funding might be tempting in the short term, but in the long term, the *real* winners would be the people who held on to the equity in their companies. Founders who didn't take funding were called bootstrappers because they pulled themselves up by their bootstraps, but Mack happened to know that Andrew had *just* a tiny leg up, having come from one of the wealthier real estate families in New York City. It was always much easier to bootstrap when your safety net was just beneath you—and super-cushy.

"Okay, let's get started." He willed himself not to look at Isabel, unless she was speaking, for the rest of the meeting. It was only then that he noticed Brandon was wearing a dinosaur onesie. *Another* fucking Onesie Day? He decided to ignore it. "First, I just want to remind everyone—and to tell you, Brandon, since this is your first Heroes meeting—that these meetings are confidential, both internally and externally. We're a very open company, as you know, but there are always going to be issues that need to be kept among a small group." He used to love that this group included Isabel; it gave the room an extra electric charge. Now he wished he could kick her out. "So. The good news is we are about to close another round of funding."

"Yes!" Jason slapped his hand down on the table and yelled so loud that Mack was sure the rest of the office had probably heard him. "Mack, you are the motherfucking *man*."

Mack smiled and gave Jason a slight nod to thank him for the show of enthusiasm. "We're still signing papers, and everyone's lawyers are still going over stuff, but I'm hoping to be able to announce the news at next week's Taking Off."

"That is stupendous," Oliver said. He was tall and thin and was wearing his typical outfit of a blue blazer, a pink button-down shirt with no tie, jeans, and loafers. "Truly stupendous, Mack. This will help us close a few deals."

"Rock on, man," Brandon said.

"It'll help with recruiting," Jon Liu said quietly. He and Mack were constantly at odds about tech recruiting—Mack was convinced that it should be easy to hire engineers, given how hot TakeOff was and all the perks they offered, not to mention the fact that the company was in New York City, while Jon insisted that the real perks and status were in Silicon Valley, and it was incredibly difficult to convince top engineering talent to move across the country, and they needed to be offering higher starting salaries, and...Mack usually tuned out the rant at this point.

"Definitely," Morgan said. "I have a couple of candidates in the pipeline who will be very pleased to hear this news."

Isabel was the only one in the room who hadn't said anything. He gave her a second to chime in, and when she was still silent, he continued.

"Good," Mack said. "Now the not-so-great news. As you can see, Brandon has taken Casper's place at the table today—because Casper is moving on from TakeOff. This is his last week here." The room was silent, as though this was news to everyone. Could Casper and Brandon really have kept it a secret? "This is going to leave us scrambling if we're not careful. We have the new beta we're pushing out in a few weeks, and with this new round of funding there are gonna be a lot of eyes on us. There's gonna be press, there's gonna be people talking about us all over, and we need to make sure we are at the *top* of our game." Everyone in the room nodded. Mack was feeling good—it was definitely smart of him to have led with the funding announcement, because it not only made people more secure in their jobs and in him, but also made them feel special that they had been let in on this secret before everyone else.

People just wanted to feel special. They wanted to feel like you *saw* them, like you could really see and appreciate what they were about. If nothing else, making people feel special was something Mack could handle.

"So let's do updates first. Who wants to start?"

"I'll start," Jon said. "We're pushing ahead to open the new version up to the public by December first—just a couple of issues we need to resolve before then."

"Like what?" Mack asked.

"Well, the most important one is figuring out how to replicate what we're doing now without saving user data," Jon said matter-of-factly.

"Wait a second," Mack said. "We're saving user data?"

Jon glanced around the room. "Um, yeah, that's been part of

the current beta since the beginning. There's just no way to get our predictive algorithms nailed down if we don't have access to the historical data."

"Are people opting in on this? I was just under the impression that nothing was being stored." He was trying to keep his voice calm, but this was a potentially major issue. He'd been confidently stating for weeks now that TakeOff was able to do what it did without storing user data. He'd even made a point of saying it to Gramercy. And now Jon was telling him that they *were*, in fact, storing the data? How was this possible? How had *he* missed that?

"Yeah, there's an opt-in," Jon said. "Anyway, that's what we're working on now. It's kind of a thornier issue than we'd anticipated, but we should be ready by December first."

"Okay," Mack said. There was no reason to belabor the point, especially not in public. But now he wanted to move on. No more surprises. "Actually, instead of general updates, I want to hear about what your department is doing to take us to the next level. And how are the rest of us going to be inspired by it?"

"*Great* question, man," Jason said. Everyone else nodded in agreement—except for Isabel.

"Isabel, let's start with you," Mack said. There was no way she was ready to go into detail on what her department was doing, let alone discuss any good ideas she had up her sleeve. *Let's see how it feels when I treat you like everyone else.*

For the first time in the whole meeting, she actually made eye contact with him. He raised an eyebrow as if to say, *I'm not kidding.* Everyone turned to Isabel expectantly, and maybe it was his imagination, but he could swear he felt the mood in the room shift. She looked away from him and across the table at Brandon. "We have several exciting initiatives planned in marketing and engagement." He had never heard her speak so formally. "We are currently partnering with Birchbox to offer a special work-pick-me-up box—"

"Seriously, Isabel, that's all you can come up with?" he said, interrupting her. He was vaguely aware of the potential minefield he was stepping into by publicly confronting her—surely she had deleted those texts?—but he didn't care; certainly Isabel had as much to lose as he did. "A partnership that you didn't even sell? That deal came through sales, right, Oliver?" Oliver nodded without making eye contact. "I asked for *new* ideas. I asked for innovation. I asked for—" He didn't get to finish the last part of the speech because Isabel abruptly stood up, said, "Excuse me," and ran out of the room.

Everyone else sat for a few seconds, people glancing at each other, at Mack. Waiting. "Well, I guess I'll need to look somewhere else for inspiration," Mack said, and he laughed. The rest of the room laughed with him. Then all of their phones trilled and vibrated at the exact same time. Mack's was on the table in front of him, facing up, and he saw that it was a TakeOff notification: Hello, friend. Don't forget: random acts of kindness are the kindest act you can do for yourself. ⚑ He waved the phone in front of the group. "Did everyone just get this random-acts-of-kindness notification?" They all looked at their phones and nodded. Mack frowned. "We need to avoid the exact same timing—these have to feel more personalized. Brandon, let's discuss." Brandon nodded.

After the meeting, Jason lingered. "Mack, question." Without waiting for Mack to respond, he continued: "I hope I'm not overstepping here—I know Isabel has been with you for a long time, but..." He hesitated. Mack hoped his face was blank. "But do you think she's really equipped for the job you have her in? It's just that I've seen this type of emotional behavior before, and it's never good. It's like I was saying earlier about Casper…sometimes when you have people who have been there from the beginning, it's hard to recognize that the company has evolved and they haven't. And we're only going to be under more scrutiny going forward. You don't want those kinds of loose cannons in positions where they can really embarrass the company."

There was no way Jason could know about him and Isabel, and yet Mack still felt like he had been caught doing something wrong. He also felt what he knew was an irrational need to defend her, even though he had just humiliated her. *Breathe*.

"Totally," he said. "That's an excellent insight. Thanks, man." He smiled. "Sometimes I still can't believe that now we can hire people with your perspective and experience. And let me just reiterate that *you. Are. Valued.*"

"Well, thanks," Jason said. "It's funny—when I was thinking about whether I wanted to take this job, I had so many people tell me I'd love working for you, and I believed them but I also had to see it for myself, you know? And now that I have, I can honestly say that these past few weeks have been the most inspiring and rewarding of my entire career."

"Now let's make sure that the rest of them are too." They fist-bumped as Mack said this, and Mack left the conference room considerably more cheerful than he'd been when he'd entered it. Isabel being immature aside, he had managed to convince a roomful of his most senior managers that the loss of Casper—probably one of the most important people at the company, and someone who was going to be tough as hell to replace—wasn't such a big deal.

He walked out to look for Isabel. She wasn't at her desk.

"Hey, have you seen Isabel?" The woman who worked directly under Isabel, Sabrina, was older—if he had to guess, he'd say thirty-two or so—and always seemed slightly nervous, like she was afraid that she was in the wrong place. She looked up at him and shook her head.

Mack went back into his office and texted her: where r u. A few minutes later, her response: not feeling well, went home for the day.

14

PRIMARY SOURCES

KATYA WAS SMOKING alone when she saw Sabrina hurry out the front door of the building and turn to walk in the other direction. She stubbed out her cigarette and ran after her. "Hey." She tapped Sabrina on the shoulder. Sabrina turned around and searched Katya's face as though trying to remember who she was. "Oh! Hey. You're Dan's coworker. Sorry, remind me of your name again?"

"Katya."

"Right. Hi. I'm just running out to grab some lunch—what's up?" It was two o'clock, when most people were coming back from lunch.

"Mind if I walk with you?"

Sabrina glanced over Katya's shoulder. "Yeah, sure." They headed toward Sixth Avenue in silence. Sabrina looked tired, Katya thought, but that might have been because she wasn't wearing any makeup. "So . . . what's going on?"

"Do you have time for a quick chat?" Katya hadn't really thought through what she was hoping to achieve with this conversation with Sabrina, but she wanted to take advantage of catching her off guard.

"Um...not really. I need to get back to the office."

"I'll be quick. Like twenty minutes."

Sabrina hesitated. "Okay. I was just going to get a salad but if you want to sit with me for a few minutes, I guess that's fine." They passed a place called Only Salad. "I don't like that one," Sabrina said, without further elaboration. Katya never frequented these choose-your-own-ingredients salad places that existed on every block of downtown and midtown Manhattan. They were overpriced, for one thing, but also so *predictable*. The people who frequented them seemed like robot salad hordes, streaming in and out of temples of rabbit food. She and Sabrina kept walking and finally reached a place that looked almost identical, except this one was called Chop't. "You've been here, right?" Sabrina asked, and Katya shook her head. Sabrina looked surprised. "Huh! Okay. Well, I usually go for the kale Caesar with chicken, but if you want something a little more substantial—wait, you're not a vegetarian, are you?"

"Oh—I'm not eating. I've been snacking all day."

Sabrina nodded knowingly. "These snack rooms, they're crazy, right?" She laughed. "Though you've probably never worked anywhere that doesn't have a million snacks, I bet." Katya smiled and didn't say anything.

As Sabrina ordered, Katya checked her phone. There was a Slack message from Dan: where'd you go? Need a smoke! She put her phone back in her pocket. When they got to the register, Katya took out her wallet. "Here, this is on me."

"What? No, no, no." Sabrina had her credit card out and was in the midst of handing it to the cashier. "Don't take her card. Use this." The cashier, a wide-faced woman with her hair pulled back into a ponytail so tight it seemed to be stretching her face, had a name tag that said LETICIA. "Leticia, really, take my card."

160

Leticia took Sabrina's credit card wordlessly and swiped it. "Declined." She held it up to her face. "Sabrina."

"Can you try it again? That card should be fine..." Leticia swiped the card again and this time Katya could hear a discordant beep when she did.

"Declined." She held the card out as though she might flick it in Sabrina's face and glanced behind them. There wasn't anyone else in line, but Leticia acted like she had expended the allotted amount of time and energy on the two of them and was now eager to move on. "You got anything else? We take cash."

"Goddamn it," Sabrina said softly. She took the card back from Leticia and put it in her wallet. She turned to Katya. "Sorry. This is so embarrassing. I actually don't have any cash on me. Would you mind..." Katya took out the American Express Corporate card that TechScene gave its reporters and handed it to Leticia. She swiped it and gave Katya the receipt.

"See, you should always come to lunch with a friend," Leticia said, grinning at Sabrina, who looked like she wanted to both punch Leticia in the face and burst into tears.

Katya and Sabrina made their way to a table in the middle of the room. Katya glanced around the nearly empty restaurant. There was a guy in khakis and a plaid button-down shirt sitting by himself at a table, a half-eaten salad in front of him, scrolling through his phone, and two women at a table near the window, both in yoga pants. The situation at the cash register had happened so quickly, Katya hadn't really processed it yet, but now that they were sitting down and Sabrina had taken the lid off her plastic bowl and was picking at the kale in front of her, Katya realized that, yes, it was pretty fucking weird that Sabrina's card had been declined. In the moment that Sabrina opened her wallet to put her card back, Katya saw at least four or five other credit cards in her wallet too. Strange that she wouldn't try to use any of those, but maybe she was just embarrassed that the one card had been declined so she didn't want to try with the others?

"Thanks for buying me lunch." Sabrina didn't quite meet Katya's eyes as she said this. "I guess it's good I ran into you. I'll have to call the credit card company, I don't know why that would have happened."

"It's fine, really. Not a problem. I was planning on buying you lunch anyway."

Sabrina nodded and took another bite of kale and chicken. "Can you not mention this to Dan? It'll just get him upset and I know he's under a lot of stress at work."

"Oh. Yeah, sure. Listen—so, I did want to talk to you about something else." Sabrina raised her eyebrows at Katya. "That party. Andrew's party. The thing we both saw on Isabel's phone."

"Yeah." Again, Sabrina just seemed tired. Or resigned. Or…something. She didn't seem surprised that Katya was bringing this up, at least. "It's been weird. At work, I mean."

"Oh yeah?"

"Yeah." Sabrina got a water bottle out of her bag and took a sip. "Can we talk just, like, casually? I don't want my name associated with anything, and also, I feel like it's already awkward that you work with Dan, and I don't want him to know that I talked to you." *Weird*, Katya thought. Sabrina was more concerned about Dan finding out than she was about Mack finding out?

"Yeah, of course. But do you mind if I take some notes? I just want to be able to remember what you say."

Sabrina scrunched up her face. "Actually, I'd rather you didn't. Just…I don't know. Being a little paranoid, I guess."

Being a reporter was like a delicate dance with a stranger where you were never quite sure whether you were leading or not, and if you stepped on someone's toes, that person might run off the dance floor crying. Katya knew she had to tread carefully. She looked into Sabrina's eyes—they were dark and revealed little. She noticed the fine lines around them, amplified by the fluorescent lighting. She wondered what it was like living with Dan.

"Right, sure, I get that. Well, let me ask you this—did you know that anything was going on between Isabel and Mack?"

Sabrina shook her head. "No way. They were very discreet. Now that I think about it, maybe he came over to our desk area a tiny bit more than he did to other people's, but honestly, I'm kind of in my own world over there. Especially those first few months when I was just trying to, like, pretend I knew what I was doing. I had barely been on Twitter, you know? It was a miracle I even got that job." Katya thought back to the day a few months ago when Dan had told her—during a smoke break, of course—that his wife ("of all people") had gotten a job at TakeOff ("of all places"). Katya was surprised that he was so surprised, but now, having met Sabrina, she kind of understood. Sabrina exuded a world-weariness that would have seemed out of place at TechScene, let alone at TakeOff.

"Why *do* you think you got the job?" Katya asked this out of genuine curiosity, not because she felt like it was germane in any way to her story.

Sabrina shrugged. "There had just been an article some-where, maybe it was in the *Times,* about how tech companies have such a horrible record when it comes to diversity, especially with older women of color." She paused. "And by *older* I mean, like, over thirty. And I'd just had an article go viral. And I'm sure I was the only person over twenty-five who walked through the door who was interested in a coordinator-level job that paid fifty-two thousand a year. I mean, that's a salary I would have been *thrilled* to make when I was your age, but to be thirty-six in New York City making fifty-two thousand is kind of sad." Sabrina took another bite of salad. It *was* kind of sad, Katya thought. She herself was making forty-eight thousand, but like Sabrina said, she was twenty-four years old and happy to live in a crappy apartment with a roommate. "I mean, I know people who do it, and I'm not saying I'm not grateful to have this job, but it's just..." She trailed off.

Katya decided to try to move on. "Do you like Mack?"

"He's fine. It's hard to know how to feel about him after all this, to be honest."

Sabrina took another bite of salad and pushed it away. "I'm finished with this, I think. At some point it all just starts tasting like rabbit food, you know?" Katya nodded. "So, wait. *Are* you writing a story?"

Katya shrugged. "Thinking about it," she said. "Trying to figure out if there's a there there. Gathering string, as they say."

"Got it," Sabrina said. "Well...I should get back to the office. And if you *are* working on a story...let's not do this again, okay? I can't help you with it. There's just too much"—she gestured in the air—"*stuff*. You know?" She gathered up her salad bowl and utensils and stood. "I'm going to walk back, but I think we probably shouldn't walk together, so would you mind just waiting a few minutes before you leave?"

Katya wasn't sure what she had been hoping to get out of this conversation—maybe some big revelation like "I always knew Mack was an ass, he sent me dick pics too!"—but whatever it was, she hadn't gotten it. "Yeah, sure. Hey, listen—do you think you could give me your number?"

Sabrina looked at her, head tilted, as though contemplating what it would mean for Katya to have her number. She sighed. "Okay. Here, let me find a pen." She started digging around in her bag.

"I'll just text you right now, and that way you'll have my number too."

"Oh—right. Of course." She took out her phone and told Katya her number. Five seconds later, there was a message notification that just said Katya. Sabrina nodded. "Okay. Got it. I guess I'll see you?"

As soon as Sabrina left, Katya got out her phone. *Didn't know abt Mack/Isabel,* Katya typed into her Notes app. *But didn't seem to think it was that big a deal? Or didn't want me to think she* thought *it was a big deal.* Sabrina might be a tougher nut to crack than she'd expected.

15

LIVING ON THE EDGE

THE CASHIER HAD handed her declined card back to her with a barely disguised smirk, a smirk that said, *You are just pretending to be a person who has it together,* and Sabrina didn't blame Leticia, really, because she probably would have done the same thing in her position. But—fuck! This was the card that she had continued to pay on time...hadn't she? Now safely far enough away from Chop't that she was in no danger of Katya coming after her, Sabrina took out her phone and went to the Capital One website and typed in her username (sabrinablum) and password (amelia!owen!). *Password incorrect,* the site spat back at her, and she realized she was shaking and had mistyped her children's names. She turned down Twenty-Second Street, a block away from the office, ducked into the foyer of a building, and typed in her password again. Immediately a screen came up that said, *Your account has been locked. Please call us immediately.* "Shit," she said at a volume that she thought was under her breath, but the security guard, an older, heavyset man whose pockmarked face could have been the Before photo in a Proactiv commercial, glanced up from his copy of the *Post.* "You looking for someone in this building?" he said in an accent that evoked the guys behind the counter at the pizza place in Coney Island that she and Dan used to go to when they'd first started dating. It seemed ironically exotic to take the D train all the way to the end of the line and ride the rickety roller coaster, and they always ended their dates at Totonno's. But they hadn't been to Coney Island in years, and last she'd heard, Totonno's had been destroyed by Hurricane Sandy.

"Uh, no, sorry, I had the wrong address," she said, and he made an indecipherable grunt-like noise and went back to his newspaper. She hadn't seen anyone actually reading a newspaper in a while, come to think of it. When she first started working in magazines, it seemed as though every other person on the subway was holding a *New York Times* carefully folded so exactly one-quarter of the page could be read at a time, and she would try to subtly peer over people's shoulders to read. Now she looked over people's shoulders to see what game they were playing or what article they had saved for later or what totally casual just wanted to say last night was fun–type texts they were composing.

She walked out of the building slowly. Why had Katya wanted to talk to her so badly? She seemed really interested in Isabel and Mack's relationship, that was for sure. But…what business was it of Katya's? *Sabrina* was the one who should have been scandalized, seeing a dick pic from the founder of her company sent to her manager, but she felt strangely calm about it—almost as though, on some level, she'd been expecting it. Wasn't this how people behaved now? Everyone was always talking about "hookup culture"—well, here it was, in the flesh. So to speak.

But now, the memory of the party had been eclipsed by a thousand other piddling annoyances of daily life, of finding Owen's shoes and Amelia's hair ties and trying to figure out what the hell she was going to make for snack day at Owen's school, which, fuck, was coming up next week, and she had to come up with something that was nut-free *and* low in sugar. Ugh. And now, if the Capital One card really was turned off, she was officially out of credit cards to use. She ran through a mental list of bills that would come out of their joint checking account on the first of the month: mortgage, Amelia's school tuition, her grad school loans. They would have enough to cover those as soon as Dan's paycheck went in. And then she could quietly siphon off a few hundred dollars to pay a couple of the cards, maybe get them turned back on.

Last night, after Owen and Amelia went to sleep and Dan still wasn't home, she'd sent off a hundred and fifty dollars' worth of old underwear. Jim from Florida got the pair that she'd actually been wearing that day. He was a repeat customer, and he was willing to pay extra for the guarantee that "Skye," the college student, had actually been wearing them while she went about her day. There was no way for him to confirm this, of course, save for her note that she had been thinking about him while she wrote a paper in the library at school, but she felt she needed to be strangely scrupulous about this particular detail. She might have a fake identity, but she couldn't bring herself to lie about whether she'd actually worn the panties or not all day. And she made him pay extra for this privilege: eighty dollars for one pair of pink lace boy shorts from the Gap. She took them off, sealed them in a plastic bag, and wrote on the bag in permanent marker: *xoxo, Skye.* Sabrina put the bag in a padded envelope, wrote Jim's address on it in what she imagined was a college student's handwriting, and put the return address as the PO box in Manhattan she'd opened last week. And there was a new customer in St. Louis who had requested that she send him a pair of underwear that she'd worn during hot yoga. Gross, but she wasn't in a position to argue.

It wasn't fair, really, that it had come to this. The underwear sales were steady, but they weren't netting as much money as she needed them to—she somehow had only seventy-six dollars in her PayPal account. If only her useless job paid more...if only Dan made more money...if only she wasn't such a sucker who had a closetful of clothes she didn't wear. People at TakeOff were always talking about their side hustles—selling their hand-knit scarves on Etsy, DJ'ing, hosting pop-up dinner parties—but she had a feeling that if she told any of them about her side hustle, they'd be horrified. And besides, she was feeling too old for a side hustle. A side hustle, when you were thirty-six, was just a second job.

Another customer last night, Paul, had asked for a white lace thong from Skye "with a strong scent." Sabrina had thought she would find her customers disgusting, or at the very least pathetic, but in fact, there was something hot about these guys who knew exactly what turned them on and were willing to go to great lengths to get it. These were guys who knew what they wanted—so what if it was smelly women's underwear from strangers? It wasn't harming anybody. And even though she knew it was fake—she was selling a fantasy; these guys were buying one—she had to admit that it was flattering to be so blatantly *wanted* by all of these men, even if they had no idea who she was or even really what she looked like.

She put on the thong and lay down on the bed and took the vibrator out of her nightstand drawer. Did Dan even know she still had a vibrator? True, she'd barely used it in the past couple of years, but it was still there, and the batteries were still working. She turned it on and held it on top of her vagina for a minute or so; even though she wasn't exactly in the mood, she still felt herself getting wet. As she masturbated, she found herself thinking not of Dan, but of her friend Natalie. They had hooked up one night in grad school; one of the other first-year students, a poet, was having a party in her parents' brownstone on the Upper West Side. It felt like high school that night, everyone getting drunk on boxed wine and making out in bedrooms, the parents at their country house upstate, the poet making a show of doing coke off their coffee table but freaking out when somebody broke a wineglass.

Sabrina thought about how Natalie's hair smelled like Clinique Happy perfume and how they'd been smoking in the garden when Natalie turned to her and kissed her and whispered, "I've wanted to do that since the first day of workshop," and now Sabrina moaned (quietly; Amelia had been getting up in the middle of the night lately and coming into their bed). It was a memory she rarely allowed herself to access, but one she remembered every detail of; they ended up in what seemed to be the poet's little brother's bedroom, with a poster of Yankee Stadium on the wall and a dresser topped with soccer trophies. She remembered the way that she and Natalie had tumbled onto the twin bed and then Natalie had unbuttoned and unzipped Sabrina's low-rise jeans—that was when her stomach had been flat enough to wear low-rise jeans—and slowly kissed her everywhere, and just when she thought she couldn't hold out any longer, Natalie had finally gone down on her and she came, hard, and moaned loudly.

She and Natalie had hooked up one other time after that, and even though she'd never dated women before, it seemed, for a minute, like maybe they would actually be a thing. But then she had met Dan and even though there was a part of her that wanted to keep hooking up with Natalie—the part that wanted to believe that hooking up with a woman wasn't exactly cheating—there was another part of her that felt like this had just been a fluke, and besides, Natalie started dating a guy not long after that too. But every so often—like now—she let herself wonder how things might have turned out differently.

16

SECOND THAT PROMOTION

THE NEXT MORNING, Mack looked up from his computer to see Jason standing in the doorway of his office. "Hey, man," Jason said. "Got a sec?"

"Of course, what's up."

Jason came into his office and sat down. Mack hadn't talked to him since the meeting yesterday. "I think we gotta make a general announcement about Casper leaving—I think people are starting to pick up on something being up and it's just gonna look weird if we act like we're not cool about it."

"Right." Mack drummed his fingers on his desk. People leaving TakeOff voluntarily was a relatively new phenomenon. He'd had to fire a few employees who were underperforming; the important thing was to subtly impart to people that they had brought this on themselves by demonstrating how unhappy they were at the company and that they owed it to themselves to find an environment that would be a better fit for their talents. It was a line, of course, but a line that Mack actually believed to be true. He kept a password-protected spreadsheet on his computer of all the employees at the company, and every three months he asked managers to rank everyone in their depart-

171

ments. People who were consistently at the bottom he put in a special column. Since the company was still small, some departments were only two or three people, so he wasn't about to fire everyone who was always at the bottom. But he noted it for later. "So we have to convey that we're really sad to see him go, and we're thrilled with all of his contributions, but also that life will go on without him? Is that the gist?"

Jason grinned. "Exactly. I can help you compose the email if you want. It should be like, you know, talking about how TakeOff has evolved and how instrumental Casper was at building this thing. But also making it clear that we will be *fine*, even though we're sad. That kind of thing."

"Okay. Right." Mack turned to his computer. "So how about..." He started typing. "'When we launched TakeOff three years ago, our first goal was to build a product that people loved and kept coming back to. We wouldn't have been able to do that without Casper Kim, who shepherded our beta design to market and came up with some of the features—predictive mood analysis, social mood sharing—that are core to the TakeOff mission.'" He looked up. "How's that sound?"

Jason nodded, and cocked his head to the side. "Someone's been lingering for a bit," he whispered, and Mack peered around him and saw Isabel sitting on top of a desk a few yards away from his office, looking at her phone.

"You ever get the feeling that people have overstayed their welcome? I just wish she'd take the hint and quit."

"You could fire her," Jason said. "That is, in fact, allowed."

"It's complicated." Mack sighed. "I wish I could just fire her but...I don't think I can, unfortunately."

"Then make her quit."

"How?"

Jason shrugged. "Things could start getting uncomfortable for her around here. You know? I mean, look, Mack, she is definitely someone whose utility has diminished."

That was a bold assessment from someone who'd been there only a few weeks, but what Jason was saying was true—Isabel's utility *had* diminished, and the fact that they were sitting here talking about her when they could be talking about something else meant that she was taking up way too much space in his brain. He hadn't texted her since yesterday, when she'd told him she wasn't feeling well and had gone home, and there was a tiny part of him that had been hoping she just wouldn't show up today so he would have an excuse to be mad at her. Suddenly, he had an idea.

"Sabrina," he said. "She works for Isabel. You know who she is?"

Jason looked out onto the office floor. "Oh—yes. Dark hair, Asian?"

Mack nodded. "Right. That's it. Let's get her in here."

Jason smiled. "Shall I go get her?" He slipped out of Mack's office. Mack wasn't totally sure what he was going to do once Sabrina came in, but he wanted to make sure that Isabel saw Jason bringing Sabrina into his office. Two minutes later, they walked in. She was pretty, Mack thought, despite the fact that she looked tired—he usually didn't like women wearing a lot of makeup, but as he noted the circles under her eyes and the general pallor of her skin, he thought she could probably use some. He realized he didn't know much about her; she was one of the quiet ones, the kind who came in and did her work and left. There weren't too many like her. Most people who worked at TakeOff were joiners, people who organized softball leagues and special T-shirt days. He had tried to encourage an atmosphere of extracurricular activities, and if the employees@takeoff.com email traffic was any indication, it was working. If you read *any* book on startups, you knew that the most successful ones had the strongest company culture. It started with a motto, something that told people why they were there, infused them with a sense of purpose. It had taken Mack a few months to develop his, but it was something he was proud of: "Do good work, and the work will help the good." He had it printed on the TakeOff T-shirts and on the mugs in the kitchen, and every new employee got a little framed letterpress placard with the slogan to put on his or her desk. He had considered writing a longer mission statement but figured that if he could encapsulate what they stood for in a few words, then why not.

"Sit down," he said to Sabrina, gesturing to the chair next to Jason, who was still standing. Sabrina sat. She was wearing a gray wool sweater whose sleeves she kept tugging over her hands, and she was barely making eye contact. He smiled, he hoped reassuringly, and said, "It's all good—you look nervous."

"Oh—I just...well, I've never actually been in your office," she said. She looked around. "I mean, I've seen it from the outside, of course." Mack smiled. Okay, she was calming down.

"We just wanted to check in," Jason said. He sat down on the couch. "You know, see how things were going."

She glanced at both of them. "They're going well. I think? I mean, do you guys not think they're going well?"

Mack waved his hand. "No, no, they're going great. Our numbers are up, we're very happy with those. We just meant more like...how things are *going*. Are you happy here?"

She smiled. "Oh yes, of course," she said. "I've never been happier, in fact."

* * *

When Jason came by to bring her into Mack's office, Sabrina had her headphones on and was deep in a series of retweets about the TakeOff app. This was part of her job: to retweet, sometimes with a funny comment, anything positive that people were saying about the app, and so she didn't notice Jason was there until he tapped her on the shoulder and she jumped and took off her headphones. "Whoa, you scared me," she said, and he smiled—a smile that she couldn't tell the meaning of. Was it a wolfish "you had lunch with Katya Pasternack and we know everything" smile, or was it an "everything's fine, I'm just randomly coming over to your desk to say hello" smile, or was it something else altogether?

"Got a sec? Mack and I want to chat with you. In his office."

"Oh—sure, yes, of course." She saw Isabel across the room, deep in conversation with someone who had his back to her. She put her headphones on her desk and followed Jason into Mack's office.

Sabrina had been hoping that everything that happened with Katya—from the moment she met her at Andrew Shepard's party to the weird, uncomfortable lunch—would just quietly go away, that Katya would forget about the photo she saw or else decide that it didn't matter. Because Dan seemed more interested in what was going on at work lately. Usually he barely asked her anything about her job, as though its very existence was beneath him, and certainly *talking* about it was not worth his time. But even just last night he had casually asked how things were going at work, and when she had replied, "The usual," he had looked at her for a few seconds and tilted his head and seemed like he was about to ask her something else, but he didn't. Then his phone vibrated and he sighed and started tapping away at it, and then Amelia had wandered into their bedroom and announced that she couldn't sleep, so Sabrina had to go sit with her and read *The Ugly Duckling*—Amelia's choice—twice and try not to wake up Owen, who was sound asleep in the same room. As she read the story, which was really a depressing and not-great-message story when you thought about it, she resolved to quietly remove the book from the shelf. She was supposed to be raising an empowered little girl, not someone who thought that people would be mean to you if you were ugly and the only important thing in life was to become a beautiful swan. Besides, Amelia *was* beautiful, she really was—she had a cherubic round face and bright green eyes—and the last thing Sabrina needed was Amelia worrying that she wasn't pretty. Or thinking that it mattered. Because...of *course* it mattered, but Amelia had more than enough time to figure that out.

Even though she could see Mack's office from her desk, she'd never actually been in it, and it somehow felt brighter inside than she'd thought it would. There was a blond wood table that was his desk, on top of which he had his laptop and another monitor, but no photos or any personal paraphernalia save for the framed slogan—DO GOOD WORK, AND THE WORK WILL HELP THE GOOD—that all the TakeOff employees got when they started. No one had ever said, explicitly, that you had to have this on your desk. But everyone did. There was a turquoise velvet couch, the only burst of color in the space, and a clear acrylic chair that she was now sitting in. She was all too conscious of having her back to the rest of the office—undoubtedly, everyone had seen her come in. What were they thinking? Why was she in his office? Was she about to get fired? Had Isabel seen her come in?

And now he was asking her if she was happy here. "Oh yes, of course," she said. "I've never been happier, in fact." She hoped her smile was convincing. Or at least convincing enough. She couldn't remember, in her previous jobs, there being such an obsession with happiness. No one at the eco-crafting magazine had cared whether she was happy; everyone seemed resigned to the idea that happiness was elusive, ephemeral, and, in any case, not suited to a life in New York City. But now, in front of her twenty-eight-year-old boss, she realized that he had only known a world in which his own happiness was of prime importance. "I love it here." She smiled and made eye contact with Mack.

"Good," he said. He glanced up at Jason. "You've been doing a great job, and we've been thinking we'd like to give you more responsibility, something that's more of a strategy role. I don't know yet what the title will be but I wanted to gauge your level of interest."

"Um, yes, of course." Strategy role? So she wouldn't have to sit there retweeting all day. She would be freed from the tyranny of the TweetDeck. She would be able to tell her husband that what she did had value. "Of course." She repeated it because she needed to believe it herself.

"Wonderful." Mack smiled and stuck out his hand. Sabrina stood up and shook it. "We'll talk more very soon. And could you send Isabel in when you leave?"

"Oh—sure," she said. "And thanks. I'm excited."

Mack watched as Sabrina walked up to Isabel, who was still talking to Oliver Brandt. Sabrina said something to Oliver, who nodded and left the two of them, and then she said something to Isabel, and—did Isabel roll her eyes? He couldn't tell. Sabrina walked back to her desk and then Isabel was standing in the doorway of his office. "Sabrina said you wanted to see me." She looked Mack straight in the eye. "What's going on?"

Jason responded before Mack could say anything. "Yeah, come on in, Isabel. Do you mind shutting the door?" Isabel shut it but stayed standing in front of it. "Have a seat," Mack said and gestured to the chair in front of him. Isabel stared at him a moment too long, and finally sat down.

"So we've decided to promote Sabrina to a more strategic role," Mack said.

Isabel's face was blank. "What does that mean, exactly."

"We're still figuring out specifics, but we think for now it makes sense for her to report to me." Mack hadn't actually thought about this until just that second, but as soon as he said it, he knew it was the right move; Isabel scowled.

"That's crazy," she said. "Sabrina...she's, like, still learning stuff."

"We've been pretty impressed with her work so far," Jason said. "We think she has a lot of potential."

"Oh, come *on*," Isabel said. "Did you guys even know her name two weeks ago?"

"That's inappropriate," Mack said. There was silence. "I'll also need you to write me a memo about your team. If you're going to continue to have direct reports, I need to have more of a vision from you about what that means and how your role could shift."

"Wait, what? Why is my role shifting?"

"Isabel." Jason sounded as though he were speaking to a small child. "We didn't say that your role *will* shift, just that it *could* shift."

Isabel's eyes went from Mack to Jason and then back again. "I just...I don't understand. Is this all because of the meeting yesterday?"

Mack tilted his head to the side, as though considering this. "Look, the meeting yesterday didn't *help*, certainly, but we've been taking a hard look at all of our teams and we're going to be making some changes. Casper's last day is Friday and it just seemed like a good time to try to shake things up a bit. This is a startup, Isabel—things are always going to be changing and evolving and iterating. If one thing doesn't work, we need to be able to pivot and start something new. You get it, right? It's nothing personal."

"Of course," Isabel said. Mack stood up, and then Jason and Isabel did too. Isabel was avoiding making eye contact with him. "Why would it be." Was she...about to cry? Mack had never seen Isabel cry, now that he thought about it. He suddenly remembered when he'd hooked up with a woman who'd cried when they had sex a couple years ago. After the third or fourth time, he told her, while they were still both naked, that he didn't really think this was going to work out and then she'd just started crying harder, and he'd rubbed her shoulders for a minute and then whispered into her ear, "I'm gonna head out," and gotten dressed and left.

Now he was feeling the same level of discomfort, and all he could think was *Isabel needs to get out of my office.* "Okay, then, we'll talk. Thanks." No one moved and he saw tears starting to well up in Isabel's eyes. *Why wasn't Jason doing anything?* He needed both of them out of his office. "Jason, would you and Isabel mind just..."

Jason understood immediately what was happening. "Yes, of course. Come on, Isabel, let's leave Mack alone." Isabel sniffled and turned around and walked out of his office, Jason behind her. Right before Jason walked through the door he turned around and rolled his eyes at Mack. *Women,* he mouthed, and Mack had to stare very intently at the floor to keep from laughing.

17

NO CHILDREN

As Katya was about to leave work, her phone vibrated with a text from Victor: hey come meet me & nilay & some other ppl @ tippler? The Tippler was a bar in the basement of Chelsea Market popular with people who worked at Google, which had office space upstairs in addition to the company's block-long building across the street. Nilay had worked at Google before he and Victor had started their company, and he was still friends with his former coworkers. Katya sighed. She didn't particularly feel like spending her evening around a bunch of Googlers. They were a cultish, secretive group, always working on some new product within Google that they were sure was going to change the world, and yet she found them strangely risk-averse. If they *really* wanted to be revolutionaries, Katya reasoned, they wouldn't be working for a gajillion-dollar multinational corporation; they'd be striking out on their own. But once you got used to in-house chefs and massage rooms, it was hard to give them up, and so there was also an edge to Googlers, a resentment that they were trapped by golden handcuffs. They all thought they had the potential to be the next Sergey Brin or

Larry Page themselves, and that their genius had not yet been fully recognized. So even though she didn't have a ton of respect for Nilay, this was one aspect of him that she did admire: he had walked away from Google and taken a leap into the unknown. It had failed, sure, but at least he had *tried*.

She could already picture the scene at the Tippler: it would be crowded, and it would take forever to get a drink, and Victor would be off trying to network, and when she'd finally found a quiet corner she'd get hit on by a junior software engineer with bad breath. But it was eight p.m., the TechScene office was deserted, and she didn't have anywhere else to be. yeah ok i'll head over there, she texted back. He responded with the fist-bump emoji.

It was about a twenty-minute walk from the TechScene office over to the bar, and Katya took the opportunity to smoke two cigarettes. She had a Google doc going with her notes about Mack and Isabel, but she'd read them over that afternoon and it felt like she didn't have much to work with. She was starting to worry—not panic, but worry, just a little bit—that she wasn't going to be able to get everything she needed to actually publish the article. Or at least, not the article that it seemed like Dan wanted her to write, which was essentially a takedown of Mack McAllister that would expose the hypocrisy of the tech world once and for all.

She stubbed out her cigarette at the corner of Fifteenth Street and Ninth Avenue and put on some bright red lipstick. She rubbed her lips together and picked up her phone and turned the camera toward her so she could see herself. "Okay," she said out loud. One block down, the Apple Store emitted a warm glow. She crossed Ninth, and halfway down Fifteenth Street, at the bottom of some stairs, there was a nondescript door that looked like the entrance to a store. There was a bored-looking guy guarding it.

"Private party tonight," he said, looking her up and down. She was in one of her standard outfits—black jeans, black Docs, leather jacket. Her nails had chipped black polish on them. Was this inspection supposed to make her feel self-conscious? It made her feel defiant. *Hey, fuck you, bouncer guy.* This was uncharitable, she knew, but private party? Since when did the Tippler have bouncers and private parties?

"Yeah, I'm here for that party. My boyfriend's in there." She said this as calmly as she could. He squinted and tilted his head at her, as though contemplating whether this could possibly be the case.

"I'll need to see some ID," he said finally. She wordlessly fished her wallet out of her bag, extracted her New York State ID—she had never bothered to learn how to drive—and handed it to him. He looked it over and gave it back to her. "All right, Katya." He moved aside to let her through.

She didn't respond, just walked into the bar. *Asshole,* she thought as she scanned the room. The bar was decorated in a kind of cozy-library-chic, with books on display above the bar, Persian rugs on the floor, and low-light Edison bulbs. Right now it was packed full of people, mostly guys. Katya took a deep breath. How was she even supposed to find Victor in this crowd? She looked at her phone—no service. "Great," she muttered. Out of the corner of her eye, she saw Isabel Taylor and Andrew Shepard. Isabel was looking at her phone in one hand, even though there was no service down here, and holding a drink in the other. Andrew was talking animatedly to the guy next to him, someone Katya didn't recognize. Should she go up to Isabel and try to talk to her? Victor would probably be pissed—he hated it when Katya did anything that seemed like she was using their relationship for work—but, fuck it, he was nowhere to be found. She took a deep breath and sidled up to Isabel, away from Andrew. Neither of them noticed her approach.

"Hey, Isabel," she said. Isabel didn't look up from her phone. Katya cleared her throat and said, louder, "Hey, Isabel." Isabel turned to her with a *Do I know you?* look on her face. "It's Katya." Isabel still looked like she wasn't sure who Katya was. "From Andrew's party the other week? I was there with Victor Vasquez?"

"Oh, *right*," Isabel said, though it wasn't actually clear if she remembered Katya or if she had just grown tired of Katya struggling to explain how they knew each other. "How's it going." She took a sip of her drink—it was clear, with a lime on top; probably a vodka soda—through the little cocktail straw.

"Oh, fine," Katya said. "How are you?"

Isabel shrugged. "Fine." She gestured with her head toward Andrew. "You know how they are. I'm basically invisible right now." Katya wasn't totally sure who *they* meant—startup guys? men in general?—but she nodded in agreement. "Do you need a drink?"

"I'm okay— " Before Katya could finish what she was going to say, Isabel was interrupting her.

"Let's get you a drink." She turned to Andrew. "Be right back." He barely nodded. She took Katya by the arm. Isabel was an expert, it seemed, at navigating crowds, or maybe it was just this particular crowd—a throng of men in their twenties and thirties wearing plaid shirts and dark jeans. She had a way of softly nudging them aside, making eye contact and smiling. It was the opposite of how Katya navigated crowds, which was to make herself seem as small as possible and try to squeeze through people so they barely even noticed her. "What do you want?" Isabel asked as they approached the bar. They couldn't get all the way to it because it was blocked, end to end, by guys ordering drinks, getting their drinks, sipping their drinks. "Excuse us," Isabel said sweetly, putting her hand on the shoulder of a guy in a Google T-shirt.

"Oh, no worries," the guy said. He gestured with his head to his friend, who was wearing a blue hoodie, and they both moved aside to let Isabel and Katya through.

"Thanks," Isabel said and smiled at them. Katya generally considered flirting with random people a waste of time—she liked to laser-focus on one person and make him (or occasionally her) her goal, and in any case, there had not been many times in the past eight or so years where she'd been single. But this was a new way of being in the world, she saw now, and it meant getting what you wanted. It was kind of the same as getting a source to talk to you, she realized. Most people, fundamentally, wanted to be liked and to please others. So that just meant putting yourself in the position of being the one to be pleased. "So what do you want?" Isabel asked. The bartender was pouring drafts of beer at the other end of the bar. Making eye contact was going to be impossible.

"I can get it." She took out her wallet. Isabel didn't know it yet, but she was going to be a source, and Katya couldn't have a source paying for her drinks. Isabel leaned over the bar and gave the bartender an almost imperceptible wave—he nodded and within seconds had materialized in front of them. "Vodka soda, please," Katya said. The bartender nodded.

"That's what I'm drinking too!" Isabel said. Katya's drink came; she paid the bartender and held her glass up to Isabel's.

"Cheers," she said, looking her in the eye.

"Cheers," Isabel said.

"So...there was actually something I wanted to talk to you about," Katya said.

"Huh?" Isabel said. It *was* really loud.

Katya raised her voice. "I said, there's something I wanted to talk to you about!"

"Oh," Isabel said. "Okay. Let's go back there." She gestured with her drink toward a corner of the room that Katya hadn't noticed before, one that did, in fact, look quieter, and once again squeezed them through the crowd. "So what's up? You wanted to talk to *me* about something?"

"Yeah. I wanted to talk to you about Mack McAllister."

Isabel's face went blank. "What about him?"

"Were you guys ever together?"

"No offense, but is that really any of your business?" Isabel wasn't looking at Katya now. "Is that why you came over to talk to me, to ask me nosy questions about my boss?"

Honesty seemed like the best policy. "Well...kind of. I'm... I'm probably going to be doing a story about Mack and, um, possible sexual harassment."

"Wait. *What?* Why are you telling me this here?"

"It was just a coincidence that I saw you," Katya said. "I was planning to call you this week, but since you were here, I figured I would at least ask."

"I'm sorry, but that's crazy," Isabel said. "Even if Mack did sexually harass me, and I'm not saying he did, why on earth would I tell you at a bar?"

Katya didn't notice Victor and Nilay until they were practically in front of her. "Hey, babe," Victor said. He smiled at her and kissed her on the lips. He tasted like weed and beer. "I was looking everywhere for you. My phone doesn't work down here."

"Yeah, mine doesn't either. And it's crowded," she said. "You know Isabel, right?"

"Of course," Victor said. He leaned over to kiss her on the cheek. "And do you know Nilay?"

"I don't think so," Isabel said. "But you look familiar."

"I'm sure we've, like...been at the same meet-ups or parties or whatever," Nilay said.

"Probably." Isabel smiled. "Well...I'll leave you all to it. Cheers." She didn't look at Katya as she walked away.

"What is this, anyway?" Katya asked. "The guy at the door said it was a private party."

"Some Google thing," Nilay said. "I think it's like...the Maps engineers' happy hour? I dunno, my friend Jamil invited me. Weird that he said that, though."

Across the room, Katya noticed Isabel whispering in Andrew's ear and Andrew saying something back to her and putting his arm around her. He leaned over and said something else to her and she nodded. Andrew handed his drink to Isabel and started walking toward them. *This cannot be good,* Katya thought.

"Hey, Victor. Hey, Nilay," Andrew said. "Hey, Katya. How's it going."

"Great, man," Victor said. "You?"

"Good, good. You got a second?"

"Me?" Victor asked. Andrew nodded. "Yeah, sure. Can you guys, uh, excuse us, I guess?" Victor gave Katya a look that said, *I have no idea what this is about.* She gave him a look back that said, *Eeeek.*

"Thanks," Andrew said as Nilay and Katya walked away.

"What's that about?" Nilay said to her as they moved toward the bar.

"Not sure." There was no point in bringing Nilay into this. She wanted to look back and see how the conversation between Andrew and Victor was going, but she also didn't want to. She was feeling hot. She had to get out of this basement, away from these people. "Hey—I think I have to get some fresh air. Can you let Victor know?"

Nilay looked at her quizzically, but nodded. "Yeah, sure."

She fought her way through the crowd—without Isabel's help, it took her almost five full minutes to cross the floor of the bar to the exit. The same bouncer was at the door as she walked out. "Taking off early?" he said.

She glared at him and stomped up the stairs two at a time. Once she was outside, she took her pack of cigarettes out of her bag, extracted one, and lit it. Her hands were shaking. She inhaled deeply and closed her eyes just for a moment. This would clear her head. When she opened them, there was a man in a security uniform standing in front of her. "Gotta move away from the entrance," he said. "Technically it's supposed to be fifty feet, but if you just move a little bit I won't say nothin'."

She sighed. "Yeah, okay." Katya walked a few yards away; she could feel the man's eyes on her as she walked. When she turned back toward the street she saw Victor exiting the building. It took only a moment for him to spot her. His mouth was set in a grim line. He came so close to her face that she thought for a moment that he might hit her. Instead, he just stared at her for a second and shook his head slowly.

"What...the...fuck," he said softly. "What the *fuck* did you say to Isabel Taylor?" He glanced down at her cigarette. "And you're smoking. Of course." He made a face.

"You know I smoke. And you smoke weed every day," Katya said. "Anyway, why do you care?"

"Don't change the subject." He was looking at her through narrowed eyes. *You're the one who brought up my cigarette,* she thought, but she kept silent. "What did you say to Isabel?"

"What did Andrew say I said to Isabel?" She took one final drag on her cigarette and stubbed it out against the building, then tossed it on the ground.

Victor rolled his eyes. "You are impossible." She didn't respond. Finally, he said, "He said that you basically threatened her, told her that you were going to publish something on TechScene about her and Mack if she didn't talk to you, and Isabel said that everything you were saying about the two of them was a lie."

Katya stared at Victor. "First of all, you're just going to believe her? I thought you were supposed to be on my side. And second of all, everything she said is bullshit. Obviously. I would never *threaten* anyone."

"Honestly, Katya, I don't know what you're capable of. Sometimes I feel like I don't even know you." She bristled at this statement. It was one that had been hurled at her before, mostly by boyfriends but also by friends.

"Oh, come on," she said. "What does that even mean? You know me as well as anyone in the world."

"Maybe you're just one of those people who's, like, not capable of letting anyone in." He wasn't as visibly agitated as he had been when he'd come storming toward her two minutes ago, but he still seemed pissed.

"You sound like a shrink. And what was that just now, anyway? Coming at me basically accusing me of threatening Isabel? What, are you worried that Andrew Shepard is going to be mad at you?" The way that Victor looked at her when she said that told her everything she needed to know. "You *are.* For fuck's sake."

"Oh, come on. I invite you out, and the first thing you do is confront the girlfriend of one of my friends? You know we have a rule. Anything related to my work is off the record. I didn't think I had to say that that included not trying to get people to talk to you at events."

"It's not something I do regularly!" She was getting annoyed. Victor was acting like she had violated some sacred rule when all she had done was seize an opportunity. "I just saw Isabel, and it seemed like it would be a good time to talk to her."

Victor tilted his head, as though trying to see her from another angle. "It's like you don't even *think* about me when you do this shit."

"That's a really rude thing to say."

"It's true! If you had stopped to think for *two* seconds, *maybe you would have been like, Hmm, I wonder how my boyfriend, Victor, who is currently trying to figure out what his next move is going to be because his company shit the bed and he hasn't had a job in two months, would feel if I went up to the girlfriend of one of the most influential guys in the whole New York tech scene and tried to* blackmail *her—*"

"Okay. Hold up. I did *not* blackmail Isabel. That is completely inaccurate. Honestly, I can't even believe that you would say something like that. It's like *you* don't understand where *I'm* coming from. I have a *job* to do. Which sometimes it seems like you don't totally take seriously."

"That is bullshit! I think what you do is amazing. I just don't want it interfering with what *I* do."

"Clearly," Katya muttered. She glared at him. "So you want to know what I really said to Isabel?"

"Yes. Yes, I do."

"I told her I was looking into whether Mack had sexually harassed her. And—"

"Wait. You *what*? Mack? Sexually harassing Isabel?"

"Yes." Katya paused to give Victor time to process this. He probably hadn't even known they were seeing each other. No one, it seemed, had known that. "And I have proof. Kind of."

"What does that mean?" He sounded wary now.

Could she trust him? She had to trust him. She felt like they were on the edge of a yawning unknown, that everything in their relationship had been leading up to this moment, when one of them was going to have to make a choice. "It means," she said slowly, "that I saw a couple of texts Mack sent her. The night we were at Andrew's party."

Victor let out a sharp breath. "So *another* thing where I *specifically* asked you not to play reporter."

"This wasn't even my fault! I just happened to see the texts come in."

"Well, what were they?"

"They were dick pics," Katya said, trying to keep her voice as calm as possible. "Mack said something like, 'Don't tell me you don't miss this,' and then there were, like, a bunch of dick pics. That I'm assuming were of him."

Victor was quiet. *He finally gets it,* Katya thought, watching him as he apparently processed it all. Then he spoke. "I mean... yeah, that's bad. I get why that's bad. But it's not like...*that* bad."

"What are you *talking* about. He sent her dick pics while she was at Andrew's party. *After* she and Andrew had started seeing each other. I mean, clearly she didn't want them. How is that not bad?"

"It's bad! I *said* it was bad. It's just like...I dunno. Forget it."

"No. I want to know why sending a woman unsolicited dick pics is not that bad. Really, enlighten me. I'd like to know."

"You wouldn't understand." She stared at him. "I mean, you don't *know* that she didn't want them."

Was her smart, kind, funny boyfriend actually saying the words that were coming out of his mouth? She shook her head. *This is not happening.*

"I think I need to go," she said quietly. "I'll see you later." She started walking east.

"Aw, come on, Katya," Victor called out. She ignored him. He hurried after her and grabbed her arm. "Wait."

"Don't touch me," Katya said, and wrested her arm out of his grasp. "See what just happened there? What if you grabbed my arm and I said don't touch me and you kept grabbing my arm?" She could see in his face that that was what he had wanted to do. That was why she had said it, to see what his reaction would be. It was clear he had never considered these questions before. *Good,* she thought. *Let him think about it.* "Seriously, though. I have to go. Don't text me tonight." They were standing in front of the entrance to the bar, and just as she said this, Nilay came out. He looked happy, drunk.

"Hey, man!" he said. He put his arm around Victor. "Hey, Katya! I was looking for you guys. Where are we going now?"

They are children, Katya realized. *They are just little boys, and they can go be little boys together.* "Nowhere," Katya said. "I'm leaving." Before Nilay could respond, she had turned and was walking away from them. This time Victor didn't call out to her.

When she was almost to the Eighth Avenue stop on the L, and the adrenaline that had been coursing through her veins had started to ebb, she felt...yes, those were tears. "Fuck," she said under her breath, and she wiped her eyes with the sleeve of her leather jacket. She squeezed her eyes shut for another moment.

What the hell was she supposed to do now? She didn't want to go home—Janelle would probably be there, making one of her beauty-tutorial videos. Lately she'd started just leaving all her makeup and equipment on the kitchen table, which was technically in the living room—"It's not like you use it, and it would just make things easier if I didn't have to set up each time," Janelle said, and Katya couldn't exactly argue because she had sat at the table maybe once in the entire time the two of them had been living together. But still, there was something about the presumption that rankled Katya. Like it was something she *should* be annoyed about, even if she actually wasn't. Except right now, when all she wanted to do was go home and lie on the couch and stare at the ceiling, and she knew Janelle would be teaching the world how to put on fake lashes.

She felt her phone vibrate. It was probably Victor, texting her to apologize. She took it out of her back pocket. It was, instead, a text from Dan: hey k, hope you're having a lovely evening. this came on my spotify on my way home & it made me think of you. if you don't know neutral milk hotel...well, you *need* to know neutral milk hotel. totally formative. Katya did not know "Neutral Milk Hotel." She clicked the link, which opened an album called *In the Aeroplane Over the Sea,* and started listening. She didn't listen to a ton of music, but when she did, it was usually whatever new hip-hop Victor was into at the moment. This was something else altogether. She listened to a minute or so of one song and texted Dan back: thx. pretty good! She hit send, put away her phone, and then took out her phone again. Before she could think about it too much, she sent him another text: i know you're already home but...any chance you feel like a drink? 🍸 As soon as she hit send, she regretted it. What was she doing turning to Dan for consolation, especially about something like this? But he was the only one who would really be able to un-derstand what had happened at the bar—Victor didn't get how hard it was to be a reporter, that everyone around you could just go on about their business but you always had to be worrying about, like, offending your boyfriend. She had barely finished rationalizing sending the text when he responded: always. name the place, i'll grab an uber.

Old Town? she wrote back. That way, she could just jump on the L at Union Square and go home afterward.

Sure, he wrote.

Half an hour later, they were sitting side by side at the bar. She had a vodka soda in front of her.

"Thanks for meeting me," she said.

"Of course," Dan said. "You're not really one to, like...cry wolf. So I knew it was serious."

She felt tears coming to her eyes again and used a cocktail napkin to dab at them before any real waterworks could start. "It just suddenly feels like nothing is going right, you know?"

"Want to talk about it?" Dan's voice was gentle. Somehow this made the tears come quicker. She rubbed her eyes with the napkin, which was getting grubby. *Ugh*. This was not what was supposed to happen. She *hated* tears. "Or you can cry too," Dan said. "That's fine."

"I don't wanna cry," she said.

"You and Mariah," he said.

"Who's Mariah?"

"Carey. You know, like the song." She didn't, actually, know the song; she was aware of Mariah Carey's existence, but she was slightly embarrassed by the huge gaps in her pop-culture knowledge, gaps that included music and movies that people her

193

age were familiar with. She blamed growing up with Russian parents but also the fact that she had trouble caring.

"Right." She took a sip of her drink. "Anyway. I dunno. I went up to Isabel at this party I was just at, and she kind of flipped out on me and then her boyfriend got involved and basically told Victor to tell me to fuck off, and then Victor got pissed, and we maybe broke up? I actually don't even know."

"Whoa," Dan said. "That's a lot. No wonder you needed a drink."

"See? And it's just like, I need to get this story. I feel like I'm so close."

"You'll get it," Dan said. "I know you will. You...have a way of getting what you want." That sentence hung in the air between them. She traced the edge of her glass with her finger and stared at it; she didn't want to, couldn't, make eye contact with Dan. Why *had* she texted him tonight? There was more hanging in the air that she didn't want to confront. Or did she? She was feeling buzzed, warm. "Do I?" she said. She still wasn't looking at Dan, but she smiled.

When she finally looked up, he was staring at her. "Let's get out of here," he said. "Take a walk. It'll clear your head." A walk *would* be a good idea, but when she opened her mouth to respond, Dan pulled her to him and kissed her, fully and unapologetically. She didn't resist, exactly, but she also wasn't a completely willing participant. "Sorry," he said when he finally pulled away. "I just...I've been wanting to do that for a while."

"It's okay," she said. Did she mean that? She wasn't sure.

"Do you want to get out of here?" Dan said softly. He put his hand on her knee. "We could go for a walk or something."

"I should get home," she said. "I'm going to get in an Uber, okay?"

"It's so early!" Dan said, almost whining. He picked up his phone and showed her. "See? Only ten thirty. You probably don't even go to bed until what, like, one?"

"It's been a long day," she said. She wriggled away from him, so his hand had to drop off her knee. "I really should go."

"I came all the way back into the city to meet you," he said quietly.

"What's that supposed to mean, exactly?" she said. She was daring him to say what she knew he was close to saying. What he wanted to say. What he thought he deserved from her.

"Oh—nothing," he said. "Nothing. I'll see you tomorrow."

18

AGE OF INNOCENCE

SABRINA HAD SEEN the subject line of the email pop up on her phone when she emerged from the subway, but she couldn't bring herself to open it until she was safely sitting down at her desk because what it said was: *Pole-dancing workshop **tomorrow** at 7 p.m.!* 💃💃💃

It was from Mackenzie Alvarez in sales. The rest of the email said:

> Heyyyy, everyone! Just a reminder that we're having a pole dancing workshop tomorrow at 7 p.m. down the street at Pole Position NYC. All are welcome but especially Oliver Brandt. ;) Wear comfortable but fitted clothes—leggings are recommended!

Underneath the text was a GIF of a woman repeatedly spinning on a pole. Sabrina stared at it for a moment, watching the woman's body twist around and around, and then noticed that there were already seventeen replies to Mackenzie's email, which had just gone out five minutes ago.

From Chelsea in product: best day evarrrrrrrrrrrrr!!

From Jenny in marketing: a GIF of Kristen Wiig on *Saturday Night Live* saying, "I'm so excited!"

From Oliver Brandt: in your dreams, Alvarez.

Sabrina sighed. If there was anything that perfectly encapsulated the daily sense of alienation that she felt from her colleagues, it was this email and the responses. People didn't used to take pole-dancing classes with their coworkers; they maybe got drunk with their coworkers, and that was the extent of it. But now you were expected to engage in forced, organized fun with people you worked with, and it seemed to her that the definition of *fun* had been majorly stretched. When she was in her twenties, people were way too jaded to think that something like a pole-dancing class, *with colleagues,* was even remotely cool.

She also felt like there was something slightly more insidious going on, about how you were now supposed to feel like your work was your everything: where you got your paycheck, yes, but also where you got fed and where you found your social circle. Everything had started bleeding into everything else. These kids—she felt no compunction about calling them kids— expected that their workplaces would provide all this for them, as if work were an extension of college, with its own clubs and student organizations. Even more disconcerting was that many TakeOff employees lived together or had roommates who were in some way connected to other TakeOff employees, and now there were even apartment buildings that were *actual dorms* for grown-ups, where you lived in a suite with a few other people and had common areas and nightly activities. It was almost like a return to the days of Henry Ford, when a company provided you with housing and meals and social events. What had happened to having to figure out life on your own?

God, she was starting to sound like Dan. She read the email again. Really, what was wrong with a little pole dancing if that was what made people happy? Just because she didn't want to participate didn't mean that other people couldn't. But people noticed when you didn't sign up for their pole-dancing classes and softball leagues and weekend dumpling crawls, and it made them think, again, about how you were *old*. To most of them, thirty-six might as well have been eighty-six in terms of how abstract it felt; they lumped her in with the rest of the "people who don't matter" population. The funny thing was, they thought they wanted to get married and have kids, but that was all far off in some nebulous future, and in the few conversations she'd ever had with any of them about it, they were almost adorably vague about how all that was going to happen.

Most of them also had this notion that they needed to get everything out of their systems by the time they were thirty, which was some kind of arbitrary witching hour, after which life suddenly Got Serious. Once, she'd overheard Chelsea lamenting, almost to the point of tears, the fact that she was about to turn twenty-eight, which meant she was only two years away from thirty, and that was when she was going to have to start figuring everything out—did she want to get married? Have kids? What about her career? Should she stay in New York or move back to Chicago? How would she ever save money?—and she *just wasn't ready for that life,* but then as soon as she noticed Sabrina walking by, she fell silent.

Maybe there was a part of Sabrina that was jealous of this version of their twenties that they were all getting to experience. Her twenties had been filled with such pathos. New York was different then too. She didn't want to say *grittier,* exactly; maybe *less sanitized* was a better way to put it. And it felt more mysterious. Your life wasn't documented on Instagram for the world to see.

"So Mack just told me the good news." Sabrina jumped; she hadn't noticed Isabel standing behind her. Usually Isabel didn't get in until at least ten thirty. Why was she here so early today? It was barely ten. This was the time that Sabrina got to have to herself. *Not today.* Sabrina took off her headphones and swiveled around in her chair. "Do you have time to get coffee?" Isabel said. "Or are you doing some hard strategy work already."

"Ha-ha-ha," Sabrina said. "You mean in the eighteen hours since Mack told me he wants to change my job? Yeah. I've actually rethought our entire social strategy."

Isabel squinted at her. Maybe this wasn't the time for jokes. "Anything's possible. So you want to get that coffee?" Sabrina didn't, not really, but there was something so pathetic about the way that Isabel—was she already her former boss?—was standing there that she felt like she had to. She got up, laying her headphones carefully on her desk. They were the big, over-the-ear kind that she usually saw teenagers wearing on the subway. She had been self-conscious about getting a pair but finally caved after she realized that if she just had earbuds in, people didn't notice them and kept trying to talk to her, and she needed the Do Not Disturb that the bigger ones telegraphed. If you looked out over the office at any given moment, approximately 80 percent of people had headphones on and were staring intently at their screens; 10 percent were walking around, either going to a meeting or getting something from the snack room; and probably only 10 percent were working without headphones or engaged in conversations. It gave the office an almost tomblike quality, despite the light streaming in from the windows and the slogans on the walls.

"Actually, can we just sit in the park?" Isabel said when they got out of the building. "Unless it's too cold for you."

Sabrina shook her head. "It's fine." They walked the two blocks to Madison Square Park in silence, stopping only so Isabel could get a coffee from the cart that was parked outside the Flatiron Building, and then they sat on a bench by the dog run. Isabel sipped her coffee and stared straight ahead. Was she going to say anything? Sabrina wasn't sure what the protocol was here, so she decided to just stay silent and let Isabel take the lead. A man holding five small dogs on leashes—a shih tzu, a Pomeranian, a Boston terrier, and two who looked like Chihuahua/Jack Russell mixes—walked in front of them and the dogs started barking with excitement, pulling on the leashes, as they got closer to the entrance to the dog run. Sabrina watched as the man opened the gate and took off their leashes, and there was a tumble of fur as they entered the dog run as one swirling, yipping mass.

"Maybe I'll just become a dog walker," Isabel said suddenly. "Doesn't that look fun, just hanging out with dogs all day and bringing them to the park?"

"I guess?" Sabrina said. "I dunno. Seems like it would be annoying in the rain and snow."

"You're right." They were quiet again. "I don't really want to be a dog walker. I'm just like...*so done* with how Mack has been treating me." She took a sip of coffee. "I mean, the thing yesterday...No offense, but it's, like, *crazy* that you are going to be reporting to him now."

Sabrina bristled inwardly but told herself to stay calm. *She's just lashing out,* she thought. *Be the grown-up.* "Why do you say that?"

Isabel turned to her. "Oh, come on, Sabrina." She sighed. "I shouldn't be telling you this, but he didn't even want me to hire you. He said you weren't a good cultural fit."

"That's crazy. I didn't even meet with him!" Sabrina felt her voice go up. She had a tight feeling in her chest—not exactly like she was having a heart attack, although she wouldn't know what that felt like anyway, so maybe it *was* a heart attack? "What does that even mean? Cultural fit?" But even as she asked, she knew: it meant not wanting to go to pole-dancing classes with her coworkers, it meant finding Mack's weekly inspirational speeches corny, it meant thinking that snacks were not going to save the world. It meant not wanting your work to be your life or your life to be your work.

But Isabel didn't respond. Instead, she burst into tears.

"What? Wait. Why are you crying?" The tightness in Sabrina's chest was replaced by a different feeling of panic, and she had a flashback to when she and Dan brought newborn Owen home from the hospital and he started screaming, and she'd thought: *Wait, oh God, what do I do now?* She rummaged in her bag—surely she had a tissue in there amid the chaos: a nearly empty tube of Kiehl's lip balm, a few Ricola wrappers from when she had a sore throat a couple weeks ago, a flyer for one of those hair salons that tried to get you to come in for a fifty-dollar cut and highlights, an expired MetroCard, the plug (but no cord) of an iPhone charger, one of Amelia's socks, a bottle of water, her wallet, the access card for the office, and three pens. But no tissues. "Sorry. I thought I had a Kleenex."

"It's okay," Isabel said, wiping her eyes on her jacket. "Sorry. I didn't mean to do that."

"Do what? Cry? It's fine." She was trying to act like it *was* fine, like it was totally normal for Isabel to be crying, like it was totally normal to have just gotten promoted, like it was totally normal that she had this job in the first place. "At least you're doing it out here and not in the office. No one's looking at us. It's fine. Besides, crying in public in New York is, like, a thing."

Isabel turned to her, almost hopefully. "It is?"

"Oh, yeah," Sabrina said. "Crying on the subway, crying in a restaurant, crying on a street corner because your boyfriend just dumped you, crying because you just walked by your ex-boyfriend's apartment building...Crying on the subway is probably the worst, though," she said thoughtfully. "Because you're, like, stuck on this car with strangers and there's nowhere to hide, you know? And people don't really know where to look, but there's always that one person—sometimes it's an old lady, sometimes it's another woman who's been there, sometimes it's a guy trying to hit on you—who tries to comfort you and you're just like, *Please leave me alone in my time of sorrow.*"

Isabel laughed. "You're funny." She wiped her nose on her sleeve. "Ugh, this is so *gross*. This is all Mack's fault. We were hooking up, you know."

Sabrina tried to look surprised. "Wow. That's...that's intense. Do you...do you think that's why he's acting out now?"

"*Acting out,*" Isabel said. "That's one way to put it, I guess. I was going to say *acting like a massive dick,* but *acting out* works. I wish someone had told me that hooking up with the founder of your company was a bad idea."

"You seriously needed someone to tell you that?"

Isabel shrugged. "I mean, no, but yeah? It's just, you work at a place like TakeOff, everyone is hooking up with everyone—

it's, like, what you do. I just happened to be hooking up with the boss, I guess." She paused, as though contemplating this anew. "*Boss* is such a funny word, isn't it? Mack never calls himself the boss, but that's totally what he is. I just never thought of him like that. He was just Mack, you know? Like, yeah, *technically* he was my boss—*is* my boss—but he never *seemed* like what I thought a boss would be like. You know, you picture a boss, like, some big fat guy chomping on a cigar."

Sabrina laughed. "That's how you picture a boss? No wonder you all have fucked-up ideas about work."

"What's that supposed to mean?"

"I dunno. Not fucked-up, I guess—just different. Everywhere I ever worked, you knew who the boss was, for one thing. Also there was maybe like *one* office hookup and it was a secret and usually some big scandal, like someone was cheating on his wife, and everyone sorta knew but not really, and usually someone ended up getting fired or quitting." Sabrina thought about this for a moment. "Although I guess it was usually the woman who left. Hm."

"Well, that's kind of what I wanted to talk to you about," Isabel said. "Last night at this party—I was there with Andrew, it was some Google party, I was pretty bored...but that woman Katya was there, from TechScene. I forgot she had been at Andrew's party."

Sabrina stiffened. Last night, right after Dan got home, he'd gotten a text and then told her that there was an emergency with something at work, and he had to leave again. She didn't wake up when he finally came home, sometime during the night, and in the morning he acted like nothing had happened. She hadn't thought too much about it, but now her Spidey sense was going off. "Did you talk to her?"

"She, like, *accosted* me. I was just standing there with Andrew and she asked if she could talk to me, and honestly I didn't even remember who she was—she looked different or something. It was dark. Anyway, almost immediately she's just like, 'I heard that Mack's been sexually harassing you and I'm going to write about it on TechScene whether or not you talk to me, but it would be better if you talk to me.'"

"Whoa. Wait. Say that again? She threatened you?"

"Basically." Isabel took a sip of coffee. "Do you think you could say something to your husband? To, like, get her off my back?"

"I don't know." This, at least, was the truth. "Dan and I don't really talk about work stuff." This was also vaguely true. "Also, I mean...I'm just curious. Are you sure you don't want her to write something? It doesn't seem like you're particularly happy."

"But that should be *my* decision," Isabel said. "I shouldn't have to quit because someone is writing an article about my private life. I didn't sign on for this. I mean, right?"

"No, you didn't," Sabrina said slowly, "but maybe you should think about, like, the big picture."

"What's that supposed to mean?"

"Well...I mean, you *were* his subordinate. I've definitely, *definitely* seen more fucked-up situations than yours. *Definitely*. But...you know, that was a long time ago." It actually wasn't, not in Sabrina's mind, but she knew that to Isabel, ten years ago was an eternity. She was in *high school* ten years ago. "Like, things that used to be normal aren't normal anymore."

"Like what?"

"It just used to be more blatant. And there were no consequences. Guys could kind of get away with anything."

"Do you really think that much has changed?"

"I mean, yes and no. I think there's less tolerance for just, like, blatant sexism. I really do. But maybe there's still the same shit going on that there used to be, it's just harder to recognize. I don't know." They were both quiet for a moment. "But, you know, even if it was just implied, the idea that you needed to stay in a relationship with him to keep your job is actually illegal."

"Right." Isabel pondered this. "Like, I *know* that. But when it's happening to you, it's hard to be like, 'Okay, I am being sexually harassed, now let me figure out what I should do.' It's more like, 'Ugh, this guy I used to hook up with who also happens to be my boss is being a total *douchebag*.' "

"I get that," Sabrina said. "I'm not, like, advocating this, but you would be completely within your rights to sue him and TakeOff for this."

"Oh God, I don't want to do that," Isabel said. "I mean, that wouldn't be fair to him. He did some fucked-up stuff but I don't want to, like, *destroy* him."

"I don't really want you to destroy him either. I don't think Mack is a *bad* person. I mean, he's not totally, one hundred percent a *good* person either, but who is? I just... " She thought about how to phrase what she was about to say. "I just think women should speak up about this kind of stuff. You know? Like what if some woman hears your story and is like, 'Oh wow, that's what's been happening to me and it's not right'?"

As she said this, she wondered: Did Isabel even know what sexual harassment was? Sabrina tried to think about what she'd thought sexual harassment was when she was twenty-six. Probably that it had to involve, like, your boss slapping your ass in front of everyone. It was such a vague, loaded term—you were supposed to know it when you saw it, but how were you really supposed to be able to tell? At some of the other places Sabrina had worked, they had been forced to sit through hours of harassment-prevention training, and she struggled to recall something—anything—from that training. But maybe it was one of those "if you have to ask..." kinds of situations. If it looks like sexual harassment, if it smells like sexual harassment, if it's making you upset enough that you have to leave work in the middle of the day and ask your much older coworker what to do, then maybe it's sexual harassment.

Isabel thought about this for a minute. "I *guess*. But why do *I* have to be that person? Isn't there, like, some other woman out there who could be that person?"

You have to be that person because nothing bad has ever happened to you, Sabrina thought. *You have to be that person because everything in your life has come easily, because you are beautiful and rich and this is one fucking thing you could do that would help people.*

She wanted to say all that to Isabel, but instead she just asked, "Did you love Mack?"

"Oh God, no." Now Isabel answered quickly. "No. It was never about love. But I thought we were both on the same page about that. We would joke about it, or at least, I thought it was a joke. He'd be like, 'When you get a boyfriend, work's gonna be so boring,' and I'd be like, 'Just make sure whoever your girlfriend is isn't prettier than me.' You know, stuff like that. But the whole time, I was going on dates with other people and I'm pretty sure he was too. But then I met Andrew and I realized how different it felt. I guess I just wasn't into Mack. And that's when he decided he couldn't handle it." She paused. "You know, I think things got really bad when I posted about Andrew on Instagram. It was like, until that moment, if I was only

Snapchatting it, he could pretend that the thing with Andrew was just as casual as we had been. Does that make sense?"

"Right," Sabrina said. She was struggling to bring herself, mentally, to this world Isabel lived in. It didn't feel like she had been twenty-six that long ago until she was confronted with the reality of *actually being* twenty-six. Certainly there was a lot that was the same—living with roommates, being able to stay out until one on a weeknight and get into work only slightly the worse for wear, thinking you were old because you were so close to being in your late twenties, which was dangerously close to being thirty. But there was this whole other element to Isabel's existence—living your life in public, on social media, before you really knew who you were—that felt wholly foreign to Sabrina, and somehow scarier.

"You're on Instagram, right?" Isabel asked suddenly. "I'll follow you."

"Um, yeah, but I don't post very much." She was suddenly self-conscious about her Instagram presence, which was a private account where she mostly posted pictures of her kids. "It's at-sabrinablum-seventy-nine."

"Seventy-nine," Isabel said thoughtfully. "That's when you were born?" Sabrina nodded. "I'm *eighty*-nine. Like Taylor Swift."

"My daughter has recently discovered Taylor Swift," Sabrina said. "Her nanny showed her some of her videos on YouTube. So now she begs me to let her watch them."

Isabel laughed. "I can't even imagine growing up right now and that being, like, a thing."

"But do you even remember a time when you didn't have internet?"

Isabel thought about this for a moment. "No. I guess not. I

mean, when I was *really* little I don't think we had it. But I was probably like six when we got AOL."

"You were on AOL when you were *six?*"

Isabel laughed. "No, no. I wasn't allowed to go on till I was probably like ten? But I would watch my mom and my older brother."

"Still. I can't imagine growing up with AOL. I mean, I was already a sentient, conscious person when you were born. I have a cousin who was born in 1989 and I remember it."

Isabel shrugged. "I mean, yeah. I'm ten years younger than you. And someday I'll be as old as you are now, and I'll be having this conversation with someone who was born in 1999." She was quiet for a moment. "Anyway. I guess we should get back. But..." She seemed to be having trouble articulating the question. "What do you think I should do?"

"About what, exactly," Sabrina said. "About Mack? About Andrew? About talking to Katya? About being twenty-six?"

"Well, all of it, but really, I guess...Like part of me just wants to quit and forget about everything and part of me wants to stay just to, like, spite Mack. But listen. Can you please say something to Dan? Just tell him that you don't think it's a real story and he should tell Katya to leave me alone."

"I...I don't think I can do that, Isabel," Sabrina said. "And honestly, I don't think you should want me to do that."

Isabel sighed. "Fine. I guess I'll just figure things out for myself."

19

STAND AND DELIVER

ON HIS LAST day at TakeOff, Casper Kim came to the door of
Mack's office around lunchtime and knocked, even though it
was open. "Come in!" Mack said, way too cheerfully. *Dial it
back,* he thought. "How's the last day treating you?"

Casper smiled and sat down on the couch. "Gotta say, it's
been a little more emotional than I was expecting. Did you
see my whole team dressed as me?" For Casper's last day at
TakeOff, his entire group had worn high-top sneakers, sweat-
shirts, and jeans. They had even gotten the thick black-rimmed
glasses he always wore, and a couple of the guys had tried to
style their hair the same way as him, with a swoop of bangs
in front. They'd all arrived at work early and were there when
Casper showed up at ten thirty, and Mack watched from his
desk as Casper grinned and high-fived all of them.

"I did." *Good. Let him feel bad about leaving them.* "Pretty
great."

"Yeah. Listen, I just wanted to say thanks for everything. I
had a great time here."

Since their last conversation in his office a couple weeks
ago—the one where Casper had quit—Mack hadn't exactly

been avoiding Casper, but he also hadn't been going out of his way to talk to him. He was wrestling with what his exact emotions were about Casper's departure. On the one hand, he knew that this was normal for companies. When people left, they hopefully carried some of your company's DNA with them to their new workplace, so you were constantly pollinating other businesses, and eventually you had this big network of people who had formerly worked for you. That was the charitable view. The less generous way of looking at it, and this was the way (despite his best efforts) that Mack had been thinking about Casper leaving, was that it wasn't fair that people you had grown attached to, whom you had confided in, whom you had grown the company alongside, whom you had *groomed,* just got to leave! Without even thinking about how it might affect you or being remotely grateful for everything you had done for them!

Still, he was throwing Casper a good-bye party that night at Flatiron Social, because that was what you did. And he wasn't going to act bitter or say anything harsh about Casper to anyone. Besides Jason, of course. But to everyone else, he was going to seem completely gracious and magnanimous: Of *course* he was sad to see Casper go, but of *course* it was a great opportunity for him, and of *course* he was welcome back at TakeOff anytime. The first was true, the second was debatable, and the third was a complete lie. There was no way Mack would let someone back who had betrayed him like that. Right before a new product launch! It was so typical of people in his generation. He hated to say it, but sometimes he nodded along when he read an article about "entitled millennials." No one had any goddamn loyalty anymore.

"Thanks, Casper. That means a lot. You ready for tonight?"

"Yeah," Casper said. "I mean, I think so. I've never had a good-bye party thrown for me."

"This was your first real job. I always forget that."

"Yeah. I mean, I had internships. I mean...I'm only twenty-three. I gotta thank you again for taking a chance on me. Letting me lead a team. That meant a lot."

"Well, thank *you*." They were both quiet. Casper nodded and stuck out his hand. Mack shook it and felt slightly mollified. Maybe his toast to Casper at drinks tonight wouldn't be quite as undermining as he had secretly been planning.

At six thirty, the office had been slowly emptying for the last half hour or so, and now he counted only about ten people left on the floor. Normally he would be peeved that people were leaving this early, but it was nice how it seemed like nearly everyone was going to Casper's good-bye. It meant that he had a strong team, that he had really built something. He pinged Jason on Slack: walk over to Flatiron w/me?

Jason responded with the thumbs-up emoji and almost instantly materialized at the door to Mack's office. "Thought you'd never ask, boss. Let's mosey." As they were waiting for the elevator, Mack's phone vibrated with a notification from Twitter that he had been mentioned in a tweet. He opened the Twitter app and found himself on the account of a Twitter user called @invisibletechman. The tweet said: Hearing that there are some founders who need to learn to keep it in their pants. @mackmcallister you know anything about this? 😉😉

"The fuck?" Mack said. He showed Jason the tweet. "Who is this person? And why the hell are they at-ing me on this tweet?"

Jason glanced at it. "Who knows, man. Probably just some jealous idiot. I'd ignore it." The elevator came and they got on. Mack didn't respond. It was all well and good for Jason to say ignore it, but he wasn't the one being tweeted at about sleeping around! "How many followers does he have, anyway?" Jason asked.

Mack clicked through to @invisibletechman's profile page. "Like two thousand."

Jason looked surprised. "Huh. That's more than I thought he would."

The doors to the lobby opened and they walked out. "That's hardly reassuring."

"Sorry." Jason grinned. "But look, there are worse things to be accused of. So you have sex. Big deal! Is that a crime? Not the last time I checked."

"It's just...I dunno." Mack shook his head. There was something weird about the tweet. It didn't exactly say that he was sleeping around; it said he couldn't keep it in his pants. Which was a little too close for comfort considering certain Snapchats he used to send. But Jason didn't need to know that. Nobody needed to know that. And nobody *did* know that. He was vaguely comforted by the idea that if Isabel had, God forbid, told anyone that they used to exchange nudes at work, she would be just as implicated as he was. There were no innocent parties here.

"Let's just go to the bar, get some drinks, say some nice shit about Casper, and forget about dumb anonymous Twitter accounts saying dumb anonymous shit. Okay?"

"Yeah, okay." The company had rented out the back room of the bar, and as they made their way there, Mack glanced at his phone again. A couple of people whose names he didn't recognize had responded to @invisibletechman's tweet—one with a 😊, one with the comment Some? lol. He put his phone in his pocket. There was no point in worrying about this now. Hopefully it would just go away.

The back room was packed. He spotted Casper in the corner talking to a couple of his look-alikes. He made a mental note to gently remind Casper about the nonsolicitation clause in his contract—he wasn't allowed to hire anyone from TakeOff for a year, and Mack would be watching carefully to make sure that he didn't. He had a feeling that the people on Casper's team were dying to continue working for him; everyone seemed to love him. Jason had disappeared into the crowd, so Mack made his way to the bar and ordered a drink. It was open bar until nine, which seemed more than generous, but as he sipped his whiskey on the rocks he hoped that people were leaving the bartender tips. He took out a five-dollar bill and left it on the bar.

He glanced around the room. He hadn't been sure if Isabel would have the nerve to show up, but there she was, chatting away with Chelsea, one of the girls on Casper's team, who was also wearing the Casper uniform. Could Isabel possibly be connected to the tweet? There was no way, he decided quickly. For one thing, Isabel wasn't conniving enough to orchestrate something like that—despite being the Engagement Hero, she personally wasn't very active on social media, except for Instagram. And Snapchat. But...still. Maybe he'd ask her. He walked over to where she was standing.

"Hi, Isabel. Hi, Chelsea," he said.

"Hey, Mack! Like my outfit?" Chelsea grinned. She was tiny, and the sweatshirt and high-tops looked ridiculous on her.

"I always said that product is the most creative team at the company," he said. Isabel was silent, and, although he wasn't looking at her at the moment, he could feel her glaring at him. "Would you mind...I just need to chat with Isabel for a second."

"Of *course*. No problem! Isabel, I'll catch up with you later." Isabel nodded and smiled. "Yup. See ya, Chels." As soon as

Chelsea walked away, her smile disappeared. "Please tell me you're not about to attempt to have a serious conversation with me at a going-away party." She drained her drink and set it on the cocktail table next to them.

"Depends on your definition of *serious*," Mack said. Isabel's face was impassive. "No, I mean, I just..." Ugh. He was still thinking about the tweet. Might as well ask her about it. "Did you see this tweet that went up a few minutes ago?"

"'This tweet,'" Isabel repeated. "Can you be a little more specific?"

He took out his phone, opened Twitter, and found the tweet. Isabel read it, her face still a blank. "No, I hadn't seen it. What about it?"

"Just seems like an interesting coincidence."

She rolled her eyes. "I have no idea what you're trying to insinuate, but whatever it is, I didn't do it. But just so you know...there's a reporter who's been asking around about us."

"Wait. What?"

Isabel shrugged. "I don't even know why I'm telling you this. It's not like you've been looking out for me."

He realized as she was talking that the sick thing was that if she suddenly smiled and said, *Hey, just kidding, I broke up with Andrew and I want us to go back to the way we were,* he would take her back. Not that there was anything to really go back to. He tried to tell himself that he just missed the sex, the texting, the charge he got from seeing her in the office and knowing that they shared a secret. But maybe he actually missed...her. She *got* him. She knew how hard he had worked to make this company what it was, had seen him start it from almost nothing. She had been there for the late nights and the app updates that crashed and the funding presentations that had bombed.

And he got *her* too—he knew how much she longed to be taken seriously. She was so pretty that people assumed that she wasn't smart, although she actually was, and that she didn't need to work hard. Even her family seemed to feel that way; he heard her on the phone with her mom once, explaining that she couldn't come home to Connecticut that weekend to go sailing with the family because she had to work, and her mother just had not understood this concept *at all*. He admired that she'd stood up to her mom like that and that she took work as seriously as she did. At least, he *had* admired that in her.

"You know," he said softly, "we could go back to the way things were." As soon as he said it, he knew it was a mistake. It was the truth—they *could* go back to the way things were—but it was a possibility that, he saw now, existed only in his own mind.

She scrunched up her face and turned to him, head cocked to one side. "The way things were," she said. "The way things *were*. I don't know what that even *means*. You and I...we weren't even really a thing! It went on as long as it did only because we work together. That's it. We weren't in *love*. The sex wasn't even that good. I don't know if we even really *like* each other. And I think the only reason you're so focused on getting me back is because I've moved on. Got that? *I've. Moved. On.*" She squinted at him. "You don't get it, do you? Because you've never not been able to have something you really wanted."

"I think you're actually talking about yourself," he said quietly.

"*Excuse* me?" she said.

"Nothing. Never mind."

She rolled her eyes. "Whatever, Mack. You know, I was trying to keep our whole thing quiet out of *respect* for you and respect for Andrew because he used to consider you a friend." *Yeah, right*, Mack thought. "But you're just acting like...ugh. You guys are all the same. You won't take no for an answer! Let me put it in terms you can understand better...we were not in beta, okay? We just *were*. Our thing was what it was. It was never going to progress to anything else. Andrew and I, we just, like, launched right away. We brought the product to market and users loved it. We—"

"Okay! I get it." He hated, with every inch of his being, that Isabel was right. Those *were* terms he could understand. "God, sometimes I wish we'd just never even met," he said. Before Isabel could say anything, he felt a hand on his shoulder. He turned around, and there was Jason.

"Hey. You ready to make that toast? I think it's time." Jason barely looked at Isabel as he said this.

"Oh—yeah, sure." They headed to the center of the room, where someone had helpfully put a chair for Mack to stand on. He hoisted himself up and handed Jason his drink. "Ahem, ahem! Could I quickly have everyone's attention?" It took a moment or two for the room to quiet down, but soon everyone's eyes were on him. "And could I get Casper Kim to step up to the, er, podium. Or whatever this is. The chair. Step up to the chair, Casper!" Everyone cheered and hollered as Casper made his way through the crowd.

"Casper, you were the Woz to my Jobs," he said. Everyone laughed. Fine, this was a little hyperbolic, but the analogy, Mack felt, was a good one; he was the outward-facing visionary, like Steve Jobs, and Casper had been the genius who worked tirelessly behind the scenes to figure out the product. "And I don't know what I'm going to do without you." This, at least, was true. He hadn't even begun to think about replacing Casper. "You've made TakeOff what it is today, and we wouldn't be the innovative, forward-thinking company we are today if you . hadn't come along."

Before he could say anything else, a voice—a female voice—piped up from the back of the room. "Could you be any more full of shit?" It was Isabel. *Fuck,* it was Isabel. Was she drunk? She had gulped that drink in front of him—who knew how many she'd already managed to down before he saw her. "Seriously, Mack. Why don't you tell everyone here how you've been treating me?"

The only sound was the bartender shaking a drink, and as soon as he realized how quiet everything was, he stopped. Now the room was more silent than Mack would have thought possible.

"Nothing to say, huh?" Isabel's voice was getting louder. "Why don't you tell everyone how you won't leave me alone? Or about the texts? Or the *sexts*."

"That's enough, Isabel." It came out sharper than he intended. He was still standing on the chair. *This is ridiculous,* he thought. He wasn't going to let her hijack this. Everyone was still silent; no one was looking directly at him, or at Isabel.

"Oh, fuck you," she said. She was crying. *"Fuck you."* And with that, she shoved her way through the crowd and ran out of the bar.

No one moved. *What do I do,* Mack thought. *What the fuck do I do now.* Before he could say or do anything, Casper came to the rescue. "I don't know what that was," he said, "but Mack, I just want to say thank you. You're a true friend and a real leader. Hey, everyone, let's give Mack a round of applause." For a moment, no one made a sound, and Mack thought, *Fuck-fuck-fuck,* but then Casper started clapping, and then a few more people did, and soon enough, the whole room had erupted in cheers and applause. Mack hopped down off the chair and Casper slapped him on the back and leaned in to whisper to him, "Yo, that bitch is *crazy*."

20

BATTLE LOYAL

SABRINA HADN'T EVEN been planning on going to Casper's thing, but then she'd gotten a message on Slack from Mack that said, See you at drinks? Important for all senior staff to be there! She was senior staff now. Despite everything she felt about Mack, this still gave her a satisfied little thrill. Dan would just have to *deal*. She texted him: Gotta go to a work thing tonight—can you be home early? Sorry last minute. She was shocked—pleasantly shocked—when he responded right away: Sure, no problem!

Thanks. Won't be too late, she wrote back, trying not to think too much about how quickly and enthusiastically he'd responded. But that was how she found herself sipping a glass of sauvignon blanc in the back room at Flatiron Social at six thirty as the bar filled up with her coworkers. She'd walked over with Isabel, who seemed distracted—maybe it was their conversation in the park that morning? Or maybe it was something else; she wouldn't say—and who immediately headed to the bar and ordered a whiskey on the rocks, drank it, and ordered a double. "Take it easy, champ," Sabrina said, trying to keep her voice light, but Isabel just rolled her eyes and said, "Whatever," and then she'd lost her in the crowd.

Sabrina just wanted to stay long enough for Mack to see her there and then head home. She got pulled into a conversation with Oliver Brandt and a couple other sales people, during which she stayed mostly silent, periodically craning her neck to see if Mack had shown up yet. She somehow missed his entrance, though, and didn't see him until he was standing on a chair in the middle of the room.

She tuned out when Mack started talking, something about how Casper had been the Woz to his Jobs, which Sabrina took to be some kind of Steve Jobs reference that she didn't quite understand the significance of, besides the fact that it seemed awfully presumptuous of Mack to be comparing himself to Steve Jobs, and she had started inching toward the door when she heard Isabel's voice, a little high-pitched, slightly frantic, interrupt him. "Could you be any more full of shit?" she said. *Oh no,* Sabrina thought. She must be drunk already. What else could have possessed her to make this kind of scene? It was precisely the *opposite* of what Isabel had said she wanted to happen. She'd said she wanted everything to be quiet, not to make a fuss. She didn't want Katya writing about what was going on, but she was willing to bring it up here? It made no sense.

As soon as Isabel ran out of the room, and Casper made his ridiculous speech that seemed to distract everyone from the fact that Isabel had accused Mack of sexual harassment in front of the entire company, she slipped out of the bar to see if she could catch Isabel. Mostly to ask, *What the fuck were you thinking?* But Isabel was already gone; there was no sign of her in front of the bar. Sabrina texted her: Where the hell are you? and waited a moment to see if Isabel would respond, but she didn't. And so there was nothing left to do but go home.

She hadn't thought that Isabel had something like that in

her. This was probably the crux of the matter: that Isabel had done something more risky and brave than Sabrina would have thought possible, and there was a tiny, *tiny* part of her that was actually jealous. As she emerged from the subway back in Park Slope, her phone vibrated; Isabel had responded to her text. It was just an audio file. She fished around in her bag for her headphones and plugged them into her phone and pressed play. First she just heard a lot of background noise. Then she heard, "Could I get everyone's attention?" and she realized, with a creeping sense of horror, that this was Mack's voice, and that Isabel had *recorded* what had happened. She hit pause on her phone—she didn't want to hear any more. She texted back, I can't listen to this. Isabel responded immediately, please. I want this to get out there. But it can't come from me.

What the hell, Sabrina thought. You're kind of sending me mixed messages, she typed back. First you said you didn't want this to be public. Actually i think you said you wanted me to talk to Dan and ask him to kill the story. So which is it?

I know, Isabel texted back immediately. Listen...think about it. I'm obviously not gonna be at work tomorrow.

Sabrina was in front of her building now. Ok. I'm home...i gotta run. Isabel didn't respond. Sabrina climbed the two flights of stairs to her apartment and opened the front door. Dan was sitting on the couch, working on his laptop. The apartment was quiet. Was it possible he had put the kids to bed all by himself? "Hey," she said. "Everything okay?"

"Yup!" he said. "Everything's great. Gave them a bath and put them to bed. How was your work thing?" Why was he being so...cheery? Something felt off.

She sat down on the couch next to him. "It was fine." Dan nodded and turned back to his computer. "What are you up to?"

"Not much, just finishing up some work stuff." He quickly closed his laptop. "So...something a little weird happened last night."

"Oh?" Sabrina felt immediately on guard. "When you went out?" They'd barely seen each other since then, Sabrina realized. When he'd gotten home, she'd been asleep, and then this morning he'd left as she was getting Owen and Amelia ready for school, giving them a quick wave good-bye as she was trying to get Owen to sit in his chair and not roll around on the floor with no pants on, which Owen thought was *hilarious*.

"Yeah. I forgot my wallet, which I didn't realize right away because I had Ubered, but for some reason I had a credit card in my jacket pocket—I was wearing that brown corduroy blazer that I don't wear that much?" She nodded. She thought she knew where this was going and she knew she couldn't stop it, and she was getting that terrible feeling in the pit of her stomach again, the one that she usually felt anytime she looked at a credit card bill. Which was why she had stopped looking at her credit card bills. "So I was getting drinks—"

"You got drinks? I thought you had a work thing."

"Yeah, they were, like, drinks with some work people."

"Okay." She briefly considered challenging him on this—he sounded like he was lying about something, although she wasn't sure exactly what.

"Anyway, so I forgot my wallet, but I realized I had that Delta SkyMiles card in my pocket, so I tried to use it, and it got declined." He paused as though waiting for her to say something. She was silent, because she was trying to figure out how she was supposed to play this. She hadn't paid the SkyMiles card in months—when the cash started coming into her PayPal account from selling her underwear, it had first gone to the Barneys and J. Crew cards, and she had been planning on getting to the SkyMiles card and the other AmEx and the Citibank Visa soon, but between everything that had been going on at work *and* her side job—because that's what selling her underwear was, a second job that she had to pay attention to—she just hadn't had the time. "Which I thought was weird, because we hardly ever use that card. I'm actually not totally sure why we even have it—it's not like we fly that much."

"We got it so we could get all those bonus miles, remember? So we could go visit your brother in San Francisco."

"Oh yeah, right," Dan said. "That was, like, three years ago, though." Sabrina nodded. She was going to try to placate him, she decided. Play a little dumb and slightly confused, not really argue, and hope that it would all go away. "Anyway, the card was declined. So I called that number on the back?"

Okay. Maybe playing confused wasn't going to work. She closed her eyes. "Just get it over with," she murmured.

"Huh?" Dan said. He shook her shoulder. "Are you okay? What did you just say?"

She opened her eyes. "Whatever you're about to say, just say it. Get it over with."

He squinted at her. "What am I about to say?"

"Don't do this, Dan."

"No, seriously, I want to know. What am I about to say? Please enlighten me."

Was she going to cry? She might cry. But maybe...maybe there was something that would feel liberating about coming clean. The burden of this secret was wearing her down. When she got married, she had been convinced that there was nothing she would keep secret from her husband; they were a team. But somewhere along the line it had started feeling more like they were like a bad physics problem: She was a train going ninety-five miles per hour and he was a train going a hundred and fifty miles per hour, and they were heading toward each other and now they were going to crash. But exactly when or where or how they were going to crash...that was what she had to solve for, and she had gotten a C+ in physics in high school.

"I don't know," Sabrina said. "Maybe...maybe something about how the card hadn't been..." She couldn't finish the sentence.

"Hadn't been paid. Is that what you were going to say? Because that's what they told me when I finally pressed the right combination of numbers to get to a representative. They said that the card had reached its limit three months ago and it hadn't been paid. Not even the minimum. And do you know what the limit is on that card?"

Sabrina shook her head. She actually truly didn't know. She'd made it a point not to know.

"It's twenty grand," Dan said. "Twenty thousand dollars. Of which I personally have spent zero, to my knowledge. So, Sabrina, tell me. Where the hell did you spend twenty thousand dollars?"

"It's...it's complicated," she whispered.

"Complicated *how*, exactly." He wasn't raising his voice, but his tone had gotten sharper. Meaner.

"It...it didn't happen all at once, I mean." She paused. "And I'm trying to pay it off. Really. I was trying to take care of it myself. I didn't want to stress you out."

"I'm just confused. And I feel a little stupid, to be perfectly honest. Like, where was I when you were spending twenty thousand dollars on...what? What did you spend it on?"

"Stuff," she said. She knew she sounded defensive, but she couldn't help it. "Just stuff. Stuff for the kids, stuff for the apartment, stuff for me...I don't know. It was nothing crazy, I swear. It just adds up quicker than you'd think." He looked around the room as though trying to ascertain what objects she'd bought with the card. "Seriously! It wasn't like one day I just went out and spent thousands of dollars. It's like, a sweater here, a vase there, a pair of rain boots for Amelia...it just adds up."

"But *twenty thousand dollars,*" Dan said. "I just don't get it."

"I don't know what else there is to get. I spent a lot of money and now I'm trying to pay it off." She wasn't going to mention the other cards. Not now. Maybe not ever. "And, like, we're fine. You have a job, I have a job, we're still paying our mortgage on time, there's food on the table. And it's over! I'm not spending money like that anymore." She believed this to be true, but she also knew, even as she said it, how delusional it sounded, especially since there was a pair of Céline sunglasses in her purse that she'd just bought last week on FlairMatch, and a Vince cashmere sweater from Saks still in its package in her closet—she didn't have to open it to know how soft it was—and a couple of things, she had forgotten exactly what, from J. Crew that were on back order and should be arriving sometime in December.

"I can't even talk to you right now," Dan said. "I'm going for a walk." She had no response to this. She watched silently as he got up from the couch, put on his coat, and walked out the door without saying anything else to her. It looked like he wanted to slam it but he closed it quietly.

"God*damn* it." Her phone buzzed again—it was Isabel. "Oh, for fuck's sake," she said. The text read, sorry to keep bugging u but srsly i could use some help. 😰

21

SECRET SERVICE

BEFORE SHE'D EVEN gotten home from Old Town the other night, there was already a text from Dan that said, good seeing you tonight. ;) She didn't respond. When she got home, Janelle was still up, watching something on her laptop on the couch in her leggings and Taylor Swift concert T-shirt. "Hey," Katya said as she sat down next to her. At least she wasn't shooting a video. She and Janelle had the kind of roommate relationship that Katya preferred; respectful, but they kept their distance. Janelle had her friends and her job and her beauty videos, Katya had her job and...well, now not much else. She had never been good at keeping friends—there were always the girls who targeted her for friendship because they thought she was cool and edgy or whatever, but they quickly realized that she wasn't interested in going to brunch or having picnics in the park or learning how to crochet and chronicling all of it on Instagram or in a Snapchat story or participating in any of the other activities of bourgeois New York twentysomething existence. Janelle tried in the beginning, inviting her out to drinks and concerts, saying with purpose that she was going to draw Katya out of her shell, whatever that meant. *My shell is me,* Katya thought every time this happened.

"What's up," Janelle said without taking her eyes off the computer. "Oh, by the way,, thanks for getting your boyfriend out of here. Though...could I have his number? He had really good weed."

"Um...yeah, sure. But can I ask your advice on something?" Before she'd even finished talking, Janelle had closed her computer and turned theatrically toward her.

"Me?" Janelle brought her hand to her chest. "*Advice?* Are you okay? Let me get this straight. You, Katya Pasternack, are asking *me,* Janelle Lewis, for advice. Can I take your temperature? I think you might be deathly ill. Or wait. Are you an impostor?"

"Ha-ha-ha," Katya said. "I'm serious. I..." She was having trouble getting the words out. *Did* she want to ask Janelle for advice? Not really, but she was all Katya had at the moment. Then the words just came tumbling out of her mouth: "My boss kissed me at a bar just now and he just texted me and I'm just like...I don't know what to do."

Janelle's eyes widened. *Fuck,* Katya thought. *I shouldn't have said anything.* "Hoo boy. Wait. What about Victor? Wait. Was he mad he had to leave?"

"No, no. Nothing like that. It was good he left. We got in a fight—it's a long story. And I ended up at a bar with Dan. My boss. And then we like...kind of made out for a minute and I feel really strange about it." She paused. "This is a new feeling for me."

Janelle laughed. "I see that. Well, what do you want from the situation? Do you *like* him?"

Katya shook her head. "No. It's not about that."

"What's it about?"

"I don't know," she said.

"Well...how did you leave things?" Janelle said.

"I was just like, I'll see you tomorrow, and I got in an Uber and came home. And he already texted me, like, 'Glad we didn't do anything else,' or something like that." She rolled her eyes. "As *if* that was on the table."

"It's *always* on the table, silly," Janelle said.

"No," Katya said. "It was a random fluke; it wasn't like we had arranged some secret rendezvous at a hotel or something. I was the one who texted him! Dan would never actually want to, like..." She trailed off.

"Fuck?" Janelle finished. "Oh, honey. You are seriously delusional if you think he isn't jerking off to you right this second and thinking about how he can get in your size twenty-five jeans."

Size twenty-four, actually, Katya thought. "That's gross, Janelle."

"Sorry, but that's just reality. Don't you know that by now? Where have you *been?*"

"You know what, forget it, I shouldn't have even mentioned it. I'm actually just going to go to bed." Janelle was looking at her in a way that Katya couldn't quite parse. It seemed like pity mixed with curiosity.

"Oooookay. You do you. I need to get back to watching Monica put a turkey on her head anyway."

"Huh?" Katya said. "Who's Monica?"

"I always forget you don't know any pop culture," Janelle said. "Never mind, it's a *Friends* thing."

That conversation had been her sole attempt to process with someone else what had happened with Dan. Since that one conversation, all she had been feeling was confused. She was relieved that things hadn't gone any further the other night, but every so often her brain stubbornly went to a place that she didn't want it to go to: thinking about him in the tiniest romantic way. There *had* been something sweet about the way he had kissed her—he had a look on his face that was so eager. Even when things had been hard in her life—having no luck finding a job after graduation, trying desperately to save enough money to move out of her dad and stepmom's apartment—she'd had a conviction, deep down, that things would work out. She was tough. She knew how to take care of herself. But now, suddenly, things were starting to feel just a bit out of her control, and she didn't like it.

And now, a couple days later, she wasn't *totally* sure, but it seemed like Victor wasn't speaking to her. She'd texted him twice and gotten no response, which was completely out of character for him. Or at least, it was out of character for their relationship. He always texted her back right away, and she didn't like this new dynamic. She didn't feel the need to tell him about Dan, maybe because she hadn't totally come to terms with what had happened with Dan. In the two days since, they'd kept their distance at work. They'd managed to avoid each other on smoke breaks, and he hadn't even come by her desk to say hi.

But he was not leaving her alone on text or on Slack. Busy after work? She felt her chest tightening. Her desk mate, Kevin, who covered transportation apps, looked over at her.

"Everything okay?"

"Yeah, why?" she said. "Does it not look like everything's okay?"

"Hey, check yourself, just asking. You just seem on edge. I was trying to be nice."

"Well...thanks. But you can be nice somewhere else today."

"Damn, that's harsh even for you," he said, almost admiringly. "What're you working on?"

"I'm working on nothing," she said. "That's part of the problem."

"Wait. So there *is* a problem."

"You're way too proud of yourself right now. I need to work."

"All righty," he said. "You do your work. I was just gonna suggest that you could look into that invisibletechman Twitter account, if you haven't already. Trevor told me about it."

Damn it; invisibletechman *had* been on her radar, and she'd completely forgotten about it with everything else that was going on. It was galling that it was Kevin bringing it up now. "What made you say that?"

He shrugged. "I keep seeing it retweeted into my timeline and no one really knows who it is."

"Aren't you kind of tired of anonymous Twitter accounts?" she said. "Like, don't they seem kind of played out to you?"

"I dunno," Kevin said. "If they're saying stuff that's like...worthy, then nah."

"I guess. I just don't get the anonymity. It's very... *Gossip Girl*," she said. *Gossip Girl* had started when she was in high school at Brooklyn Tech. She hadn't known anyone personally who lived on the Upper East Side or who went to private school. She knew that these people existed; she saw them occasionally when her classes went on field trips to the Met or the Guggenheim, these girls with long smooth hair and bags that probably cost more than the rent on both her parents' apartments put together.

Kevin laughed. "It was literally just a suggestion—oh, *shit*," he said.

"What?" she said.

"'Hearing that shit went down at TakeOff drinks the other night—anyone know anything?'" Kevin read out.

"Where is that from?"

"Invisibletechman. See? I *told* you it was something."

"Fuck," Katya said. "Dan's gonna kill me."

"Why?" Kevin asked, but before she could respond, another Slack notification from Dan popped up that just said, You see this? with a link to the @invisibletechman tweet.

"How the fuck did he see that already?" Katya said.

"Probably the same way I saw it?" Kevin said. "Looking at Twitter?"

"I get that," Katya said. "I dunno. I'm just surprised he saw it so quickly. I'm usually faster than him."

And now Dan was actually at her desk. "You weren't responding!" he said. She saw Kevin smirk and turn back to his computer.

"Sorry, I was busy," she said.

"Did you see what I just sent you? Something went down the other night, apparently."

"Yeah, actually, Kevin told me right before you Slacked me," she said. "What do you think it could be?"

"That's your job." He grinned; he seemed jittery with excitement.

"If only my best source at that company wasn't your wife," she said under her breath.

"Hm?" he said.

"Nothing," she said. "I'll look into it."

"Great." He lowered his voice. "Did you, uh, see my other message?"

"Yeah," she said. He looked at her expectantly. "I'll... respond to it."

He smiled. "Great. And yeah, if we could have something on that today, that'd be...well, that'd be great. Maybe see if Mack has any comment."

"Okay," she said, thinking, *Please go away now*. He stood there for another moment as though waiting for her to say something else, and then, after a few more awkward seconds, he said, "Great. And let me know if you want to"—he pantomimed smoking—"later."

"Will do," she said. He finally walked away. She clicked on Slack and went to Dan's direct messages. I'm busy tonight, she wrote.

He typed back:

Dan: ☹ I feel like you've been ignoring me since the other night
Katya: huh? how have I been ignoring you?
Dan: we haven't talked at all
Katya: idk what to say to that. I'm just trying to act normal and not make other ppl think something's up btwn us
Dan: i get that but...i guess i just miss you

I'm literally right here! she typed, and then deleted it. How can you miss me, I'm right here, she typed, and then deleted that. Don't be silly, she typed. That, too, got deleted. *Fuck,* she thought. The way Dan was acting...it was starting to feel like he did *not* think of the other night as just a onetime fluke that had happened because Katya was feeling really fucking vulnerable and—selfishly?—knew that he'd be there for her. Wasn't it supposed to go without saying that *nothing else was going to happen between them?* He was married! *Wait,* she thought. *I am a cliché! I'm the young woman hooking up with her boss.* She corrected her internal monologue. *I'm the young woman who kissed her boss one night when she was drunk and sad. Fuck, still a cliché.*

Katya: k
Dan: don't "k" me
Katya: sorry
Dan: are you upset about the other night?
Katya: not upset. Just feel like it probably shouldn't happen again.
Dan: :(
Katya: i have a ton of work to do so i'm gonna close slack for a little bit
Dan: k. see what i did there?
Katya: good one

She closed Slack and squeezed her eyes shut for a moment. The way Dan was acting was officially Not Good. He wasn't supposed to *actually* like her! Or want this to be a thing! He was like, what, fifteen years older than she was? It wasn't that she had never been with older guys, but if she was going to have an affair with an older man, it wouldn't be with a depressed Park Slope dad of two whose life was so boring that he was trying to hook up with one of his reporters, who was ambivalent about him at best. *Definitely* not going to be that guy.

In the meantime, she had to assume that she wasn't going to be the only reporter trying to figure out what the hell @invisibletechman was talking about. It had been only twelve minutes since his tweet, but there were undoubtedly people already planning on writing posts that didn't even really say anything but just speculated about what it could be. There would be levels of depth to the various posts; there would be one that was just an embed of the tweet with a headline like "What Went Down at the TakeOff Party the Other Night?" Or, if the reporter wanted to play it a little safer, something like "Anonymous Twitter Account Alleges That 'Sh*t Went Down' at Recent TakeOff Party." That post would go up within minutes, Katya was sure of it. Then there would be another post in an hour or so from someone who'd gotten a statement from TakeOff, probably an official denial. It was possible this post would also have a quote from someone who worked at TakeOff. And each of the stories would get tweeted and retweeted and so it would go, on and on, until everyone forgot about the story and moved on to something else. But this was her job, to get into that scrum at some point, to somehow come up with the quote or the angle that no one else had found.

She was just about to send Isabel a text when an email came into her inbox. The sender was Mack McAllister. "Whoa," she whispered. She clicked it open. It said:

This isn't really Mack McAllister, but I wanted to get your attention. You should probably listen to this and then judge for yourself what went down the other night at the TakeOff party.

Attached was an audio file. Now that she looked at the email header, she saw that the address was actually notmackmcallister @gmail.com. Someone had just made Mack McAllister the name that showed up. She was slightly wary about clicking on an audio file from an unknown sender, especially one who admitted that he (or she) wasn't the person the email had purportedly been from, but she put on her headphones and clicked anyway.

She heard a man talking, but she was having trouble figuring out exactly what he was saying because there was a lot of background noise. She turned up the volume and heard a voice that was unmistakably Mack's saying, "Casper, you were the was to my jobs." *Huh?* She went back a few seconds and listened again. "Casper, you were the Woz to my Jobs." *Oh.* So now Mack was comparing himself to Steve Jobs? These guys were unbelievable. "And I don't know what I'm going to do without you. You've made TakeOff what it is today, and we wouldn't be the innovative, forward-thinking company we are without you."

So far, so boring, Katya thought. Could Mack be any more generic if he tried? Then a voice—a female voice—that came through much more clearly. This person was either holding the phone doing the recording or was standing very close to it. "Could you be any more full of shit? Seriously, Mack. Why don't you tell everyone here how you've been treating me?" Then there was dead silence. All the noise of people talking among themselves that hadn't really stopped when Mack was speaking had now stopped completely. Katya realized it was Isabel's voice. "Nothing to say, huh? Why don't you tell everyone how you won't leave me alone? Or about the texts? Or the *sexts*."

Then Mack's voice came back. It was easier to hear him, now that there wasn't anyone else talking. "That's enough, Isabel," he said. He sounded pissed but also, maybe, nervous.

Isabel's voice again: "Oh, fuck you." It sounded like she was crying. *"Fuck you."* Then there was some muffled noise and the recording stopped.

Holy shit, Katya thought. *Holy shit holy shit holy shit.* She needed to listen again. She went back to the beginning of the recording and clicked play. Mack's voice again. Isabel's voice. The silence. Mack. Isabel. Crying.

The logical thing to do, of course, was to post the recording. This was explosive. This was the scoop to end all scoops, and whoever this notmackmcallister@gmail.com was, he (or she) had chosen *her*. There was no reason to send something like this to a reporter if you didn't want it disseminated, right? And yet, there was always the chance that this was some kind of elaborate hoax. You could never be too skeptical. She would need to contact Isabel and Mack and verify that the recording was real. She also wanted to know where it had come from. *Thanks for sending this,* she wrote back to notmackmcallister @gmail.com. *Where did you get this? Can you verify authenticity? Who are you? Thanks, Katya.* Then she messaged Dan on Slack: Check out what just landed in my inbox, she wrote, and uploaded the file.

Three minutes later he messaged her back: holy. fucking. shit.

22

FALLOUT SHELTER

As soon as Isabel had run out of Flatiron Social, Mack just kept going like nothing had happened. He was surprised, and annoyed, and embarrassed about it, but also just a little impressed that Isabel had done it. She had more balls than he'd thought. And so far, three days later, no one at TakeOff had said anything about it—even though he could sense that there was a different, not altogether positive, charge in the air. It was like nothing had happened and yet everything had changed.

Jason's advice had been *not* to fire her, that firing her was only going to antagonize her more. Instead, he should either wait for her to quit or fire her if she stopped showing up for work, because then he could say he was firing her for *that* reason instead of for her outburst. "This is just a blip," Jason assured him. "In fact, this is probably good, because it makes things reach their logical conclusion faster than they would have. We don't want this to drag on and on, but she kind of put us in a terrible situation, and now she's done us a huge favor."

Mack nodded. "I shouldn't contact her, right?" Jason laughed and didn't even respond. But even if Mack did contact her, he wasn't sure what he would say to her. What he *wanted* to say was something to the effect of *I can't believe I was actually attracted to you, I wish I had never met you.* Isabel had become a distraction, one that was starting to permeate too many aspects of his life. He wanted the distraction gone.

Which was when Jason pinged him with a link to a tweet from the @invisibletechman account, saying something about stuff that had "gone down" at their drinks the other night. *Again?* Why was this guy totally on his ass? There were always going to be people—or anonymous Twitter accounts—who were going to try to bring good people down. That was just a fact of life. It just sucked that right now the focus had to be on him and his company. That was the thing about people like this. He would be willing to bet hundreds—actually, make that thousands—of dollars that not only did this person not work in tech, but whoever was tweeting from this account had never started anything on his own. He'd never known what it was like to pull an all-nighter because you had a new release you had to ship the next morning or what it was like to have dozens of people relying on you for their livelihoods. It was a shit-ton of responsibility! And sure, it was easy to sit there and be critical and think you knew everything about everything if you had never actually *done* anything.

Let's get ahead of this, Jason wrote on Slack. Mack was about to respond when his phone rang. It was an unfamiliar number. "Mack McAllister," he said as he looked at Twitter on one computer monitor and read TechScene on the other.

"Hello, Mack, this is Katya Pasternack, from TechScene," said the female voice on the other end of the line. She had a faint accent that Mack couldn't quite place.

"Hey, Katya, I was just looking at your website," he said.

"What a coincidence," she said. "So I'm calling because, I don't know if you've seen it, the invisibletechman tweet? Saying that something had gone down at a TakeOff event on Friday night?"

Oh, for fuck's sake, he thought. How was TechScene already on the case? The tweet had literally *just* gone up like fifteen minutes ago.

"Okay." He sent Jason a message on Slack: on phone w Katya from TechScene—she's asking about the tweet. To Katya, he said, "What about it?" *Stall, stall, stall.*

Jason replied right away: Don't tell her anything.

Roger that, he responded to Jason.

"Can you tell me what happened the other night?" she said.

"It was a private TakeOff drinks event," he said. "Beyond that I can't really comment."

"So you're confirming that there was a TakeOff event on Friday night." *Oh, fuck,* he thought.

"You know what, Katya, I'm going to have to have you talk to our PR department. How did you get my cell number, anyway?"

"I'd rather not say," she said.

"Okay. I'm going to hang up now. If you have additional questions, you can direct them to our PR team." He ended the call without waiting for her response.

Jason materialized in the doorway. "How'd that go?" Mack shook his head. "Not well?"

"Not well," Mack said. "I managed to confirm that we had an event the other night."

"Huh." Jason contemplated this. "Maybe that's not so bad."

"Explain."

"Well...like I was saying before, we want to get ahead of this. Or at least, get our version of the story out there."

"Which is what? She hasn't even written the damn story yet and I already feel like this is all over. Everything is over."

Jason shook his head vigorously. "No, no, *no!*" he said. "That is the *wrong* attitude. This is just the *battle*. We are going to fight a *war*. There is no fucking way that bitch is going to ruin everything you've built with some bullshit accusation."

Mack was a bit taken aback by Jason's vehemence, but he tried not to show it. As much as he hated Isabel right now, he was still sensitive about *other* people criticizing her. Even if things had gone badly, it was still a reflection on *him* that he had been with her. At the same time, he didn't want Jason to be able to tell that it bothered him. "Right," he said. "But how do we do that?"

"Well…there's a way of framing this. Having a 'source' call up Katya and tell her the 'real deal' about what happened. You know, that an employee who is a little…*unstable* went a little crazy at an event the other night, and we're all worried about her and we're going to try to get her some help."

"I knew there was a reason I hired you," Mack said. "That is fucking *genius*."

Jason smiled. "This isn't my first rodeo."

"I probably don't want to know about your other rodeos, do I."

"Let's just say that I am familiar with the dark arts of media manipulation. The key is making reporters think that they're getting a scoop or, like, the *real story*. It's just a game to them."

"They're the worst," Mack said. "It's not a fucking game to me! This"—he gestured to the entire office—"is not a game. It's like people don't understand that."

"There are always going to be people who don't understand," Jason said. "Fuck those people. We don't need those people. Those people have nothing else in their lives worth living for, so they just exist to tear people like us down. It's bullshit."

Mack smiled a sincere smile for what felt like the first time that day. Thank God at least Jason understood him. "You're

right," he said. "This *is* bullshit. I know it's bullshit. You know it's bullshit. So wait. Who's going to call Katya back?"

"I'll handle it," Jason said. "I can even do it from your office, if you want."

"I mean, sure," Mack said. "Want to do it now?"

"Yeah, let's get 'er done. What's her number?" Mack gave it to him and he dialed. He set the phone down on the desk and put it on speaker. "Hello, Katya?"

"Hello, yes, this is Katya. Who's calling?"

"Yes, hi. This is Jason Schneider from TakeOff. I understand you had some questions about an event we had the other night?"

"Yes, I did, and—"

Jason interrupted her. "Okay. I'm happy to talk to you, but everything I say has to be attributed to a source at TakeOff. I don't want my name anywhere near the story. Is that understood?"

There was a pause. "Can I ask why?"

"When you hear what I have to say, you'll understand why it wouldn't be appropriate for me to put my name in the story."

"I'd really prefer to speak on the record."

Jason rolled his eyes at Mack as if to say, *Can you believe this shit?* "It's unfortunately not a negotiation. Either you agree to my terms or I hang up the phone."

There was silence from the other end of the line, then: "Okay."

Nice, Mack mouthed, and he high-fived Jason silently.

"Great," Jason said. "So listen. Things got a little wonky the other night, but let me give you some background. The event was a good-bye drinks thing for one of our core employees, okay? And Mack got up to speak, you know, to toast this employee, and—"

"Who was it?" Katya said. Jason glanced at Mack, who raised his eyebrows. Did it matter if she knew it was drinks for

Casper Kim? Probably not—the news that he'd left was going to be out there soon enough. And telling her might make her feel like they had given her a useful crumb of information.

"I'll tell you off the record, okay? Like, you can't publish his name in the piece—it's not fair to drag him into this story."

"Okay, fine," Katya said.

"It was for Casper Kim, our head of product, who's leaving."

"Why is he leaving?" she asked. Jason glanced at Mack, who shook his head.

"I'm unfortunately not able to comment on confidential personnel matters," Jason said.

"Can you tell me where he's going?" she asked.

"Unfortunately, no," Jason said. There was silence. He cleared his throat. "Anyway, so Mack got up in front of everyone to toast Casper, and then there was this…*outburst* by one of our employees. I'll get to who it was in a moment, but first I want to make something clear: this particular employee has been a problem for us for a while."

"A problem?" Katya said. "Can you be more specific?"

Jason sighed. "I can, but off the record. I just need to emphasize, again, how this *cannot* be coming from me. This is highly confidential information that is actually illegal for me to be sharing with you."

"I get it," Katya said. "And I appreciate your candor."

"Okay. So it was Isabel Taylor, who has been an Engagement Ninja here for a couple years now. Her performance had been under review—she was showing up late for work or not at all, her work hadn't been up to par, et cetera. We finally decided to layer her with one of her direct reports, which I think is what sent her over the edge."

"Layer her?" Katya said.

"It just means that like…instead of firing someone, you hire or promote someone over them."

"Ah. I see. Got it."

"Right. So she seemed unhappy about that, but instead of dealing with it in a productive manner, she chose to lash out at Mack in a public setting. Which of course is highly inappropriate."

"What did she say, exactly?"

"I don't really remember every word she said. Something to the effect of 'Mack sucks and I'm outta here.'"

"Hm," Katya said. Jason looked at Mack. What did that "hm" mean? "So she didn't say anything about, like, sexting or anything like that."

Shit. How the fuck did Katya know about this? Mack waved his hands frantically and mouthed, *No.* Jason smiled and held up his hands and mouthed, *I got this.*

"No, nothing like that," Jason said.

"Okay, I see," Katya said. "Does she still work at TakeOff?"

Jason glanced at Mack. "We're currently discussing her employment status."

"Got it," Katya said. "So none of this has anything to do with the fact that Isabel and Mack had a relationship, is what you're saying."

What the hell. How did Katya even have an inkling about what had happened between him and Isabel? And how was Jason going to get them out of this?

"Katya, can you excuse me for just one moment? Thanks." Jason put the phone on mute before she could even respond. To Mack, he said, "Dude. How the fuck does she know about that? I thought you said no one knew."

"I have no fucking idea," Mack said. "Unless…I mean, it's possible she's been talking to Isabel. But how would she even know to go talk to Isabel? And why would Isabel talk to her? It makes no sense."

Jason shook his head. "Well, I think we just deny at this point, right? Or...do you want to say that you had a consensual relationship, it ended amicably, you don't know where this is coming from? Et cetera."

"Maybe that's a better way to go," Mack said. "Makes Isabel seem jealous, right?"

Jason shrugged. "I think it just puts us in charge of the narrative a little more. I'm going to get back on the phone with her before she starts getting suspicious that she's been on hold too long." He unmuted the call. "Katya? Hey, sorry about that. Yeah, so, listen—Mack and Isabel had a brief, adult, consensual relationship that ended amicably. That's all I can say about that."

"I see," Katya said. There was something in her tone of voice that Mack didn't like. It was a tone that said *I know you're lying*. "All right. Is there anything else you'd like to add about what happened or about Isabel?"

Mack shook his head. Jason said, "No. If there are specific things that end up in your piece that you think Mack or someone else at TakeOff should respond to, I'd appreciate it if you gave us a call back."

"Yes, of course," Katya said. "I appreciate your time."

"Thanks." Jason hung up. Mack was having trouble reading his face. He certainly didn't look as confident as he had before the call.

"What do you think?" Mack said.

"I think...I think that we just continue to deny, deny, deny. Look...at the end of the day, people are going to believe what they want to believe, but I think that our story is a more convincing one. Who's Isabel Taylor? She's nobody. You...you're Mack McAllister. It's just, like, not even a question!"

Mack smiled. He needed this affirmation. For a long time, he had felt invincible, and maybe this was, actually, a good way for him to check himself. It was so important to stay humble, to remember that everything he had worked so hard for could be gone so quickly, that he was only in control of what he could be in control of. How did you know what the light looked like if you never saw the darkness?

"Hey, by the way..." Jason said. "Any word from Gramercy?"

Gramercy. No, there had not been any word from Gramercy, not since they'd sent him the term sheet. Should he be worried? He didn't *think* he should be worried, but then again...Jason knew as well as he did how much runway they still had left, and it wasn't a ton. Mack was visualizing their cash on hand getting depleted in front of his eyes, the numbers turning into gibberish, like that weird numbers display in Union Square that didn't make any sense. "Yeah, just waiting on lawyers. You know."

Jason seemed satisfied with this response. "All right, man. I have a coffee with a potential product guy at the Ace. Friend of a friend." He fist-bumped Mack. "We got this. Don't forget that." Jason started to leave the office.

"Hey, I just thought of something," Mack said. "Sabrina."

"Sabrina?" Jason said. "What about her? We'll figure out exactly what her role is, don't worry."

"No. I mean, her husband works at TechScene," Mack said. "Remember?"

"*Oh,*" Jason said. "Right. Of course. It's probably time we had a chat with her about this, don't you think?"

"I do," Mack said. "I really, really do."

23

TO SMELL THE TRUTH

HE'S LYING, KATYA typed to Dan on Slack. he is a lying liar.

Just try to keep him on the phone, Dan typed back. As soon as Jason called, she ran into a meeting room for privacy, and now she was sitting in front of her computer with her phone on speaker, taking notes in a Google Doc in one window and Slacking Dan in another. Dan seemed a little disappointed that it was Jason, not Mack, who had called back, but Katya could tell that she was on speaker and told Dan, I think Mack is probably listening to the call, so I'm going to behave accordingly.

She had already asked Jason specifically about what happened the other night at the drinks for Casper Kim, and he had deflected. Or not exactly deflected but given her a very subjective version of events. He was calling what Isabel had said an "outburst" by an employee who was a "problem," which had almost made her laugh out loud. *Isabel* was the problem? That was an interesting way to frame it. And now he was trying to tell her that Isabel was upset not because she had been on the receiving end of harassment from her boss, but because she wasn't doing a good job and they had "layered" her. Katya didn't know what this meant, but she figured there was no harm in asking. "Layer her?" she said.

"It just means that like...instead of firing someone, you hire or promote someone over them."

Classy move, she thought. She typed to Dan on Slack: they're acting like Isabel is just pissed bc she got layered.

Weird, Dan typed back.

She asked them what, specifically, Isabel had said the other night. She was trying to get them to reveal the contents of Isabel's speech in some kind of meaningful way, but then again, their denials about what had happened were useful as well. She wasn't exactly sure yet how she was going to play this with Isabel. Should she reveal that she had this recording? She wanted to tell her Jason's version of events, because it deviated so wildly from what seemed to have actually happened that maybe Isabel would get so angry that she would say something incendiary. It would all make for a better story in the end.

As they were talking, she wondered: Was it possible that this was what Jason and Mack actually believed? Could it be that their version of events, which was so clearly at odds with reality—she had the tape! what more could you ask for!—had become their truth? But how delusional would you have to be to construct this version of truth?

And if this was their version of *this* truth, then how could she possibly believe anything else they were saying? She decided to try to catch them in as many lies and half-truths as possible—not to challenge them directly as they were speaking, but collect them all like a nice Christmas stocking of lies.

"So what did she say, exactly?" she asked. To Dan, she typed: asking him exactly what Isabel said. They still don't know i have the recording.

Good idea, he typed back. Get him to make as many dumb statements as you can. Do they think we're idiots? Katya typed back: ¯_(ツ)_/¯.

"I don't really remember every word she said," Jason said. "Something to the effect of 'Mack sucks and I'm outta here.'"

Katya had to suppress a laugh. *Mack sucks and I'm outta here?* Who was he kidding with this? She wrote this down in her Google Doc and next to it wrote: TOTAL BULLSHIT. To Jason, all she said was "Hm." It was a "hm" that was meant to telegraph *I know you're full of shit, and I'm going to give you one more chance to suddenly remember something, but really, I think you're full of shit.* She let the "hm" hang in the air for a few more long, awkward moments. Still, no one said anything. When you were interviewing someone, you were supposed to get comfortable with pauses, because most people weren't, and they'd just do your job for you by filling up the pause. Jason wasn't taking the bait, though. So finally, she said: "So she didn't say anything about, like, sexting or anything like that?"

There was another pause. *Bingo,* she thought. She had revealed *just* enough to let them know that she actually *did* know more than she was letting on.

"No, nothing like that," Jason said. To Dan, she typed, My eyes are rolling so far back in my head that I might go blind.

Hahaha, he wrote back. You got this.

When she asked Jason if Isabel still worked at TakeOff, she thought his response was interesting: "We're currently discussing her employment status." If Mack really had nothing to hide—or nothing to fear—wouldn't they have fired Isabel by now? It didn't make any sense to keep someone on who was as much trouble as Isabel allegedly was. She decided to scare them a little bit more.

"Got it. So none of this has anything to do with the fact that Isabel and Mack had a relationship, is what you're saying."

Jason asked if he could put her on hold. *Oh, they know they are truly fucked,* she thought. Got 'em, she typed to Dan. They can't get out of this.

You are a fucking champ, he wrote back. I'm going to have to insist on taking you to drinks after this.

Ugh. She didn't really want to get drinks with Dan—hadn't she made that clear? Hahaha, she typed. Let's see how the rest of this conversation goes. I'm on hold now because now they know I know that Mack and Isabel were actually a thing.

God, you're good, he wrote.

Jason's voice came back on the phone. "Katya? Hey, sorry about that. Yeah, so, listen—Mack and Isabel had a brief, adult, consensual relationship that ended amicably. That's all I can say about that."

"I see," Katya said. Should she call them out more? Or was this enough? "All right. Is there anything else you'd like to add about what happened or about Isabel?" Jason said no, there wasn't anything else he wanted to add, and that if there were specific things in her story that he or someone else at TakeOff should respond to, could she give them a call? Of course, she told them.

Well, that was interesting, Katya wrote to Dan.

You're off? he wrote. Want to chat IRL, talk about next steps?

Not really, Katya thought. She knew what the next steps were: call Isabel and get her version of events, and try to get the person who had sent her the recording to tell her who he or she was. And—actually, she had another idea of who to call right now.

Gonna make a couple more calls, she typed back to Dan.

She texted Teddy Rosen. Got a sec to chat? she wrote. Have a qq for you.

He responded right away: Always have time for you. What's up? Calling now, she wrote.

"Katya!" he said when he picked up the phone. "How the hell have you been? Did Victor tell you we had a good chat the other day? I like where he and Nilay are going with their new thing." *Victor has a new thing?* It had been, like, three days since they'd spoken, and already he had a new thing that he had met with Teddy about? Or—and this was more troubling in retrospect—maybe he had been at work for a while on a new thing that she hadn't known about. She racked her brain—had Victor mentioned something and she'd just forgotten about it? He *had* been spending a lot of time with Nilay again since they'd patched things up. She certainly didn't want to let Teddy know that they'd gotten in a fight. Or broken up. Or . . . whatever had happened. She still wasn't sure.

"It's cool, right?" she said. "Really proud of him."

"You should be," Teddy said. "And it seems like they've really learned from what happened with StrollUp."

"Yeah, I think so," Katya said. She was dying to get more details out of him about the new company, but she worried that if she asked any questions, it would be obvious that she was missing crucial information. But also, in what world was it possible for a person to have a company that totally failed and then, literally weeks later, get someone to contemplate giving him money for a new thing? People thought this was normal. It wasn't normal.

"Anyway. What's up? You said you had a question?"

"Yeah, I do. I've been looking into some stuff about TakeOff, and I know you'd said that you guys were close to a deal with them. So I wanted to get your, uh, *take* on a couple things. Sorry."

"Hit me," Teddy said.

"So at their good-bye drinks on Friday night for Casper Kim—"

"Wait. Did you say good-bye drinks?"

"Yeah," Katya said. "His last day was Friday."

"Well, that's interesting," Teddy said. He sounded not exactly thrilled to learn this information.

"Why?" She wasn't intending for the conversation to go this way, but that was sometimes how you got your best stuff—by just letting your sources talk and then subtly guiding them back on track.

"We're off the record, right?"

"Always," Katya said. She wasn't about to burn one of her best sources.

"So...when Mack came in and did his presentation, we really grilled him about the product, because they had a release that was a little buggy, and he was going on and on about the new release and how great it was going to be, so we were asking him who he had in charge of product and he just starts talking about this guy Casper Kim who's some kind of genius product wunderkind, and honestly that made a big difference for us. We want to know that people have a strong team behind them, you know?"

"Totally," Katya said.

"So if Casper left, and Mack didn't feel the need to reveal this information to us...that's—well, that's problematic."

"Right," Katya said. "Do you think this will change anything for you guys?"

Teddy paused. "I mean, I want to say no? I *want* to say that we have faith in Mack and his vision for TakeOff and that we're impressed with the work he's done so far and have total confidence in him for the future." He paused again. "I *want* to say that."

"Ha," Katya said. "Well, let me ask you something else. Have you heard anything about what happened at the drinks the other night?"

"Is this about that invisibletechman tweet?" Teddy sounded annoyed. "James sent it to me and asked if I knew anything about it. I told him I didn't. But now you're saying...well, what *are* you saying?"

"What if I told you that Mack's biggest problem right now probably *isn't* Casper Kim leaving?"

"I'm almost afraid to ask you what you mean by that," Teddy said. "Should I be afraid to ask you what you mean by that?"

Katya laughed. "I'm not sure. Are you afraid of sexual harassment?"

Teddy emitted a low whistle. "You're shitting me," he said. "You're fucking shitting me right now."

"I am not, in fact, shitting you," Katya said. "I'm sorry to say."

"Fuck," Teddy said. "Sexual harassment? Are you sure? Do you have proof? Who? I need to know everything."

"I actually can't go into too much detail," Katya said. "I just wanted to know...well, theoretically, would this have an impact on your investment?"

"Katya, you need to fucking tell me if this is something real," Teddy said. His voice was tight. "We are literally like a day away from signing this deal and I am personally fucked if this comes out after the deal is signed. Okay? So, like, as a friend, just *tell me* what the problem is."

"I'll tell you if I can get a quote I can attribute to a Gramercy employee," Katya said.

"Everyone will fucking know it's me!" Teddy said. His voice was high-pitched now. "I can't give you a quote!"

"Well, it's your call," Katya said.

There was silence on the other end of the line. "What kind of quote do you want?" he said finally.

"I'd like a quote about whether this news, combined with the news of Casper Kim leaving, will in any way affect Gramercy's potential funding of TakeOff."

Teddy sighed audibly. "You're killing me here, Pasternack."

"Just doing my job, Rosen," she said.

"Your job kind of sucks right now," he said. "No offense."

"None taken." There was another pause. "So . . . a quote?"

"How about this," Teddy said. "I give you a quote and you can attribute it to 'someone with knowledge of the situation at Gramercy.' Okay?"

"I can live with that," she said. People who paid attention would know that it was obviously someone at Gramercy who had spoken to her, and if putting it that way was what tipped the scales to make Teddy talk to her, then so be it. Life was a series of tradeoffs. "So, hit me. What's your quote?"

"Okay. Gimme a sec." Katya waited. There was something about being able to have Teddy Rosen by the balls, even briefly, that she liked. He would probably become a partner at Gramercy soon, start pulling in millions of dollars a year, buy a condo in Tribeca, marry a beautiful blond publicist named Lauren or Whitney who would quit her job and have three perfect babies, and live happily ever after. This whole TakeOff incident would end up being a tiny blip, if he even remembered it at all after, like, a week. Maybe Gramercy would pull their investment in TakeOff, maybe they wouldn't. Either way, life as he knew it would go on for Teddy Rosen.

The stakes were just higher for her. She couldn't afford to lose this story. She couldn't afford to lose this job. People like Teddy, people like Mack—they could afford to make mistakes. They were forgiven. Young women with immigrant parents who went to college on scholarship and were one paycheck away from not being able to pay rent—they couldn't.

"Okay," Teddy said finally. "So you have to tell me first, because I can't really come up with a quote about something that I don't know about."

"Fine," Katya said. "Okay. So the other night at Casper's drinks, Mack was giving a toast to Casper and Isabel interrupted him and was like, 'You're full of shit, why don't you tell everyone how you fucked me over and sent me sexts and you suck.'"

"Whoa," Teddy said. "Is that, uh, a direct quote?"

"Not exactly, but that was the gist," Katya said.

"I see," Teddy said. "What happened after that?"

"Apparently Isabel ran out of the bar—they were at Flatiron Social—and everyone continued on like nothing had happened?"

"Whew," Teddy said. "That's...that's intense. I mean, she's crazy, right?"

"Who? Isabel?"

"Yeah."

"I dunno," Katya said. "Is she? She doesn't seem crazy to me."

"Well, you have to be a little crazy to do something like that, don't you?"

Do you? Katya thought. There was a time when maybe, *maybe* she would have conceded this point. But not now. Now it seemed like these guys had all gone to the same school of "call women crazy whenever they do something that makes you uncomfortable." But she didn't want to get into a fight with Teddy over this. The idea was to get him to say *more,* not hang up on her. So she just said, "Hm, maybe."

"Does Andrew know that she did this?"

"I have no idea," Katya said. "Does Andrew really have

anything to do with this?" *Andrew*. If fucking Andrew hadn't confronted Victor, then Victor would still be speaking to her!

"I guess not," Teddy said. He sighed. "Okay. Here's my quote. 'They're figuring out what to do—they had been prepared to make a substantial investment, and now they're getting cold feet. It's not off the table, but they're reexamining everything.' How's that?"

"Perfect," Katya said.

"Wait," Teddy said. "Change it to 'They had been prepared to make a substantial investment, but now they're reexamining everything.' Okay? Take out the *cold feet* and the *off the table*."

"Fine," Katya said. "Anything else?"

"No," Teddy said. "Nothing else."

She had one more person to talk to. As she dialed Isabel's number she thought about everything that had led up to this phone call. What if she had skipped Andrew's party and just gone home? What if she hadn't started talking to Isabel and Sabrina at the party, or what if Isabel hadn't left her phone on the table? What would have ended up happening between Isabel and Mack? she wondered. Maybe things would have just petered out between them. By pursuing the story, had she actually influenced its outcome? She shivered involuntarily. She couldn't deny that it gave her a rush to know that she possibly had.

She didn't have time to contemplate this anymore, because Isabel picked up. "I've been waiting for your call," she said.

"You have?" Katya was genuinely surprised about this.

"Mm-hmm," Isabel said. She sounded almost giddy.

"Why is that?"

"Why don't you tell me why you're calling, and then I can tell you why I thought you were going to call me."

Katya felt thrown off. Her whole modus operandi was to take people by surprise. Maybe she had underestimated Isabel. "Well..." At this point, she might as well tell her everything. "I'm going to write that story about you and Mack that I've been working on for a while. Even though Andrew tried to get me not to write it."

"I *know*," Isabel said. "Wasn't that weird? I guess he thinks I can't take care of myself."

"Well, I think Victor and I broke up because of that."

"You did? No way. Wait. Seriously? Andrew didn't really mean anything by that."

"Yeah," Katya said, realizing that she was confiding in Isabel when she was supposed to be interviewing her. "Um. Anyway. I was just saying that I'm going to write that story. And...I need to confirm something with you, and this might be a little awkward."

"I'm ready," Isabel said.

"Did you interrupt Mack's speech the other night at Casper's going-away party?"

"I did!" Isabel said. She sounded triumphant, almost smug. "I sure did."

"You seem...enthusiastic about this," Katya said. This conversation was not going badly, but it also wasn't going the way Katya had thought it would. "Can I ask why? You seemed so reluctant to talk before, let alone make a dramatic gesture like you did at Casper's."

"I know," Isabel said. "It does seem like I've done a total one-eighty, doesn't it."

"Um, yeah, it does," she said. Maybe this was some kind of trap or trick, and Isabel was just saying this to fuck with her?

"Let's just say I had a conversation with someone I work with who made me see why I was being dumb about this," she said. "And that Mack deserves whatever is coming to him."

"Whoa," Katya said. "You mean that?"

"I mean that," Isabel said. "This person said to me, 'Think about it this way, if you don't speak up he will continue to get away with this stuff forever, and you owe it to, like, *womanity* to expose him.'"

"Wow. I mean...I think that's true," Katya said. "And just so you know—I will absolutely treat your story with respect."

"Oh, I know," Isabel said. "I'm not worried about that. So was there anything else you wanted to know?"

Katya took a deep breath. "Actually, there is," she said. "You might have wondered why I wanted to write about this in the first place."

"I kind of did, actually," Isabel said. "I wondered how you even knew that Mack and I were a thing. Or had a thing. Or whatever—you know what I mean."

"Right," Katya said. "Remember Andrew's dinner party a few weeks ago? You left your phone with me and Sabrina at one point, maybe you were going to the bathroom? I don't remember. Anyway. That was when you got a...let's say, NSFW text from Mack. And I saw it on your phone, and I took a picture of it with *my* phone." As soon as she said these words—ones she'd thought she might never say—she felt lighter, freer. Even if Isabel flipped out now, at least she had said them. She hadn't realized just how much keeping this secret from Isabel had been bothering her, and then she asked herself why she was so consumed by this. This was what she—what journalists—did; they accumulated information and gathered intelligence and put together something that resembled the truth. At the very least, it had to resemble a truth that the journalist herself believed.

"You did *what?* No way," Isabel said. Katya couldn't tell if she was angry or admiring or a little bit of both. "That is badass. I mean, it's fucked up, but it's also kind of badass. I can't believe...wow. So you've had that this whole time, then?"

"Um, yeah," Katya said. She squeezed her eyes shut. *Please don't stop talking to me,* she thought. She was so close to getting this story.

"Fucked up, right?" Isabel said, and Katya exhaled. "Like, can you believe he'd do that?"

"Do what, exactly," Katya said. "Send you nudes?"

"Well...it's a little more complicated, I guess," Isabel said. "Look—I don't know if I want this in the story, but we used to send each other nudes all the time. But on Snapchat. It was, like, kind of a joke. Or I mean, not a *joke,* exactly, but like, just kind of a fun thing we'd do during the day. It helped pass the time." *Interesting way to pass the time,* Katya thought but didn't say. "But after a while, it got a little boring. I just wasn't that into him anymore. It wasn't like we were exclusive either—I had definitely hooked up with other guys during that whole time, but no one seriously—but then it got to the point where I was like, Am I going to be the girl who just, like, hooks up with her boss? I dunno. It just wasn't who I wanted to be anymore."

It wasn't who I wanted to be anymore. Where did Isabel Taylor get the idea that identity was so malleable? Not that Katya *wanted* her identity to be malleable, but it was fascinating how some people thought that the world would just go along with whatever they decided their lives were like at any given moment. "Right," Katya said. "And...Mack disagreed?"

"You could say that," Isabel said. "I tried to just gradually taper off, and this was even before Andrew and I started seeing each other. But he just, like...didn't take it well. First he tried to pretend that nothing had changed, like just kept texting me and trying to get me to come over and stuff, and I would try to blow him off politely, and then I met Andrew and we just, like, fell for each other so quickly. I hadn't felt that about someone for so long." Isabel was quiet for a moment. "So then it was just over with Mack. It shouldn't have even been a big deal, you know? Like *he* was always so clear about this not being a serious thing! But of course the second Andrew shows up on my Snapchat, it's like, he can't handle it."

"Men are all the same," Katya said.

"Ugh," Isabel said. "Anyway, honestly, I wouldn't have even really thought it was *harassment* until you said something. Did I tell you how he completely humiliated me in a meeting? It was like he was *waiting* to embarrass me in front of people."

"So what are you gonna do now?" Katya asked. "Have you quit TakeOff?"

"I'm about to. And then I'll file a lawsuit." She paused. "Look, I didn't *want* to quit my job. I loved TakeOff. I even used to love working for Mack. But no one should be treated the way I've been treated."

"Wow," Katya said.

"Wait, don't put that in the piece," Isabel said. "That I'm going to file a lawsuit. I haven't, like, talked to a lawyer yet or anything."

"Can I say that you're considering legal action?"

"Umm," Isabel said. "Oh, fuck it, sure. Why the hell not. At this point it's not like I have anything to lose."

24

CATCH AND RELEASE

"DON'T LET ME interrupt," Dan said.

Sabrina's eyes popped open and—desperately, pointlessly—she pulled the covers up over herself. "I didn't hear you come in," she said, even though that felt like the most clichéd and inane thing to say, and she watched him look around the room and thought: *Fuck-fuck-fuck.* She was still holding the vibrator. She swallowed.

"Clearly." He smiled, a funny little smile. "But really, don't let me interrupt. I don't think I've seen you masturbate since...maybe not ever, actually. It was kind of hot."

Her face was bright red, she could tell. "Uh...thanks." That was when he noticed the envelopes on the bed.

"What're these?" he said, picking one of them up. "Jim Lowry, Daytona Beach, Florida." He felt the envelope. "What's in here, Sabrina?"

"It's..." She wanted to melt into the sheets and disappear. When had her throat gotten this dry? And her palms so sweaty? "It's underwear."

"Underwear," Dan said. "*Your* underwear?"

Sabrina nodded.

"Why is my wife sending her underwear to Jim Lowry in Daytona Beach?" His voice was soft.

"Because..." Where to even begin? If she really wanted to tell him why she was sending her underwear to Jim Lowry in Daytona Beach—one of her best customers—she would have to start way, way back, with that very first $125 perfect white cotton Acne T-shirt that she ordered from Barneys. Because when it came time to check out, a message popped up on her screen offering her 10 percent off her purchases all day if she got a Barneys credit card, which seemed like the logical thing to do, and then it seemed to only make sense to add a few more items to her cart to take advantage of the discount, and by the time she finally clicked *purchase*, her grand total for the afternoon was $2,617. She winced but also felt a rush of joy, and it was that rush of joy that she was trying to replicate every single time she bought something. But it was getting harder and harder to find it, and now, selling her underwear, she was getting that same charge, that same rush, that she'd felt originally.

How was Dan ever supposed to understand that?

Whatever. Dan didn't need the backstory. Actually, Dan didn't *deserve* the backstory. "I needed some cash," she said. *What are you going to say to that,* she thought.

"Does this have anything to do with the credit cards?" he said. Sabrina felt sick. This was when he would piece everything together. He would piece everything together, and then—she was sure of it—he would leave her. He would just walk out the door and leave her, and their life, behind. And for all the times she had wished that she wasn't married to him anymore, she suddenly, clearly, didn't want him to leave. "Does this have anything to do with the credit cards," he said, louder. "Are you doing this to pay off the credit cards? What the fuck, Sabrina?"

"Shhh," Sabrina said. "You'll wake Owen and Amelia."

"Excellent point," Dan said. "What if it had been one of them who walked in on you just now?"

"Oh, come on, Dan. They'd have no idea what was going on."

"They'd know that something was fucked up." He sat down on the bed, facing away from Sabrina. "Jesus. Really? You're selling your underwear?" His voice sounded normal now. "Who's even...who buys this shit?"

"You'd be surprised," she said. "I mean, I haven't actually met any of them, but they seem normal. Ish. No one's gotten super-creepy."

"Wait." He turned around. "How long have you been doing this?"

"Just a couple of weeks." *Plus a couple of weeks,* she thought. *Close enough.*

Dan shook his head. "What a world." They were both quiet for a minute. "Really? This is how you decided to make some cash? It's just so...gross."

"I don't know," she said. "I read about it on this Facebook moms' group I'm in. It seemed relatively painless. Someone—not me!—asked if anyone knew a good way to make some quick cash working from home, and someone else responded and said she'd been selling her underwear."

Dan whistled quietly. "Wow," he said. "The secret life of moms."

"I guess." She glanced at him. "I thought you'd be more pissed. Not that I was hoping you'd find out, but, you know."

"I mean, I'm not *thrilled* about it," he said. "But I do wonder..." He paused. "Nah."

261

"What?" she said.

"Nothing," he said. "It's a dumb idea."

"Tell me." She couldn't believe she was actually sitting here having a somewhat normal conversation with her *husband* about the fact that she was selling underwear on the internet to strangers. She hadn't really allowed herself to think about what Dan's reaction would be if he ever found out, but it wasn't exactly...this. Had she been secretly hoping he'd find out? Had she *wanted* to provoke a confrontation with him, something that would end in screaming and tears, something that would jolt her out of her constant low-grade misery?

"Well...I'm just thinking, you know...this is kind of a fascinating way-we-live-now story, right?" Dan said. "Like—you used social media to find out about it, in this world of private Facebook moms' groups that I didn't even know existed."

"You're barely even on Facebook."

"I know, it's kind of a time suck," Dan said. "Anyway. I'm just thinking...what if you wrote something about it?"

"Huh? You mean, like, post about it on Facebook?"

"No, no," Dan said. "An essay. 'How Selling My Underwear for Cash Improved My Marriage.'" He smiled. "Or, you know, something along those lines."

"That's rather premature," she said.

Dan shrugged. "I mean, things couldn't really get worse, could they?"

So he had noticed, then. "If you thought things were so bad," she said slowly, "how come you never said anything?"

"I don't know," he said. "I guess I thought things would just get better on their own. They used to before. Or maybe it took catching you selling your underwear for me to realize how bad things had actually gotten."

"How bad have things gotten?" She couldn't look at him.

"Well," Dan said, "you've stopped being interested in all the stuff we used to love to do. We haven't gone out to eat with another couple in months. We haven't gone away together in probably two years. We *never* have sex. We barely even speak to each other! It feels like we have nothing in common anymore. We even work in the same fucking building and it just feels like we're operating in different universes."

Sabrina could feel the rage boiling up inside of her and willed herself not to scream or do what she really wanted to do, which was claw his face off. "Fuck you," she said. "Why is that all on me? Why do *I* have to be the one making the plans to go out to dinner or go away for the weekend? Why can't *you* be interested in *my* day? You have this assumption that whatever it is you're doing is more interesting than whatever it is that I'm doing."

"I think that objectively, yes, my day is more interesting than yours," he said. "I'm not saying it's more important, but I think it is more interesting."

"Oh, really, fuck you," she said. "Maybe I'm *trying* to make mine more interesting, how about that? Maybe I'm sick of going to work and coming home and taking care of the kids until you decide you feel like showing up."

"Maybe I'm sick of you not understanding how stressful my job is."

"Give me a fucking break," she said. "You want to know what's stressful? Stressful is your boss asking to talk to you today and telling you—nicely, but telling you—that you should really have a talk with your husband about the story his site is trying to write about him."

"Wait." Dan sat down on the bed. "He actually said that?"

"He actually said that," Sabrina said.

"Can we write about that? That's fucked up. He shouldn't be trying to use you like that. Or can I at least say something to him about that? Privately?"

"I'd prefer that you didn't, actually," Sabrina said. That was all she needed—her husband confronting her boss in some kind of misguided chivalrous gesture.

"But you *know* he's such a douche," Dan said.

Sabrina shrugged. "Is he really any better or worse than any other guy in tech?"

"He's pretty bad, Sabrina. I mean, before you started working for him, I knew he was bad, but he's even worse, and his app is so dumb and pointless—like, why do we need something telling us how to cheer up, as though man's preferred state of being at all times is to be *cheerful* so that you can do better work or be a better you—which, by the way, is *such* a startup way of thinking. It's like they can't imagine a world where people have actual *emotions* or feel sad or angry or frustrated; everything has to be *fixed* immediately—anyway, this guy just sucks."

"But...what's wrong with trying to be happy? I wouldn't mind trying to be happy, to be perfectly honest."

"It's not that being happy is bad," Dan said. "It's the fetishization of happiness and productivity above all else that I take issue with."

"Okay." She thought for a moment. "But it's not like you don't want the people who work for *you* to be productive too."

"That's not the point." *It's kind of the point,* Sabrina thought. But suddenly she was so, so tired. They were silent for a minute. "So will you consider writing that essay?"

"Oh—um," Sabrina said. "I don't think so."

"It could be totally anonymous," he said. "You wouldn't have to worry about your name coming up in a Google search or anything like that."

That was something that hadn't even occurred to her. But also, was he saying that he wanted her to write it—for *him?* "Wait. You mean write it for *you?* For TechScene?"

"Why not?" Dan stood up. "We publish first-person stuff. And we're trying to do more—just as long as it has something to do with technology or social media or the internet, you know? Boom. That stuff shares really well too."

"No way. Even if it was anonymous. It just feels...gross. And weird. And what if someone figured it out? No."

Dan laughed. "That seems unlikely." He lay down so that his head was near her knees. He looked up at her. "Sorry. I'm just...well, now I'm thinking about seeing you masturbating." He smiled. She could tell he was getting hard. He turned toward her and scooted up a little farther, and she slid down toward him. He started kissing her ear, then her neck. She thought about the stacks of cashmere hidden deep in her closet as one of his hands moved under the vintage Velvet Underground concert T-shirt (which she'd bought for seventy-five dollars on eBay) and found her right nipple while the other hand slipped under the band of the thirty-six-dollar Cosabella boy shorts she'd ordered ten pairs of last week. Her vagina was moist; whether it was still from getting herself off or the way he was rubbing her clit, she couldn't tell. All she knew was that the last couple times they'd tried to have sex, she'd been so dry that even copious amounts of lube hadn't helped. "You like that?" he whispered into her ear as he rubbed her clit harder, and she moaned. She *did* like it, she did, and he flipped her over and pulled her up toward him so he could thrust into her, holding her small, firm tits in one hand and one of her hips in the other. She thought of Natalie.

All of a sudden, right as she was getting close, he came inside her with a jolt, no warning. "I'm sorry," he whispered, flipping her back over. "Here, let me…" He started moving down her body, but one of their phones vibrated, and she wriggled up. "It's okay, Dan," she said. He didn't protest.

"Be right back," he whispered in her ear and went into the bathroom. She lay on the bed for a moment, listening to him pee, and then glanced down at her phone. Nothing. Then she noticed Dan's phone on the bed. It must have fallen out of his pants. She didn't think twice about what she was about to do, just picked it up and looked at the screen. It said: *Katya Pasternack—iMessage.* Dan must have had his notifications set so you couldn't read the actual message on the lock screen. She thought for a moment—now the water was running—and typed in Owen's birthday, Dan's numerical password for everything. She quickly opened his messages tab, and, without opening the actual message, she read the first couple lines of Katya's text: hey def can't meet up later, sorry. See u tomorrow. She heard the water stop running, put the phone on the lock screen, and tossed it back to where it had ended up on the bed. Dan came out of the bathroom, glanced at her, and smiled. She half smiled back.

25

KEEP YOUR FRIENDS CLOSE

"WE HAVE A little problem," Jason said. He was standing in the doorway of Mack's office, and his face was scrunched into an expression that Mack couldn't quite figure out. It didn't look good, though.

"What's that," Mack said.

"Invisibletechman," Jason said.

"Again?" Mack said. "What the fuck, seriously. What does this guy have against me?"

"Honestly, I have no idea, but it's fucked," Jason said.

Mack went to @invisibletechman and read the tweet at the top of the page. Y'all gotta listen to this—told you shit at TakeOff didn't smell right. Mack clicked on the link and immediately heard sound coming out of his computer.

"You, uh, might want to turn that down," Jason said. "Or put on headphones." Mack rolled his eyes but plugged in his headphones and listened. It was a recording from Casper's good-bye party of Isabel's outburst.

"You've got to be fucking kidding me," Mack said. "Someone recorded that?"

Jason nodded. His face was grim. "Yeah. And this is officially not good for us," he said. "People are going to start calling and emailing—so just pass everyone on to me. I'm going to say we're investigating and have no comment, and I'll tell people off the record that we suspect that it's a doctored recording."

"Wait. *Do* we think it's a doctored recording?" Mack said.

Jason shrugged. "It *could* be a doctored recording. We just don't know yet."

"Ah," Mack said. "Well, what the fuck am I supposed to do in the meantime?"

"There's nothing you really *can* do, unfortunately."

At that moment, Mack's phone buzzed. He glanced at it—an unknown number was calling. He held the phone up to Jason. "Look," he said. "It's already starting."

"Don't answer it, obviously," he said. "Sit tight. Don't stress about this too much—I know that's easy for me to say, but really. Don't." He leaned over Mack's desk and fist-bumped him. "We got this."

Mack gave him a weak smile and then watched him go. He wanted to believe that everything was going to be okay—but how was that possible? He thought back to the first day in this office. He'd started the company in one of the incubator spaces on the third floor, but after hiring five people, they had officially outgrown it, and coincidentally, there was a photo-retouching app that was moving out of the seventh floor. The new office had seemed impossibly, gloriously big. That first day, when it was just the six of them still, he bought Nerf guns and that afternoon they had a huge Nerf gun fight. He remembered that Isabel had gotten really into it, shooting the balls and laughing hysterically every time she hit someone. As the space had filled up with tables and computers and people, they'd had fewer and fewer Nerf gun fights, and now he wasn't sure where the Nerf guns even were.

His phone was vibrating not just with phone calls and texts but also Twitter notifications.

Can't believe this news about @mackmcallister.

If allegations against @mackmcallister are true, entire NYC tech scene should be asking itself some tough questions.

@mackmcallister accused of sexual harassment by employee in public. Is this the end for @takeoffapp?

Isabel still hadn't been identified, he realized. Well, *that* was fucked up. Why should he have to bear the brunt of this?

And then, just when he was about to ping Jason about this injustice, he got an email from Katya Pasternack.

Hi, Mack, given that this recording leaked this morning, I decided to go ahead and publish my story. Here's the link. Let me know if you have any additional comment—I'd be happy to update or even write a new piece.

Oh, fuck yourself, Mack thought. He clicked the link.

TakeOff Founder Mack McAllister Accused of Sexual Harassment by Ex-Employee

Isabel Taylor is currently exploring legal options.
By Katya Pasternack

The female employee heard on an explosive recording accusing TakeOff founder Mack McAllister of sexual harassment that has been making the rounds of startup Twitter this morning is McAllister's former assistant Isabel Taylor, TechScene can exclusively reveal. McAllister, the 28-year-old founder of one of the hottest companies in the New York startup scene, was accused by Taylor in front of the entire company at a recent event for a departing employee. Taylor told TechScene she is considering filing a lawsuit against McAllister. She agreed to allow her name to be published.

"Mack and I were in a casual relationship for a few months, but as soon as I started dating someone else"—reported to be Magic Bean founder Andrew Shepard, who did not respond to TechScene's request for comment—"he suddenly started freaking out."

Taylor claimed that she was forced to quit her job after McAllister "humiliated" her at a meeting with several colleagues in what she said was retribution for rebuffing his attempts to get back together with her—which allegedly included sending unsolicited sexually explicit text messages. "I didn't want to quit my job. I loved TakeOff. I even used to love working for Mack. But no one should be treated the way I've been treated."

When reached for comment, a TakeOff representative denied Taylor's claims and said, "Isabel and Mack had a brief, adult, consensual relationship that ended amicably."

TakeOff is reportedly close to closing a round of Series A funding, led by Gramercy Partners, that sources say would value the company at $600 million. A source close to Gramercy Partners said that the firm "had been prepared to make a substantial investment, but now they're reexamining everything" in light of the news. A spokesperson for Gramercy had no comment.

Photo: The texts that McAllister allegedly sent to Taylor. Click to reveal.

Audio: The recording of Taylor's accusations.

Mack pinged Jason. I'm calling an emergency all-hands, he wrote on Slack. I need to nip this in the bud before it gets too out of control. Before Jason could respond, Mack had sent an email to employees@takeoff.com, instructing them to meet in the canteen in an hour. He knew he had to speak from the heart or nobody was going to believe him, so—uncharacteristically—he decided not to even think through exactly what he was going to say. Jason finally wrote back: Okay. Whatever you want to do. Not exactly the enthusiastic go-ahead he had been hoping for, but this was an emergency. He had to go with his gut.

Exactly sixty minutes after he'd sent the email, he stood up in front of the team and cleared his throat. He was going to speak without a microphone—it felt more authentic—and he launched right into it, without any kind of preamble. "I know by this point you all have probably seen the story that was written about TakeOff—about me—in TechScene today," he said. "I've never wanted to be anything but transparent with everyone here—you all are the most brilliant, most inspiring, most creative, most hardworking people in tech. And it's only fair to all of you that you know the truth." He paused. No one was talking or checking their phones. He had never stood in front of a room of people so rapt. "The truth is that Isabel Taylor and I *did* have a relationship. I'm sure many of you can relate to falling for someone you work with, and maybe some of you can even relate to falling for Isabel." The room was silent. "That was a joke, everyone," he said, and people laughed as though they had been waiting for his permission, and suddenly the mood seemed to lighten. "And yes, we broke up. These things happen. Was I upset? Sure. Wouldn't you be?" Again, slightly nervous laughter. He breathed in quietly through his nose and out through his mouth. "And I'm just disappointed that her interpretation of events is so wildly different from mine. But I'm prepared to fight this. I owe it to you all, to fight this. I'm not going to take questions right now, but if you have any, please come see me. I'm happy to discuss this more." He paused again and looked out into the room. These people, everyone looking at him right now with what seemed to be a measure of approval, or at least acceptance—*he* had gotten them here. *He* had built this. And no one, least of all Isabel Taylor, was going to take it away from him without a knock-down, drag-out fight. The room was silent for a moment, and then he saw Jason nodding, and then Jason was clapping, and then a few other people started clapping, and soon the whole room was applauding wildly. "Thank you," he said.

His phone vibrated as he was walking back to his office. He was feeling good. At least his company was still on his side. They believed him, and that was all that mattered right now. He looked at his phone—it was a Slack notification from Jason. Hey, man, I have Teddy Rosen coming up—he wants to chat. Cool to do it in your office?

What the hell, Mack thought. Teddy Rosen was coming up? And why was Jason coordinating the meeting?

A couple minutes later, Jason walked into his office with not only Teddy Rosen but also James Patel. "Nice space," James said. "Mind if we sit?" He gestured to the couch.

"Uh, no, go ahead," Mack said. Did his voice really sound hoarse? And...were his palms sweating? His palms were sweating.

"Thanks for meeting with us on such short notice," James said. "Just...given recent events, we felt it would be best if we, you know, nipped this situation in the bud. Given that we are about to make a substantial investment in your company." James smiled. Mack nodded. "Jason mentioned you just spoke to the staff—that's good. But we need you to also make a public apology, own up to what happened and be *contrite*. It was a lapse in judgment that will never happen again, you apologize, maybe we have you make a donation to some women's organization. Maybe something that works with girls in tech? My wife can probably help with that. Anyway, in the meantime, we need to reach out to Isabel and offer her a settlement."

"A settlement?" Mack said. "That seems crazy. Isn't that just an admission of wrongdoing?"

"We don't need to admit to the specifics, but if she has the texts, this isn't going away," James said. "It's not a 'he said, she said' situation. Your other option is to claim you were hacked, which, frankly, no one is going to believe."

"Yeah, no. We're not telling the world my phone got hacked. That would just be embarrassing." Mack suddenly remembered something. "What if we just went full scorched-earth? Something like this happened at the company my buddy founded and he fought it tooth and nail, and the girl who brought the suit ended up *completely* regretting it. Like...technically, yes, I think she got a settlement, but this girl was *destroyed*. She'll never get another job. Her boyfriend dumped her, I think she moved back home to Minnesota or wherever she was from. And she even admitted after that if she had to do it over, she never would have gone to trial. My buddy was like, we *told* you! We said this is not going to be good for you to go to trial, there are going to be things that come out that you're not going to like, and we are not going to hold back. And she said, Bring it on. So they did. And so everything she had texted, emailed, said in front of people was admissible. Her behavior in past relationships was admissible. They got her ex-boyfriend to come on the stand and testify that she'd stalked him after they broke up—it demonstrated a pattern of irrational behavior." He looked at everyone excitedly. Surely they understood that this was a viable option. "There's all *kinds* of shit you can do."

Jason, Teddy, and James glanced at one another. Finally, James spoke. "I'm not sure that's necessarily the most prudent tack right now," he said carefully.

"Fuck prudent!" Mack said. "I'm *done* being prudent. Being prudent is what got me here."

"Is it, though," Teddy mumbled. James shot him a look. Teddy shrugged.

"What the hell is that supposed to mean?" Mack said.

"As I said, I would not advise that we go that route," James said smoothly. "And...there's actually something else we'd like to discuss." He paused a millisecond longer than felt comfortable and then said, "We've discussed this with the rest of the partners, and we think that what's best for TakeOff right now is if you step down as CEO."

His heart felt like it was falling—actually *falling*—into his stomach. He gulped. Was *this* why they had ambushed him like this? Was this whole thing a setup? They didn't really care what he thought they should do, he realized suddenly—they were just trying to rile him up to make him look bad. What a crock of shit. "*Excuse* me? Step down as CEO? That's...no. No. I'm sorry, that's just not an option." He shook his head. "No."

There was silence again. Finally, Teddy spoke. "You have to understand," he said slowly, "we are about to make a *sub-*

stantial investment in this company, and all of this *stuff*"—he gestured around him—"is a huge, huge distraction. And whatever the merits of the case are, even you must be able to see that the optics of it are *terrible*."

"We're in a very male-hostile moment," James said matter-of-factly. "I'm sure you're aware of it."

"What do you mean, 'male-hostile moment'?" Mack said.

"It's social media. It's regular media. It's everywhere. People are just very, very ready to be suspicious of men and men's motives right now," James said. "Look, you were in our office. How many women were in our meeting with you?" He didn't wait for Mack to answer. "We hear about this *constantly*—that there aren't enough women in tech. That there aren't enough female founders. That there are three VC partners in all of New York City who are women. And it's not like these things are my fault, or your fault! It's really a pipeline issue, and that's something that I can't fix today, or tomorrow, or next week. But people want it to get fixed *yesterday*. That's the problem." James sighed. "I'll be perfectly honest with you. It's just *not* a good time to be a straight white guy getting accused of sexual harassment."

"I guess I should jump in my time machine, then." Mack laughed halfheartedly at his own joke, but everyone else was silent.

"It's no joke, Mack," James said. "Guys with bigger companies and more funding at stake than you have lost everything. *Everything*. Think about it—*anyone* can be accused of sexual harassment! By anyone! You barely even need to have proof! Because once people find out that you've been accused, it's all over Twitter, it's all over the blogs, it's on cable news, and you're presumed guilty until proven innocent. And even when you're proven innocent, that's still not enough. These people, they will go *after* you." He paused, as though he hadn't expected himself to unleash this tirade, and seemed to gather his thoughts. "Look, Mack, we still believe in you. We just think that it's better for the company if you step aside as CEO."

Breathe, Mack told himself. *Count to three and exhale.* "That is *bullshit* and you know it," he said. James looked surprised. Teddy and Jason were both very much *not* looking at him. "Why should I have to pay because the world is messed up? The fact that there's no female partner at Gramercy has *nothing* to do with my situation. And I'm going to deal with it! I'll make the public apology. We can put together a settlement for Isabel. I'll do whatever it takes. This is going to go away, and when it does you're going to be sorry that we even had this conversation. I'm not going to be bullied into giving up my company."

"This is, unfortunately, not negotiable," James said calmly. "Either you step down as CEO, or we rescind our term sheet."

Mack looked at each person in the room. Surely one of them would be on his side, but none of them, not even Jason, met his gaze.

"And one other thing," James said. "We'd like Jason to take over as CEO immediately. You are welcome to stay on in a senior-level role to be determined."

Oh. So that's what this was. A *coup.* He realized Jason hadn't said anything in the entire meeting so far. He must have known this was coming. "You asshole," Mack said to Jason. "All of that stuff about how we were going to get through this—what *was* that? Just total bullshit? Or...or what?"

"I'm sorry, Mack," Jason said. "I really meant that. But I need to think about not just what's best for you or me, but what's best for TakeOff. You understand that, don't you?"

26

LIFT EVERY VOICE

KATYA HAD NEVER seen her mentions column on TweetDeck scroll as fast as it did in the minutes after she published her story about Mack. First it was people just retweeting her story. Then comments like damn @katyapasternack out here with the killer scoops about sleazy founders is 🔥 and why am I surprised but not surprised that @mackmcallister is a total sleazebucket. Thanks @katyapasternack! But soon, she started to see other tweets from people whose avatars were the Twitter egg or a cartoon. Tweets like typical TechSleaze story by @katyapasternack that doesn't even consider that @mackmcallister's accuser is a lying slut. FALSE ACCUSATIONS DESTROY LIVES #justice4mack. She pinged Dan.

Katya: The Twitter eggs are starting to come out against me
Dan: block block block
Katya: yeah I know :/ just wish it didn't have to be this way. do you think they actually believe what they're saying, or they just do it to see what kind of reaction they're gonna get? bc some of the stuff they're saying is really crazy

Dan: welcome to the cesspool we like to call "Twitter"
Katya: thanks. I've been here before, it's always a pleasure.
Katya: jk. duh.
Dan: smoke?
Katya: yeah sure
Dan: actually...i'll come by your desk in a sec

Ever since the other night, when she told him she couldn't meet up, he hadn't asked her to hang out after work again, and she was hoping they had reached a cautious equilibrium, one that tacitly acknowledged that something had happened between them but that there was really no need, at all, to talk about it or think about it or reference it ever again, and they could just go back to being normal, or at least normal-ish.

She was still looking at her TweetDeck when she felt a presence behind her. She turned around. It was Dan. He had his hand behind his back. "Hey," she said. "Are we going to smoke?"

He took his hand out from behind his back and produced a small bouquet of daisies. "Ta-da!" he said. "I just got you these because, well, you're kicking ass."

So much for cautious equilibrium. Against her will, Katya felt herself blushing. Victor had gotten her flowers once, and she had laughed and told him that she wasn't really the type for flowers and he should save his money, and he had gotten offended and pouted a little bit, so finally she'd found a pint glass from Social Media Week—it must have been Janelle's—in the kitchen cabinet and put them in water in there, and then by the time she remembered to check on them, they were dead. But she meant it—what did she need with flowers? They were just a reminder of mortality, the way that they were vibrant and beautiful one day and withered and dry the next, not to mention a waste of money.

She couldn't say that to Dan. Even after everything, he was her boss. And he meant well. So she smiled and said, "Wow, thank you, that's very nice, I guess I should find something to put them in, right?"

"They're just from the bodega down the block," he said, a little too quickly. "I think there might be a vase in the kitchen—I'll get it."

"Well, thanks," she said. Dan nodded, smiled, and walked toward the kitchen.

"Flowers, huh?" She now realized Kevin had watched their entire exchange and was smirking.

"Yeah," she said. "For the Mack story."

"Mm-hmm." Kevin grinned. "Dan Blum has never gotten anyone else in this newsroom flowers. *Lit-er-ally* never. Even when Christina broke that story about Uber." Christina's Uber story had been one of the biggest scoops of the year; she had even gone on CNN to talk about it.

"Well, he really wanted me to do this story." *Not that it's any of your business*, she added silently. She started typing an email, hoping Kevin would take the hint and stop talking to her.

He didn't. "How *did* you get the story, anyway?"

"You know I can't tell you my sources," Katya said.

"Whoa-whoa-*whooooooa*," Kevin said, throwing up his hands in mock surrender. "No one's asking you for your *sources*. Chill."

Katya rolled her eyes. "Chill," she mimicked. "Do you know how much I hate that word? It's just so...*ugh*." She shook her head.

"Damn, you have been *cranky* lately," he said. "It's really not that bad, you know."

She rolled her eyes. "Okay, whatever you say," she said. "Actually, I'm really busy. Do you mind?" She gestured to her computer.

"Yeah, you know what, so am I," Kevin said as Dan returned from the kitchen with a mason jar filled with water.

"Thanks," Katya said. She put the flowers in the jar.

"Still want that smoke?" Dan said. Katya nodded. She *did* want a smoke, even if she now felt a little awkward having it with Dan.

"Gimme a sec—I'll meet you downstairs," she said. At least she'd be able to avoid having people see them walk out together. When she got outside, he had already lit a cigarette. "So? How you feeling?" he said. He squeezed her shoulders. "You just fucking *killed* it. We were just ready to *go* with that story. Deanna and Rich have both told me how great you did."

"Yeah, they emailed me too," she said. She lit a cigarette and took a long drag, and allowed herself a small smile. "The whole thing feels pretty good."

"It's amazing," Dan said. "Really, really amazing." They were silent for a moment. "What's the day-two story here?"

"Hmm," Katya said. "Not totally sure yet. I feel like I need to see how things sort of shake out, you know?"

"Yeah," Dan said. "But let's not wait too long. There are going to be other outlets on this, and we don't want to let the story get away from us."

"Right, right," Katya said. "I was also thinking, maybe it'd be a good time to pick up the invisibletechman story. Feels like the moment is right for it, you know?"

Dan nodded. "Yeah." He took a long drag of his cigarette. "Listen...before you do, there's something I should tell you."

"Okay," Katya said. "I'm listening."

"Actually...I'll just show you." He took out his phone and swiped and tapped on it a few times and finally turned to show her. It was the @invisibletechman account in the Twitter app.

"What about it?"

Dan looked at her meaningfully. "Watch," he said. He held the phone so she could see as he clicked on the little feather icon in the app. The "What's Happening?" screen, with @invisibletechman's avatar in the corner, popped up. Then he typed: Can't believe the news about @mackmcallister...oh wait, yes I can. He added 😂😂😂 and hit the bright blue tweet button. "Voilà."

It took Katya a moment to process what she had just seen. Dan...Blum...was @invisibletechman? No. No no no no *no*. It made no sense. It not only made no sense, but it was wrong on every level. Completely wrong. This could *not* be real. "Wait. What? *You've* been running invisibletechman? But...what? You're not even—"

"Black?" Dan said. "I know." Now he was smiling in a way that was way, *way* too self-satisfied. "I just figured it would seem more authentic if people assumed that the owner of the account was black. I never actually *said* I was black. I might have *implied* it, but go back through my tweets—I never actually *said* it."

"Oh, come on, that's bullshit and you know it," Katya said. "And that's so fucked up. Why would you even do that? Like...to what end? It doesn't make sense. Just to, like, cause trouble?"

"I was commenting on the insularity and myopia in so much of the tech industry," Dan said. "A place rife with sexism, racism, and probably every other ism in existence. It felt like this was the most effective way to do it. I could give people in this industry a *voice,* someone people typically don't hear from. Don't you think I succeeded? Like, now people are talking about this stuff! They weren't before."

"You're an asshole," Katya said. "I didn't say you could speak for me or for, like, Trevor or anyone else in this industry who's not a white man like you. *God,*" she practically spat. "It is *so fucking typical* that a fucking forty-year-old white dude would be the one running this account. What a fucking joke."

"Okay, first of all, I'm thirty-nine, and—"

"You're a *fraud.*"

"Jesus, Katya, I thought you'd be excited that the mystery had finally been solved! You're blowing this *way* out of proportion."

"Solved? You fucking told me. How was I supposed to solve it?" It was true, she was upset, but she had every right to be pissed. Suddenly, something else dawned on her. "Wait a second. *Wait* a second. *That's* how he—*you*—tweeted out the recording of Isabel! Because I had sent it to you. Sent it to *you,* not to your dumb parody Twitter account. How could you even do that to me? I could have lost the whole story."

"It's actually not a parody," Dan said. "More like a satire."

"Whatever the fuck it is," Katya said. Dan had never seen her get really mad, she realized. Well, now he was going to. "Don't mansplain your fake Twitter account to me, okay?"

"Whatever, Katya," he said. "You probably wouldn't have even published your story if I hadn't tweeted out that recording. That blew this whole thing *wide* open. I was really hoping you'd pick up on my hints that we *really* wanted the story, but you were just moving so slowly. I needed to get things going. You'd been, like, sitting on your ass about it for weeks. Even *after* you knew how important these impactful stories were to us."

"I had *not* been sitting on my ass!" Katya said. She was practically yelling now, and the people walking by them on the sidewalk were giving them looks. "You *know* I have not been sitting on my ass."

Dan took one last drag of his cigarette and threw it to the ground. "You know what," he said, "I think maybe just take the rest of the day off. Just...relax. We can pick your story back up again tomorrow." She was silent. "I'm going to go back inside now." He squeezed her shoulder. She flinched. "Hey, it's fine, just take the rest of the day off, okay?" He patted her shoulder and went inside.

She wanted to scream or break something. *Preferably Dan's face,* she thought. What an asshole! She squeezed her eyes shut. *Do not cry,* she thought. *Do. Not. Cry.* She wanted to take the rest of the day off, but she was annoyed that Dan had suggested it, and she also didn't want to go back inside to get the rest of her things. When she opened her eyes, Sabrina was standing in front of her with a smug look on her face. "Lovers' quarrel?" she said. Her tone was cold. Triumphant.

Katya felt herself blushing. "Hardly. Your husband is an ass," she said. "I don't know what he told you, but he's not my lover.' He never was. He won't leave me alone, though."

"I'm supposed to believe that?" Sabrina said. "Come *on,* Katya."

"Believe what you want to believe," Katya said. "But I'm telling you the truth." She almost felt sorry for Sabrina, who seemed to think she was finally going to get her big, dramatic showdown. But of *course* a woman like Sabrina would think her husband was so irresistible that he could have his pick of lovers. (Who said *lover*, anyway?) As *though* Katya would want that.

Sabrina's face crumpled. "Ugh," she said. "So much for my brave confrontation of the other woman. I can't even get *that* right." She sighed and stared up at the sky. "Can I bum one of those?" She pointed to Katya's cigarette.

"Uh, yeah, sure," Katya said. She took the pack out of her back pocket and handed one to Sabrina. "Need a light?" Sabrina nodded. She handed Sabrina her lighter. It took her a couple of tries, but she finally managed to light it.

"Sorry," Sabrina said. "I just...I had this fantasy about confronting you about Dan, so when I saw you two fighting out here and then he stormed back inside—I don't even think he saw me—I thought, *Aha, I got them!* It seemed perfect."

"Confronting me about Dan?" Katya said. "How—I mean, *why* did you need to confront me about Dan?"

"I saw a couple of texts," Sabrina said. "He was trying to get you to come meet him for a drink, and, look, when you've been with someone for more than ten years and you have two kids—there aren't a lot of late-night texts to other women about getting drinks." She took a long drag on her cigarette. "Though I guess, now that I think about it, you're right, he was the one trying to get *you* to go out."

"Yeah. *Exactly*," Katya said. "He's my *boss*, you know. It's not, like, the most straightforward thing to just say no to him. I mean, *he's* probably the person you should be confronting. Not me."

Sabrina nodded. "I know." She seemed, suddenly, miserable. She took another drag on the cigarette, and coughed. "Damn," she said. "I haven't had one of these in ages. They're so delicious and gross."

"That is a perfect description of a cigarette," Katya said. "Where are you headed? I can walk you." Even if she wasn't going to take the whole rest of the day off, she could at least take a break from work.

"I was actually on my way to Isabel's apartment," Sabrina said. "She's kind of freaking out, as I'm sure you can imagine."

"Oof," Katya said. "Yeah. I can imagine." Suddenly, she had an idea. "Hey...this might be weird, but would it be okay if I came with you to Isabel's? I wouldn't mind just having, like, a normal conversation with her about what's been going on."

Sabrina tilted her head at her. "I don't know if that's such a great plan," she said. "You know, Isabel's a lot more sensitive than people think. She's taking all of this pretty hard. I know it was just a story to you, but this is, like, her life. She's saying stuff about how she'll never get another job, her life is over, that kind of thing. She's not in a good place. You're probably the last person she wants to see right now, to be honest."

Katya nodded. "Yeah," she said quietly. "I can see that." She stubbed her cigarette out against the wall of the building and dropped it on the ground. "But...maybe just text her and ask? Tell her it's not for a story or anything. I just want to talk. Completely off the record."

Sabrina was quiet for a moment. "Okay." She took out her phone and sent a text. "Let's give it a couple minutes. But if she doesn't respond, then I'm just gonna go." Katya nodded. But they didn't have to wait long—within thirty seconds, Sabrina's phone had vibrated. She looked at it and seemed surprised. "She says sure. Okay, let's go."

27

THREE'S COMPANY

WHY HAD SHE agreed to let Katya come along to Isabel's? For that matter, why was *she* even going to Isabel's? Sabrina needed to be working on making her life *less* complicated. Neither of these decisions was going to help her do that. She glanced over at Katya, sitting next to her in the backseat of the Uber they were taking to Isabel's apartment in Williamsburg. It was only four thirty in the afternoon, but the sun was starting to go down, and as they went over the Williamsburg Bridge, the light glinted off the shiny tall buildings next to the East River, giving the whole neighborhood a warm, dusky glow. Even when she was of the age when one was supposed to go to Williamsburg often, Sabrina hadn't come to Williamsburg very much, and she certainly didn't come to Williamsburg these days. But as the driver eased his Honda Civic off the bridge and into the streets, she noticed how even the older, shorter buildings she vaguely remembered had been torn down to make way for structures of glass and steel. They seemed to be telegraphing that New York was nothing if not a molting snake, regularly shedding its old skin to reveal a new body underneath—except that the new body usually looked nothing like the old one. She recalled a night sometime in the middle of the previous decade—before marriage, Park Slope, kids—when she and Dan had gone to a rooftop party somewhere around here, probably in one of the buildings that didn't exist anymore, and stayed out until the sun was coming up. It felt like a different person had gone to that party. Every now and then as they sped through the neighborhood she'd get a glimpse of something—a deli, a coffee shop, a bar—that looked vaguely, *vaguely* familiar. Maybe she had stopped at that deli for a Gatorade and a bacon, egg, and cheese after that rooftop party—or maybe not. Geographic nostalgia for somewhere you had only faint memories of was such a mind-fuck.

The driver pulled into the circular driveway of one of the shiny buildings by the river—this one was called Williamsburg Montage—and they got out of the car. Katya and Sabrina were both silent for a moment as they gazed up at the building. It had to be at least thirty stories high. "I live pretty close to here," Katya said. These were the first words she'd uttered since they got in the Uber. "In Greenpoint. But I've never been to this building. I always wondered who lived here."

"Isabel, apparently," Sabrina said. She was also momentarily quieted by the building's luxury. She could see the doorman from out here. It didn't seem fair that she would never get to live in a building like this one. Not that she *wanted* to live in a luxury building in Williamsburg, but it was thoroughly out of her reach now. They gave their names to the doorman and took the elevator to the seventeenth floor. Sabrina noted the elevator buttons for the pool and the yoga/meditation room and the fitness center. This wasn't an apartment building—this was a hotel.

She knocked on the door of Isabel's apartment. "Come in, it's open," she heard Isabel call out. She opened the door. Isabel lived in a studio that was around the size of Sabrina and Dan's apartment minus their bedroom. Everything was brand-new: the stainless-steel appliances, the ash-gray hardwood floors, the furniture that looked like it had all come straight from the CB2 catalog. Isabel had a gallery wall of photos and prints above the couch, where she was lying, her head propped up on a pillow facing Sabrina as she walked in, Katya trailing a little bit behind her.

"Hey," Sabrina said. She and Isabel hugged. "Katya's here too." Katya waved. Isabel waved back.

"Sit, you two," Isabel said. She gestured to the pink velvet armchair across from the sofa and sat up. "Here, someone can sit next to me." She patted the space next to her. Sabrina sat. Katya sat in the armchair. "Thanks for coming over," she said. She reached for a mug that was sitting on her coffee table and took a sip. Sabrina glanced out the window, which looked out on the Williamsburg Bridge.

"No problem," Sabrina said, even if she wasn't sure she actually believed that. "Great view, by the way." How *did* Isabel afford this apartment? She couldn't be making that much more than Sabrina—whenever you started somewhere as an assistant and worked your way up, your salary was never exactly what it should be. Then again, Isabel didn't have two kids and a shopping addiction.

"Thanks. Yeah, I love this place. Who knows how much longer I'll be able to stay in it, though." The three of them were silent for a moment. "Do you know what you're gonna do yet?" she asked Sabrina.

"Do?" Sabrina said. "In what sense?"

"Like, are you gonna stay at TakeOff after all this?"

"Oh," Sabrina said. "I don't know. I mean, shit, I'd love to quit with you in solidarity, but...God. You know, if I was your age, I totally would. I would *totally* quit, and take a stand, and tell everyone to just fuck right off."

"Yeah!" Isabel said. She sat up straighter on the couch and grinned. "That's the spirit."

"I can't, though," Sabrina said quietly. "My life is just... more complicated right now. I *wish* I still had only myself to think about. But...I never told you this, Isabel, because it didn't seem appropriate since you were, like, my boss, but now that you're not—I'm in a lot of debt. I really fucked up and just, like, started buying stuff online and it got completely out of control, and I basically don't have any credit cards I can even use anymore, and Dan just found out and he's so pissed at me...It's not the best time for me to quit." She cringed, wondering how Isabel was going to take this confession.

"No, I get it," Isabel said. She sounded like she actually did. "I understand. Just like...knowing that you *would* quit, that's what matters to me."

Sabrina reached over and took Isabel's hand and squeezed it. "You're a good person," she said. "No matter what happens, remember that."

"There are a lot of people right now who don't think so," she said. She glanced at Katya. "You've seen the shit that people are saying about me, right? It's like...*bad*. There's a thread on a men's rights subreddit about me that has, like, over twelve hundred comments. And I had to just delete Twitter from my phone because I was getting so many notifications, mostly from guys who are telling me I'm a slut, I deserve to be raped, Andrew is a cuck, whatever that means..." She trailed off. "People are so fucked up."

Katya nodded. She looked uncomfortable. She hadn't said anything since they walked into Isabel's apartment. *I wonder what's going through her head right now,* Sabrina thought. She was so inscrutable. Was she mentally cataloging everything in the apartment, everything they were saying, to use it against them later? Or had she truly come in peace? "I have seen it, yes," Katya finally said. "And...I'm sorry." Everyone was quiet again. "Look, Isabel...I don't regret writing the story. I don't. I think it's important for people to know about Mack. But I guess...I just wasn't totally expecting everything to play out the way it did. And if I'd known that people were going to be so horrible to you..."

"You would've done what?" Isabel asked. "I don't think there's actually anything you should have done differently. That's the sad part."

The three of them were silent for a moment. Then Katya glanced at Sabrina. "You know that Twitter account invisibletechman?"

"Yeah," Isabel said. "They were the ones who tweeted my recording. Which I still don't know how they even got."

"Well, they got it because I sent it to them," Katya said.

"Huh?" Isabel said. "Why would you do that?"

"Well...I didn't *know* I was sending it to them," Katya said. "I thought I was sending it to my editor. To Dan." She paused to let this sink in. "I thought I was sending it to *Dan,*" she repeated.

"Wait," Isabel said. "Dan sent it to invisibletechman? Why would he do that?"

"No," Sabrina said. She was putting something together that she didn't love. At all. "Dan *was* invisibletechman." She watched Isabel's eyes widen as she processed all of this. "And I was the one who sent *you* the recording, Katya, because Isabel asked me to." Isabel nodded. Sabrina felt sick. "My husband is..." She couldn't even finish the sentence.

Katya nodded. "Yeah," she said. "He said he was giving a

voice to marginalized people in tech by creating the account." She rolled her eyes.

"God, that is so gross," Sabrina said. "I guess being married to someone Korean makes you qualified to pretend to be a black person on Twitter."

"Oh, he was very emphatic that invisibletechman never actually *said* he was a black person," Katya said.

"You have *got* to be kidding me," Sabrina said. "I'm...I mean, I know I had nothing to do with it, but I feel like I need to apologize for my husband's ridiculous actions."

"It's okay," Isabel said. "We don't have to hold ourselves responsible for the dumb shit men do."

"I'd drink to that," Sabrina said.

"Do you want a drink?" Isabel said. "I can open a bottle of wine."

"Sure," Sabrina and Katya said simultaneously. Isabel hopped up from the couch and went to the fridge and took out a bottle of white wine. Sabrina noticed there was little else in the refrigerator—just what looked like a takeout container, a bottle of kombucha, and another bottle of wine.

"I wish I had champagne," she said, setting the bottle down on the counter. "It feels like we should be celebrating, in a weird way." She took three wineglasses out of the cabinet and opened the bottle. She poured glasses for all of them and handed one each to Katya and Sabrina. "Well, cheers, ladies," she said. "To doing our own shit."

"To doing our own shit," Katya and Sabrina said. The three of them clinked glasses. As Sabrina took a sip of the wine, she looked out the window. The sky was a dusky orange-red; in the distance, the Williamsburg Bridge was illuminated. And she knew—more clearly than she had ever known anything— exactly what she was going to do.

ACKNOWLEDGMENTS

As a journalist, I found that there were moments during the writing of this book that I panicked, believing that I wasn't allowed to be writing fiction, much less getting it published. Fortunately, I have many people in my life who are experts at encouragement, starting with my one-of-a-kind agent, Alia Hanna Habib, and her colleagues Leslie Falk and Susan Hobson at McCormick Literary, who have been *Startup* fans from day one. Of course, *Startup* would not be what it is without the enthusiasm and guidance of my wonderful editor, Reagan Arthur, and the whole team at Little, Brown: Matt Carlini, Katharine Myers, Julie Ertl, Lauren Passell, Craig Young, Pamela Brown, Jayne Yaffe Kemp, and Kaitlyn Boudah. Copyeditor Tracy Roe's sharp eyes saved me from many mortifying mistakes and allowed *email* (no hyphen) to stand, and designer Lauren Harms came up with a jacket that makes me hope people judge this book by it. And Kassie Evashevski and Jason Richman at UTA are the best people in Hollywood to have in your corner.

I never would have finished if not for my two-person writing group with Kate Spencer, who was both a cheerleader and an astute reader over the year and a half I was working on *Startup*. I'm also grateful to Laura Dave and Alex Balk, who read early versions of the manuscript and offered invaluable comments; to genius twentysomethings Katie Heaney and Arianna Rebolini, who went above and beyond in making sure that I didn't completely embarrass myself by saying Snapchat when I meant Instagram and vice versa; and Danielle Nussbaum, who paid me the highest compliment possible when she told me she read the manuscript in less than twenty-four hours. And huge thanks to Elizabeth Olson for being my on-call design expert and who saved us all from a potential kerning disaster.

Thanks to friends Emily Fleischaker, Marc Kushner, Chris Barley, and Chrysanthe Tenentes for giving me places to write in Santa Fe and New York, and thanks to my friends who were working on books at the same time who were always available to commiserate: Anya Yurchyshyn, Saeed Jones, Isaac Fitzgerald, Emily Gould, and Anne Helen Petersen.

Thanks to the founders and employees who generously offered their insights into startup life: Caroline McCarthy, Matt Weiler, Peter Bell, Nick Gray, Su Sanni, Ally Millar, Matt Lieber, Jason Klein, Soraya Darabi, Daniel Hoffer (who filled me in on life as a venture capitalist), and of course the incomparable Melanie Altarescu. This is a work of fiction, but their experiences and perspectives helped ensure my characters' world felt authentic.

Countless friends have been so supportive and excited for me over the past many months. You know who you are, and you are greatly appreciated and loved. Same goes for my brilliant colleagues at BuzzFeed, many of whom have become friends during my five years there. You inspire me daily, and you manage to both keep me young and make me feel old. (In a good way.)

I'm so lucky to have a family that I not only love, but also actually like: Roberta Steinberg, Avishai Shafrir, Michael Shafrir, Alyson Luck, Sam Shafrir, Karen Vladeck, Steve Vladeck, and

Maddie Vladeck. Thank you for being family *and* friends, and for being there always.

Before I moved to L.A., someone said to me, "You're going to go out there and marry a screenwriter and live happily ever after." That person was close: I married a TV writer and podcaster, and I'm so thankful to have his love, support, and creativity in my life. I love you, Matt Mira, and thank you for never letting me give up.

ABOUT THE AUTHOR

DOREE SHAFRIR is a senior culture writer at BuzzFeed News. She has written for *New York, Slate, The Awl, Rolling Stone, Wired,* and other publications. A former resident of Brooklyn, she now lives in Los Angeles with her husband, Matt Mira, a comedy writer and podcaster, and their dog, Beau.